SEASON OF MIST

Mc. Donald Dixon

Tony Boxall
31 March 2009.

Copyright © 2007 by Mc. Donald Dixon.

Library of Congress Control Number: 2007903815
ISBN: Hardcover   978-1-4257-6946-8
               Softcover   978-1-4257-6943-7

All rights reserved. No part of this book may be reproduced or transmitted in any form or by any means, electronic or mechanical, including photocopying, recording, or by any information storage and retrieval system, without permission in writing from the copyright owner.

This is a work of fiction. Names, characters, places and incidents either are the product of the author's imagination or are used fictitiously, and any resemblance to any actual persons, living or dead, events, or locales is entirely coincidental.

This book was printed in the United States of America.

To order additional copies of this book, contact:
Xlibris Corporation
1-888-795-4274
www.Xlibris.com
Orders@Xlibris.com
39613

CONTENTS

Prologue 7

Chapter One 9
Chapter Two 22
Chapter Three 31
Chapter Four 41
Chapter Five 54
Chapter Six 68
Chapter Seven 85
Chapter Eight 100
Chapter Nine 110
Chapter Ten 124
Chapter Eleven 133
Chapter Twelve 146
Chapter Thirteen 160
Chapter Fourteen 167

Epilogue 175
Glossary 181

DEDICATION

TO MY MOTHER LETITIA
AND FOR THOSE COUNTLESS OTHER WOMEN
WHO MOTHERED AND FATHERED US.

PROLOGUE

The period may not have been of any particular significance when viewed in retrospect against the colourful history of the Colony; depending on what side of the fence your die was cast. Except for an occasional burst of musket fire in the hills, and the scream from a wild pig caught in the path of hot lead, nothing of importance appeared to be happening. It was a period of transition from a government that cared little for the life of its citizens, once there was a profit to be made from the fruits of the land, to one spawned from the hatred and vengeance of a bloody revolution. There was a pall of silence about the streets, thick like the mist on La Sorcière at the height of the rainy season. Every man wore a traitor's face and the guillotine was as active as a well-oiled rat trap. Citizens confronted their maker for the slightest indiscretion against the State. It was a means to end the sudden outburst of treason that had infested the colony from coast to coast. Fear lurked in the corners of eyes and men went about their daily chores afraid to glance over their shoulders, dreading the shadow of the hangman on their tails.

The pounding of hooves on cobblestone stirring dust storms large enough to smother a small village as they galloped through the streets in hot pursuit of an unseen enemy, the harsh uneven blares from a bugler's horn, at street corners, rallying the faithful to the flag, were the only reminders that war was simmering in the parliament halls of faraway lands. To those who lived in the colony their fortunes remained unchanged, while they remained oblivious to the signs and rumours around them. Sugar prices were good and victor and vanquished drank from the same tankards in the little alehouses that sprang up overnight in the back streets, despite a noose of foreboding tightening around the neck of towns. They drank to the silence, allowing their fears a moment's reprieve, to ingratiate with the new order. Brother had drawn sword against brother in the name of causes they never understood, enemies were hatched in the questioning look on a face. It was the time of the brigands' war; a king had lost his head in France. Words muttered in ignorance brought the *inquisiteurs* to your door. Citizens vanished without trace in the dead of the night. It was the edict of the revolution. It had no friends . . .

To an old woman caught in a cough of wind buffeting her*driette* as she raised her head to gaze at the burnt out shell of the fortress on the hill overlooking the town, squinting to protect her eyes from wisps of gray hair that carelessly flashed across her face, it was the season of remembrance. Forty years had rolled over these memories, had smoothed their raw edge with the persistence of the sea over its stones. She had worn well under her weight of years, immaculate in her strides. She remembered events to the last detail as though they had happened yesterday and they flared vividly like sunset, over the hilltops, in her mind . . . A red tunic, the colour of boiled crayfish shells; the sun dazzling off the brass buttons stuck to a chest in the form of a cross . . . A whiff of English lavender turned her nose to the green thicket where she had heard a faint rustling between the leaves. She aimed her musket from the hip—a flick of flint—fired—It was her first kill . . .

CHAPTER ONE

 Madelienne Des Voeux was as black as a moonless midnight, with skin smooth as treacle especially when sweat enveloped her body after slogging for a full day in the sun. Tall, standing six feet, barefooted, she towered over most—if not all—of her male companions in camp, always musing and mumbling a soundless narrative as she went about her chores. She had survived on instinct as early as her first memories. She was a child of the bush, not pampered by *dahs* in the cabins, like the children reared on the estates, a product of the wilderness and had mastered the art of foraging before she had learnt to crawl. Her father, Desolee, was a maroon chief who was feared by man and beast living within the ambit of his domain. He had built his camp deep in the forest at the base of Morne Gimee, a full day's ride from the sleepy town of La Convention. Children mumbled his name in their sleep and drew cold sweat, imagining him at the head of his small band of hunters. He would swoop down on the small plantations, particularly those close to the edge of the forest, like Xenon, Diamant and Ventine, rattling through the chambers of their great houses with the padded precision of mice, plundering their storerooms of every ounce of food without harming members of the households. After each attack he left his mark in the form of a large cross, drawn with his cutlass, on their front lawns. It was his idea of a joke. He remembered as a boy, on the Xenon plantation where he grew up, a visiting missionary reminding him that the Lord gives and the Lord takes. The symbol of the cross became for him, his signature to that testimony. In time his mark became well known among slave and freeman, between mulatto and overseer, much to the annoyance of the planters, who were forced next day to venture into town to replenish supplies at substantial cost, in the full glare of smiling black faces, pretending to snooze, perched on empty hogsheads outside the merchant shops.

Memories of her father distributing the spoils, first among the aged and the infirmed, then, among the able bodied members of his camp, brought feelings of sadness to Madlienne's eyes. It softened the hard caste that had covered all of her like a crab shell. There was an aura of kindness about him despite his harsh looks, a benign gentility that only those close to him were ever allowed to experience. Madlienne never knew her mother. She had died within days of giving birth, despite the superhuman efforts of all in the camp, notwithstanding their collective knowledge of bush medicines. Desolee had met Solitaire as a young buck, flexing his dazzle on the Xenon plantation. When the plantation was sold to a man whose only interest was sugar-cane, it was time to run away and he took Solitaire along with him. But she was a delicate child, fair skin, a *shabeene,* daughter of some mulatto overseer and a young belle, who brought water and food for the cane cutters during crop time. Solitaire never grew accustomed to the ways of the wild. Her skin swelled from mosquito bites and when the rains came she shivered with fever. She bore the pains for three years but eventually succumbed to yellow fever.

The old wizened countenance crisscrossed with wrinkles, plastered with tearstains and dry sweat, bore close resemblance to a tattered mask, hewn from ebony, buried and forgotten for half a century in a new world where only hope was reason enough to survive. Her eyes peeped through sockets set deep in her skull and her nostrils covered more space than was normally allotted to a face. Her body, however, defied the stoop of age and a subtle arrogance appeared whenever she was forced to use a walking stick, as a measure of last resort, to cross the streets after a shower. She cursed nature for making her a woman. She wished she had been born a man. She had done everything a man could do without the freedom naturally ingrained in them from infancy. It was that freedom she craved, one that had always been denied by custom and practice, despite her formidable reputation. She had gained her colours fighting by their side. She had led them into battle, rescued them from the jaws of the cannon; poured medicines into their wounds and healed them, yet in their eyes, she felt that she was never considered their equal. She remembered in camp how she envied the men going around half naked, only in pantaloons, when the sun scorched the earth in Lent; the frequent groping and pawing when she slept with them in bivouac; watching them plunge naked into the rivers to clean their bodies after a fight, yet for her, there was always to be the secluded spot, away from the rest like a leper. Age had changed many things but not the chemistry of self.

She was returning from her evening stroll through her flower garden, meticulously tended ever since she had retired to her little cottage at Trois Piton overlooking the fort. She knew every flagstone; she had set them in place herself, even the wayward pieces that were loose and threatened to catapult her into the bougainvillea's thorns when she absentmindedly stepped on them. More painful, were the colonies of biting ants that had invaded her sanctuary, for which there was no remedy. There was the occasional pot of boiling water, poured with religious fervour, only to watch helpless as they migrate to her ornamental shrubs within a matter of days. From there they would mount their sudden attacks on her bare feet as she stood squarely in their midst . . . She grimaced as she heard the wind rustling through the mango trees. She looked up, focusing on a solitary ripe fruit, high up among the branches. She prayed for it to fall, curling her face into a smile. She had relived this experience on a mountain of occasions. In her younger years she would have had that mango on the ground in a flash, either by climbing, or by dropping it with a stone. Her aim was superb. A flicker from childhood pranced before her eyes in the quivering rays, as the sun's light filtered through the leaves. She saw herself walking along the shaded footpath towards the river, Theodule, Argos, Jean, Ti Frère and Constantin in tow. Wherever she went, it was always with the boys. They came towards a mango tree close to the river; they heard the water rushing across the stones. It's the clammy month of August when sweat piles on sweat and sticks to the skin like syrup. The boys outpaced each other to climb the tree. Madlienne collected stones. While they raced upward to where the fruit was golden ripe, she was already picking—one stone, one fruit. They were accomplished hunters, with one musket shared between the six of them a satchel of gunpowder and a few rounds of grapeshot. The gun and ammunition was usually carried by Madlienne, not only because she was the eldest, but was also a crack shot, although barely twelve. Haversacks filled with *ramier, agouti* and other small game, was ample evidence of her skill. Sometimes they killed a boar and quartered it among them to share the load . . .

The cool afternoon breeze wrapped in the sickly scent of frangipani from the neighbour's yard filled her nostrils. Her breasts heaved as she inhaled the pure air, shuffling towards the doorway to the rocker that had become her throne. Her mind swayed backward and forward with the wind reaching further into the past rather than dwelling on the present. For her, the future held no surprises only the hour of her death, but she was not ready to die, at least not yet. There was something she had to do before death came. It had become an obsession, one that obliterated the clarity of thought. It began when an old white priest, Abbe Petorne, wandered into her father's camp to bring salvation to their lost souls. The revolutionaries had burnt his church and had strictly forbidden his congregation to worship under threat of the guillotine, having labeled them as conspirators against the State. They had changed the seven day week to one of ten and had removed Sundays from the new calendar. They called the week the *decade* and three weeks had become the month. She remembered her father on his knees, prostrate at the feet of this priest who, with his long hair, white robe and flowing beard, bore close resemblance—although she had never seen a portrait of him—to a foreign god that her father had told her was the god of the planter. He had more power than all the gods of Guinea. In his satchel, Abbe Petorne had brought along with him bits and pieces of the body of this god, (who had died to absolve the world from evil) to distribute after they had knelt at his feet and confessed their sins. They would eat the bits of the body of this god and it would make them strong. She did not at the time grasp the significance of these events. She found them quaint but it was not in her place to question. On the instructions of her father, whose taciturn looks could not be disobeyed, she too knelt at the feet of Abbe Petrone and received her first and last holy communion. He left as suddenly as he had appeared with a supply of fruit and dried meat, sufficient to last him for weeks. Within days of his departure, a band of vigilantes surrounded the camp and slaughtered all the inhabitants, including her father who was asleep in his hammock at the hour of the siesta. A bullet fired at close range pierced a soft spot in his skull, above his left ear. Powder burns had singed his hair; his eyes wide open, staring blankly, in disbelief . . .

She had left camp with her little group—Theodule, Argos, Jean, Ti Frère and Constantin—to hunt *ramier* in the white cedar grove on the other side of Morne Gimee, a fair five miles away. Later they searched for the iguana, after it had eaten and was resting on its branch in the cool of the day, knowing by instinct it would soon be night. The sun was kissing the mountain slopes good bye, making room for dusk. Long shadows from the surrounding hills had spread across camp. It was already dark when they returned, their haversacks over brimming with meat and wild yams from the forest. Madlienne was the first to feel the strange unnerving silence as she entered the clearing leading to the huts from where she could see them huddled in a cluster, silent and foreboding . . . Nothing moved, not even the usual curl of smoke from Maitre

Charle's fireplace, in anticipation of the bounty. Her instincts, natural in the wild, were aroused. They circled camp advancing cautiously, like the wild boar they had wounded once in the forest, but had not killed, each forward step heavier than the last, weighed by a disconcerted fear, infectious between them, until they entered the first hut. Heartbeats quickened, beating in unison. Inside, blood quailed. A mother still clutching her infant in a protective stoop to ward off machete blows, was hacked beyond recognition; the child, without its head. They fanned out among the huts, bursting through cabin by cabin only to be held in check by the faint knot of nausea gripping their bowels. The scene in each cabin was the same. Young and old in varying stages of undress were either shot or hacked to pieces, where they lay, caked in their blood. Madlienne entered her father's cabin unprepared for what she found. A stifled scream forced through her lips. Her father's body was lying in its hammock, eyes wide open, staring dumbstruck at the roof, face rigid in death. There was a cynical smirk pasted to his features which said, his death would be avenged.

The attack had been thorough, planned with clock-like precision. No one had escaped. Madlienne counted thirty-two bodies, including four infants. Maitre Charle, her old mentor, who on moonlight nights told stories around the fireside while he roasted the birds they brought home from a day's romp through the forest, was among the dead. He was shot and pinned to a post in his shack like a pig, butchered and hung, to drain its blood. There were no signs of resistance, except for two mulattos with gaping holes in their chests. The man who had killed them was still clutching his cutlass in death, the back of his skull blown off; a musket ball had savagely seared through taking a chunk of bone, scalp and brain. His eyes glazed, under the same icy pall that had spread its halo around the camp. He was once Argos' and Ti Frere's father.

Night was fast approaching. In the morning they would bury their dead. Grief had paralyzed her thoughts. The simple grief of seeing her people decimated, their bodies lying still, stiffened by the paroxysms of death made something inside her snap like a fragile strand of thread. Tears flowed freely down her cheeks, angling across her pronounced cheekbones to drop like a waterfall to the floor. Notwithstanding the enormity of this event and the lasting effect that it would have from that moment on the rest of her life, it could not hold back the fatigue weakening her limbs as she welcomed sleep. Next morning when the sun came up with the birds, they knew they were alone in the world, the last of a people, molded by murder into a tribe. They had stayed huddled together under the coverlet of night, in the bushes, under the shadow of the trees a safe distance from the camp, fearing the vigilantes return. They were concerned that the vigilantes would have observed that two among them were missing and comeback to rescue their own. But they did not.

"What kind of animal they is?" Madlienne thought. "They don't bury their own dead?"

She already knew the unwritten rules of engagement; you must take care of your own, nobody will do it for you. She found the vigilantes' behaviour reprehensible. Being the daughter of the chief, the shawl of leadership now covered her shoulders. The time for mourning, for her, was past. It was now time to act. She was not much older than the rest, except Theodule, who was not more than a year older. She did not know the exact date of her birth, but from events she had seen and remembered, she guessed that she had left her teens behind. She directed that a large trench be dug in the soft loam of the pasture where her father had attempted once unsuccessfully to grow corn. It was close to noon when they completed the task. Madlienne helped to carry the bodies and they lined then up as best as they could in the common grave. Desolee was carried by Madlienne with the help of Theodule and was laid at the head of the trench, apart from the rest, perhaps remembering Maitre Charle's fables about the burial of Kings, in that far off land (of his) that had always fascinated her. The dirt was warm and it lay lightly on the bodies, so still and rigid in the noonday sun, resembling in her mind's eye the stone monuments of which he spoke. It took more than an hour to complete the burial as Ti Frère and Constantin broke down and wept as they lifted the cold slabs of flesh that were alive when they last saw them, moving about their cabins in the early morning, the previous day before they left.

Madlienne had done her crying in the night. Her eyes, except for two red rings around their lids, were dry. The wreath of vengeance was drawing circles around her mind. She ordered Argos and Ti Frere to bring out the bodies of the two Mulattos in their father's cabin:

"You not burying them with my father!" Argos exclaimed angrily.

"Not in that hole!" Ti Frere said, "I not helping you put them in there."

"No." Madlienne replied calmly, "I will help you build a bonfire with wood from our huts and we will put their bodies on top it and watch them burn to coals, in hell."

Hatred was usurping the seat of sorrow in her heart. They inhaled the acrid stench of burning flesh. It seemed to fill them with an unholy power, transfiguring their earthly features into glowing orbs of extraterrestrial light. When they were finished, they washed themselves in the river, without bothering to take off their clothes. The hand of death had left its imprint. It was a dark stain on their conscience, darker than the blood clots that had already congealed, attracting the ant.

Madlienne had heard her father and the other elders of the camp speak of the *Negre Marron*. They roamed in gangs throughout the forest, but in all her escapades their paths had never crossed hers. They were the armies of the dispossessed, who, generations ago, had fled the estates when life became unbearable, their people regarded slightly better than the wild beasts that roamed through the imagination of children to devour them in their sleep. They killed without mercy and drank the blood of their victims, she had heard. An idea was forming in her mind. She called the group together, like her father would have done when he summoned his council of braves.

"We have no where to go," she said. "We cannot stay in this camp. They may come back and find us. I will go to find the others like us living in the forest. You don't have to follow me."

They looked at each other. Their eyes spoke. She did not have to beg, they would follow her to the end. They waited along the riverbank until the sun had set; each in their own little cocoon, independent of the other, struggling to overcome the grief that had fed their bodies and had remained chained to their hearts. Following tracks that had been permanently scratched along the slopes by feet that no longer walked the earth, using night and the coverlet of trees as a shield, they began the long journey towards the east, the direction where the sun rose. Without light, not wanting to attract attention as they plodded through this unknown territory, they journeyed for most of the night, uphill, downhill, along a mountain ledge, then down into a valley, without stopping to rest. As they entered the valley, the strong stench of purified molasses alerted them to the existence of a still. They followed their nostrils.

They did not know where they were, only that they were following a trail that led to the east. They had never followed it before and did not know where it went. They walked all night without pausing for breath. A few crimson streaks stained the sky ahead.

"It would soon be morning again." Madlienne broke the silence. "We must take heart."

They stumbled on the still before morning broke: It was an old ramshackle building that seemed to spring from the trunk of a huge fichus tree, whose aerial roots had enveloped the structure and was crushing it like a tinder box, in the hands of a child. As they got closer, the smell carried by the wind in their direction became unbearable. They held their nostrils. Inside, two men were fast asleep on a cushion of straw, close to a log fire which had been burning all night. In the red afterglow, their skins assumed the complexion of the fire. Madlienne, who had carried the musket all night, poked them in the ribs, one by one. She had realized from the kinky tufts of black hair on their heads, they were neither mulatto nor white. She had no quarrels with her own. It took some serious poking to awaken the two men. Their eyes were permanently glazed and appeared unaccustomed to being awake.

"We are looking for the camp of the *Gens Libre!*" she said. It was the polite name for the *Negre Marron*. No one was known to call them *Negre Marron* to their face and live. The bush had its own laws. There, only the cunning survived.

"We are *Gens Libre!*" The elder of the two replied. His speech was heavy and slurred. "We are *L'Armée Française dans les bois*," the younger one added.

"Who are you?" The older one enquired; (addressing Madlienne) they had not yet observed her other companions, who stood in the shadows waiting.

"Orphans," Madlienne replied.

"Orphans?" Repeated the older one. "I don't see anybody else."

"You haven't look hard enough," replied Madlienne.

The younger one peered into the shadows behind her but could not see beyond the dark.

"The Militia rode through here yesterday. They were in a hurry," the older one said.

"How come they didn't see you?" Madlienne asked. "This place stinks for miles!"

"We heard the horn and we hid," the older one explained. "They were in a hurry to get to town before dark."

"We have people in the hills that watch," The younger one chipped in.

"Shut up!" The older one yelled, "You don't know who you speaking to!" He was beginning to sober up.

"All black people under the bush is friends," the younger one remarked. "Your skin is your password," he added, sniggering.

"You not laughing at me because I blacker than you?" Madlienne taunted him, lifting the musket to his mouth.

"No! No!" he replied, "I am only a rum maker. Me an my brother make rum for the whole damn army in the bush."

"Where is this army?" Madlienne asked, "we looking to join."

"They everywhere," the older one replied. "*Bettes a feu* is their lamp. The bush is their eyes."

"You say the militia pass through here yesterday?" Madlienne asked the older one.

"Yes, I was hiding in the bush when they pass, me an my brother."

"How many you see?" Madlienne asked.

"See?" The younger one exclaimed, "We was too afraid to show our face." Madlienne smothered her smile with a frown.

"You had to hear something, their horses perhaps?"

"Yes!" The younger one exclaimed, "I hear them. It did have about twenty or thirty of them," he said.

"It had more," the older one said. Madlienne made a mental note of the number—twenty to thirty. She had surveyed the ground around the camp herself and from the hoof marks she had observed, twenty to thirty was right.

"You say you have people in the hills that watch. I want to see them." Madlienne was hoping to extract more information from the younger one; he looked across at his older brother and back to her again.

"What is your name?" Madlienne asked the older one.

"Emile Des Voeux," he replied. "My father worked at Xenon. He die." Xenon, a name she would always remember; it was also the birthplace of her father. He had met her mother there. She turned to the younger one and without her having to ask, he said;

"My name is Paul, Paul Des Voeux. He is my big brother," pointing to the older one who poked at a breadfruit roasting in the dying embers under the huge copper still that disappeared into the roof. He poured some coffee from a blackened percolator into a battered pewter cup and gave it to Madlienne, attempting to appear hospitable despite his fears.

"I told you, I was not alone," she said, signalling to her other companions, who calmly walked out of the shadows into the pale light of the oil lamp, straining through its soot to light the room. On seeing them, both brothers cringed in fear. It was not difficult to understand why they had been assigned to their posts. They had no stomach for a fight.

"Don't kill us! Please! *Su plais*!" exclaimed Emile, his whole body shaking with fright, "we don't have nothing to take."

To Madlienne he appeared comical. She was yet to see a grown man drivel. She brushed past him and snatched the breadfruit from the fire. Without wincing, she broke and shared it among her five companions, who sat around the fire to dry the dew that had dampened their clothes. She poured out more coffee, filling the cup to its brim and passed it around. After they had warmed their entrails with the brothers' coffee and completely devoured their breadfruit and had extracted the night air from their bones, Madlienne asked the brothers for directions to the camp of the *Gens Libre*. Again they looked at each other, eyes struggling to remain firmly rooted in their sockets, then, without uttering a single word Emile pointed east.

They followed the trail through the valley, along the banks of the big river, larger than any river they had seen, following its eastward flow, their eyes glued to human footprints embedded in the sandy loam. Suddenly, the river veered south, but the tracks remained riveted to its banks, clear in the daylight, it guided them along. All morning they heard a conch shell blare from the hills. It was always at a distance, it appeared to encircle them with its sound. It measured their footsteps as they foraged deeper and deeper into unknown territory. Apart from the footprints in various stages of wear along the riverbank, the first signs of life they stumbled across since leaving the still that morning was an abandoned campsite, where the ashes were still warm and ants had not yet infested the bits of bone littered about, on the grass. There was no evidence of horses present; no hoof marks, no dung. Like them, this party had left on foot and could not be more than a few hours away. They moved on, following the footprints away from the river, plodding through some low lying hills, winding for miles through shrub and grazing lands, but no cattle or sheep were seen, although the grass was closely cropped to the earth like a manicured lawn where a gardener had spent a lifetime tailoring. Shortly after noon, the path led up a steep ridge. Close to its summit, they came to the mouth of a cave, disguised with wattle and vines. They spotted it instantly, as it was different from the rest of the vegetation. There was only one musket between them and eight rounds of lead.

'What if this is a trap?' Madlienne thought, 'I would be leading the rest of my people to their death.' Her leadership instincts honed from hunting in the wilderness bristled to the fore. She had acquired a feel for danger, and smelt it in the air, even when it disguised itself. She would admit later that she felt afraid, not for herself, but for the others. She unbuckled her large rawhide belt that kept her pouch of powder securely fastened to her waist and gave it to Theodule along with the musket.

"I am going inside," she said to the group. "If I don't come back by the time the sun move over this hill" (which was about in half an hour's time) "run from this place as fast as your legs can make."

Theodule placed his hands on her shoulders, but quickly looked away. He was the only boy she had allowed to get close to her. They had grown up together under the bush. They had experienced hardship together, foraging for food soon after they had learnt to walk. She often thought of him as the brother she had always wanted but never had. She took his knife; a large crude implement he had whittled from an iron stave, ripped from a discarded wine cask, which her father had brought to the camp from one of his sorties. It was sharp on both sides, and pointed like a dagger. Without further debate or a final glance over her shoulder, she disappeared through the wattle and vines.

Light vanished quickly on entering the cave, like the moon's sudden shift, behind a cloud. She closed her eyes and waited for her pupils to adjust before stepping forward cautiously into the meandering chamber. The walls were damp and water was seeping through stone. It felt cold under her bare feet. The tunnel twisted and turned like a corkscrew, but was large enough to allow her to walk through without having to stoop. It was slippery in parts and to balance her footing she walked close to the sides, groping the rough edges.

'Who had the patience to dig this place out of the hill,' she thought. 'It must be a special people.' She knew the cave was man-made as her fingers wandered over the coarse journey of an adze through the sandstone walls in amazement. She was fascinated by this discovery and was happy to have entered alone. Subconsciously, she knew that this cave would become an ally one day and hoped to find many more at other strategic points in the forest.

She had traveled a fair distance into the cave, when she spotted a speck of light ahead. At first she thought it was a firefly, but as she moved towards it, it grew brighter and larger. Her eyes by then had adjusted to the poor light; she was beginning to discern objects that she had not noticed before. First she found a gourd half filled with drinking water neatly placed in a niche carved in the rocks next to the remains of a tallow candle wasted down to its base. Both felt damp, further on she found three musket balls that may have dropped from someone's pouch. She picked them up and placed the cold lead in her bosom. A short distance away she almost tripped on a hunting knife, probably discarded on account of its dull blade. She picked it up, knowing that it could still serve as a useful weapon in her armoury. She trudged on cautiously measuring her steps, armed with evidence of human existence, until she came to a carefully chiseled stairway, hewn from the folds in the rock that formed the walls of the cave.

'Whoever built this cave had given a great deal of thought to its construction'. She could not help but reflect. In the faint light she saw marks left by several tools, their even indentations into the soft stone betrayed the skills of trained craftsmen. The walls were recessed to allow steps to protrude from the sides, deliberate, like a sculpture, leading towards that speck of light she had used as a compass to steer her through the maze. She climbed; the light was now streaming through the roof of the cave, reflecting in a pool of clear water that provided further illumination within the chamber.

'There's something sacred about this place,' she thought, as her body absorbed the light. The water was crystal clear. She cupped her hands and drank. She looked up at the shaft of light beaming from an opening in the roof the size of a man's shoulders directly above her. She had seen the sky reflected in the pool as she drank and knew that light she saw was from the sun. A sensation of weightlessness invaded her body, she felt as light as a bird without the urge to fly. Effortlessly, she climbed towards the opening. She emerged through a crevice in the rocks; the full force of the afternoon sun slapped her face. It almost blinded her. She covered her face with her hands, peeping through her fingers.

She was looking down on a mountain valley she had never seen before. The river, squirming like an old boa limped along between green hems of grass, covering the valley like a skirt, a silvered mirror reflecting mountain and sky. Her eyes followed the river's flow, until it came to an abrupt end, frothing in a large basin of blue that stretched far away into the east until it shook hands with the sky. She had never seen this before, but knew, from the stories Maitre Charle had retold, she was looking at the sea. That large expanse of blue that was the same colour as the sky with its white lace trimmings was the same body of water that stretched to that faraway kingdom that haunted him all his life. Her mind wandered across the landscape, imagining the feel of the sea on her feet with its compass that would steer her to the safe shores of that faraway land of her ancestors. Seeing it now at a distance, in all its chopping splendour, the urge to cross it some day to discover heaven on the other side, was tickling every fibre in her body. She turned looking back across the land. Not faraway, there was a hill pointed like an eyetooth. She thought she recognized it, but was not certain. Her surroundings were new. After careful consideration, chewing the total landscape in her mind, she decided to walk back in the direction of the hill, from there she hoped to find her bearings and return to the cave's other entrance where Theodule and the rest would be waiting for her. The sun had moved from overhead and was slightly to the west. She waded through clumps of Guinea grass, which appeared to be the primal vegetation. In some places it was taller than her and knotted over her head as she breezed through. Keeping the hill always in view as her compass, she was steered towards a footpath that was still in use, for the grass had retraced its steps to the sides. It led her around the peak whose summit resembled an incisor, from where she could see the river she had crossed that morning, but not the sea, for other hills were blocking her view from that angle.

She spied them before they spotted her. She saw the broad frame of Theodule with musket in hand peeping through the wattle and vines, shouting her name, his other four companions at his heels, peering over his shoulders. Madlienne crept up slowly on them, treading lightly on the dried twigs, fearing they'd snap to betray her presence. She was obliquely above them when she shouted:

"Aye Theodule! Argos! Jean! Ti Frère! Constantin!" Calling them all by name in a single breath. She grinned as the shock of surprise registered simultaneously on all their faces. She opened her arms, seemingly to embrace the clouds, sliding down the steep slope to join them. The significance of a cave with two entrances eluded and consciously puzzled her. It stuck to the back of her mind. In time she would understand.

'Who carved this tunnel through the hill? What purpose did it serve? Was it the *Gens Libre*, or some ancient chamber of worship built by another race from a distant past?' Madlienne's mind slowly rehearsed the questions battling with the mystery. She would draw her own conclusions. One day she would come to know every escape tunnel in the hills, every safe house in the town and villages. This was the first cave she had discovered, instinctively she felt there would be many more. In her quest for vengeance, she knew they would be used effectively when required . . . She would see to it.

CHAPTER TWO

The old woman sat in her rocker, feeling the pale light of the afternoon sun on her skin. No matter the time of day she felt cold. Threading through her nest of memories with the ease of an embroiderer weaving delicate patterns on calico, her brain labouring through the labyrinth of consciousness and sleep, through the lenses in her mind's eye she saw the sky ablaze; a crimson shade of hell. The ground trembles under her feet as the recurring sound of big guns pound her ears; the grass stiffening with fright. Adrenalin flows through her veins. Her eyes alight with sparks from a thousand fires. The stifling smell from burning powder clogs her nostrils. She longs to breathe. The air is thick with the stench of cordite. She hears the bugler's call arching above the dying arc of flares. Redcoats march towards her, their bayonets fixed thirsting for blood. Their drummers, in unison, taunt her with their kettling beat. Her nerves are on edge. Suspense is driving her mad. She waits, holding her breath until the frenzy of kettledrums mutate to heartbeats hammering against their chests; closer, closer, closer, until the earth screams hearing this sound. She bobs over the tufts of grass, weaving from a crouched position with the sudden fury of the wind, screaming at the top of her voice, "*Attaque! Attaque!*" The enemy had marched straight into her trap . . . The night was alive with hundreds of swirling machetes and pike-bearing demons. To every shadow a lance, a spear with a broken body twitching at the end where the point, once sharp and gleaming, sliced the air. The buglers and standard bearers were the first to fall; then the front lines began whittling away like golden apple leaves in a pale November sun. Their numbers were thinning, but they kept on coming, in perfect square formation, the living stumbling across the dead, using their bodies as a shield to prop the crutch of Empire. When it was over her clothes was crimson with their blood . . .

She looked down at her skirt, holding it up to the light by its outer seams. It was only a vision. It was not reality but a recurring dream that visited her on afternoons when her mind failed to submit to loneliness or despair. The mango that she longed to pick was still hanging from its perch, high up in the tree. It had survived the wind. There were other evenings, less sombre, when only tender moments from her past dropped by, moments when her heart opened its pages to love. She remembered Theodule—tall and strong. She could have loved him had it been a different time, but hate like an ingrown toenail had pinched a sore nerve in her mind, where only vengeance lived. The rule of the day, wanton murder, pillage and destruction had not helped, besides, there was the alchemy of her own body, she never clearly understood, not during her youth. She could not understand the natural urges that surged through her, making her breast swell at various changes of the moon, twisting her bowels into a knot until she bled. Although these urges dissipated as swiftly as they came, there was something in lying on her back for a man she found repulsive, degrading almost, to the point where she felt a loss of power. Her femininity was her strength. It may have been the strange look in their eyes, she had seen at the moment of death, after she had dealt that final blow, after she withdrew her bayonet from their bowels; that look of fear mixed with surprise, unmasking a fragility that surfaced only at the point of death. It was that weakness, she perceived, which made her strong. She admired their boldness, their bravery and cunning. They were not afraid to advance their cause under the cloak of ingenious disguises. One sweep of her eyes at the curve in their crutch was enough to reduce their dashing flamboyancy to a mere stutter. The thought of a man withdrawing his phallus from her, tired, limp and useless, his body lacerated with beads of sweat, induced fits of laughter. Her heart thumped. Her mind skipped to Louise. With her it was different. Her earthy smell, like *vétiver* root oozing through every pore in her body had sent wild dreams racing through her head. She had touched her once while she was asleep. Her hand straying to rest on her velvet mound, lost in the uncombed confusion of her short curls, lingering there until Louise turned suddenly perhaps distracted by a dream. It was a strange compulsion that drove her to do this but her whole body sang with new unnerving sensations, her head spun, like the day she discovered the sea.

In war, feelings turn like a door on its hinge. In peacetime, she would have grown up to cook and bear children for a man of her father's choice.

It could have been Theodule. He was her father's favourite. In the raids on the storerooms, on the estates, Desolee had begun grooming him for the post—he called for him from the ranks to be at his side when he entered the great houses. Madlienne had observed this, but never questioned her father. His tribal instinct pure and primitive, was the only creed he knew, a world where men grew up to be hunters and progenitors of their race, where women served as vessels for their passion, ground the maize and bore their children. During her own sorties into the wilderness to hunt, she had exercised her own brand of authority, honing her senses into a fine tipped blade to pilot the group with a fair degree of prudence and caution. She had learned to earn their respect by example. Never shying from the risks that lay before them, alone in the wilderness, helping with the burden of spoils they had pillaged miles away from camp. Her gender was never an excuse. It was the prop that made her all the more defiant, impervious to adversity and unyielding in the face of defeat.

From the time she began observing signs in her body when the moon changed, feeling her stomach churn every time Theodule looked at the knobs blossoming on her chest into the full pride of womanhood: his eyes piercing through her bosom soured like lime in her mouth, she knew she was different. This feeling which was often accompanied by nausea and a churning in her stomach, felt unnatural. They had hunted the iguana together side by side and weathered through the perils of the wilderness together, particularly hunger and fatigue. Theodule was the first to observe what she lacked in facial appearances, nature had more than compensated in the rest of her body. From childhood they had bathed in the river together, unashamed of each other's nakedness. That wistful innocence had clung to them like damp clothes and had remained with them well into their adolescent years, until one afternoon, late, after delivering the day's kill to Maitre Charle, when the two of them, alone, went down to the river. While he was scrubbing the grime from her back with *savonnette* leaves, as they had always done for each other and she had done for him moments before, she felt a strange animal like an eel squirming between her thighs. She knew what it was and its warm head caused her body to tremble. His hands, dripping green, from the leaves, came around and found her nipples . . . She could have loved him, she knew, but something snapped inside her. The feeling was draining her strength. Her head felt like a feather. He was about to possess her will. Without it she was powerless. She could not allow it to happen . . .

The wind continued to blow unabated, slamming the hurricane shutters against their frames, cooling the house at the end of the hot day. Madlienne loved the wind. It filled her with vigour. It refreshed her lungs as she drew it in with long deep breaths. She was a child of the wilderness, where the wind was a ruffled balm that soothed her nerves. She always loathed the rain. It brought its sharp needles arousing the rheumatism in her knees, reminding her of old age. Her mind continued to flick through its pages, not in chronological order, but with a precision that was the gift of longevity. She remembered the long trek through the Quillese Valley, across the Blanchard ridge to Des Mailly estate where she met Citoyen Goyrand, who was at the time recruiting his "Army in the Woods." Though she did not know it then with her mind still clouded with grief, the meeting would prove to be the first step in her long and bloody battle for the liberation of mind and body, fought against enemies both real and perceived.

It was late afternoon when they arrived at the burnt out ruins of a *maison blanche* on an abandoned estate. The cane no longer grew in orderly rows, having returned to its original uncouth state, wild like Guinea grass, writhing in the wind. The owners had abandoned the place and the slaves that once nursed the long stalks in expectation of a harvest, may have fled to freedom after torching the great house. The walls that were once the foundation stones were standing like solitary sentinels against the weather, without the staves that once held the roof in place about the height of a man, too short to prop the sky. Its wooden structure, except for a few stubborn posts that still kept vigil over the lot, had disappeared. Soot marks ingrained in the masonry spoke of its fate. They climbed the stairs that once led into its grand hall, surveying the ruins for a safe haven to outlast the night, oblivious to eyes beaming from the lengthening shadows of the evening that was racing across the landscape, faster than the black storm clouds floating in from the sea. Silence, a close companion, all day was growing unbearable. The unnerving stench of danger oozed from the charred walls encircling them, like guards waiting the command to pounce. They felt the weight of eyes; they knew they were being watched. Madlienne instinctively fingered the trigger on the musket slung over her shoulder. Theodule tapped the handle of his knife reassuring himself. Argos, Ti Frère, Jean and Constantin grouped together. The soft clammy mound around the crab holes in the ground melted between their toes, cold like a dog's nose, increasing the intensity of their discomfiture. It would be risky to rest there. It was safer under the trees.

They climbed the stone battlements, with day-light a bare whisper, hinting at footholds in what was left of the masonry, still solid like the walls of a fort. They reached the landing which skirted the building; it was once the floor of its covered verandah They descended another flight of steps, on the opposite side, to the south, without looking back. Their eyes were focused on a copse of logwood trees, forming a hedge between the open ground and the taller trees behind. They felt they would be safer there. They did not reach very far into the underbrush, perhaps distracted from having to avoid the logwood's thorns, which though minute, pierced the skin with the ferocity of a wild boar's wild teeth, when they were surrounded by a band of ruffians, who appeared to materialize from below the ground. Their ravenous unkempt features gave them a strange sub-human appearance, like a pack of wild animals that had never seen a human soul before and would not be opposed to having Madlienne and her merry band for supper. Each had a loaded musket aimed at the group. Madlienne knew she was outnumbered and outgunned. Not a word was exchanged. Surprise had drained the final ounce of fighting energy from Madlienne's body; besides, it would have been a senseless battle. It was over before it began. Madlienne laid down the solitary musket they had shared between them and followed instructions fanned from the barrel of the guns pointed at them. They assumed that Theodule was the leader and forced him to walk ahead of the group with his hands clasped cupping the back of his head. Madlienne and the others were allowed to walk in single file behind him with their hands at their sides. To them the others were not a threat. Theodule's huge frame and muscular torso conjured in their minds the epitome of the warrior in the fabled tradition of their forefathers.

They trudged up hill for a further two miles, until they reached a plateau with a large savannah. The first thing that caught Madlienne's eye in the faint light, was the huge red, white and blue flag fluttering from a bamboo pole over one of the tents. They had been taken to a large camp, where they saw several other men similar to their captors milling about in various stages of undress. The entire perimeter of the camp was protected by an outer canal that encircled it with fortifications at various points along its circumference. To enter the camp they crossed a plank hewn from the trunk of *bois d' almond*, a local hardwood, highly prized by the French planters for cabinet work and varnished panels for the interiors of their great houses. Madlienne knew all the important woods in the forest by their grain. Her father, in peaceful years, had been a sawyer and had hewn the timber to fortify his own camp almost single-handed. He had taught her well. She had also observed that her captors, despite their rough appearances, had not ill-treated them. They had made no attack on her person, being a woman alone, surrounded by men. Except for the occasional prod to Theodule's rib prompted more from fear rather than cruelty and the need to establish authority, they had scarcely touched anyone. 'This is a strange bunch.' Madlienne thought, 'could this be the Army in the Woods?'

A small band of curious observers had surrounded them as they entered the camp, following them to a large makeshift table in the field, where a white man sat, studying a large ordinance map unfolded across a table. Neither Madlienne nor the rest of her group fully understood what was happening, but they were not intimidated by his presence, particularly after he had looked up at them and smiled. He was undoubtedly the chief of this ragged band, judging by the manner in which those nearest to him behaved. Madlienne saw a benign air of reverence like a phlegm envelope their eyes as they approached him, with their bodies crouched in caricatures of subservience. One of her captors had broken away from the band and ran up to him at the table, ahead, busy filing a verbal report. He was very excited and gesticulated using every muscle in his body, his hands flying in all directions over his head. The man appeared to listen attentively to the speaker and waited until he was finished before beckoning the rest of the group to come forward. Madlienne, growing impatient, eager to know her fate, broke ranks and strode ahead of the band. She was anxious to speak.

"I want to know why you bring us here and who are you?"

"What are you doing poking your nose so deep in the forest?" The white man asked. His tone was gentle, almost fatherly, exuding an air of concern. Somebody inside told her, go gentle, he could be trusted.

"I am hunting the men who killed my father, and theirs," she replied, pointing to her comrades who were standing behind her. They had broken from their captors and followed her forward. The men around the table laughed. Citoyen Goyrand remained unperturbed.

"Vengeance makes good soldiers," he said, without the sign of a crease coursing his face. Madlienne glanced across the table at the other faces. They belonged to men of every conceivable shade and colour, a motley crew of disciples, well nourished, by the flush in their cheeks, although their bodies were lean and supple, without any trace of fat. She could find nothing in their looks to betray a quirk in character, except their eyes, piercing through her clothes like balls of lead, immune to any form of tenderness or feeling.

"I am Citoyen Goyrand. I am here to build an army in the forest to fight for the liberation of your people."

A light suddenly flared in the faces around him. The words "army" and "liberation" provided the match. Madlienne felt the breath of Theodule, Argos, Jean, Ti Frère, and Constantin, collectively warm the back of her neck. They had drawn closer behind her. Her mind was bent on her mission, to find the murderers of her tribe. In this quest she needed allies; she may have stumbled on them . . .

This fight for freedom is something that would take them a long time to understand. They had been free all their lives. Madlienne had heard of slavery in snippets from her father, but had never experienced it. Theirs was a mission of vengeance, which Madlienne was prepared to pursue alone, if she was unable to find allies for her cause, for in her mind her cause was just. Time would not be an impediment.

"Against who you will fight?" she asked, betraying her naivety on the subject, but more, to reassure herself that theirs was a common enemy. Her question encouraged further laughter from the group around the table. Citoyen Goyrand raised his hand. His gesture stifled their chuckles.

"We fight the men who killed your father, the murderers who slaughtered your people." He was serious. A genuine swell of anger shook through his body, which was immediately transplanted on the features of the men around him.

"We fight for the same side." The man continued reassuringly as if he had already heard their story from the lips of someone else.

"We will fight with you," Madlienne did not hesitate to say. Intuitively the words came to her mouth: "These are my people. All we have left. We will face the devil himself if you let us."

In the silence of that moment Madlienne felt a calm relief sweep across her mind as she waited for the next question. Citoyen Goyrand surveyed the six of them, fixing on the tall muscular figure of Theodule.

"Who is your leader?" he asked, almost anticipating the answer to come from Theodule whose voice he was yet to hear.

"I am!" Madlienne shouted proudly. Citoyen Goyrand was slightly startled. He was never wrong about such things. Guerilla warfare had sharpened his senses and he judged men by their girth and the mark of knowledge that lurked in their eyes. His eyes skimmed over the six faces again, searching for something he may have missed. His eyes turned to Madlienne, sweeping her from head to feet.

"You are a woman!" He said, almost in disbelief.

"I see you have women in your camp," Madlienne replied. She had seen them gazing at a distance when she entered the camp.

"They are not soldiers," he said; "they are following their men."

"I can shoot straight; I hunt," Madlienne said.

"Have you ever killed a man?" Citoyen Goyrand asked.

"Give me the men who kill my father and I'll show you," Madlienne replied without blinking.

"Give her back her weapon!" He ordered. One of the scruffy guards, who had long ceased to level his musket at her, tossed the other weapon he had carelessly slung across his shoulder moments before and she caught it effortlessly, with both hands. She checked the flintlock and nodded with approval.

"You say you can shoot straight. I will test you." Citoyen Goyrand smiled as he looked up at the late evening sky. The sun had already disappeared behind the hills to the west, but its afterglow reddening in a clear patch in the heavens had been fighting a losing battle with the fast approaching storm from the east. There was sufficient light, however, to see a chicken hawk silhouetted against an orange sky, gyring over the tents, its keen eyes patrolling the perimeter for stray chicks even at that late hour. It was riding the breeze with the full span of its wings extended like a sail.

"If you are as good as you say, bring it down!" Madlienne took a lead ball from her bosom, the scruffy guard who had returned her musket, handed her his powder horn. She poured some powder into the breach, stoked, nimbly loading the musket. She looked up at the chicken hawk. It had soared higher in the sky, swiftly floating out of range, perhaps sensing danger. She aimed and pressed her finger lightly against the trigger without bothering to hold her breath. The bird folded its right wing under its breast and swayed through the air like a drunk. The silence around Madlienne was deafening. When it fell to the ground, everyone who had witnessed the event, including her captors, some of whom had faded to a discreet distance behind her, applauded. Citoyen Goyrand had followed the bird through the sky; he gripped his chin in amazement seeing the flapping bundle of feathers hit the ground less than a hundred feet from where he stood. The legend of Jeanne d'Arc, drummed in his head both at home and at school came sharply back to his memory with a ring of truth.

'Could this be a reincarnation?' He asked himself, softly, without moving his lips.

Madlienne and her group that night dined on roast pig and wild fowl around a raging bonfire, in the company of Citoyen Goyrand and several of the senior combatants in the camp. In the morning all six of them were issued with new muskets, fifty rounds of lead and an ample supply of powder.

"This is no ordinary fight," Citoyen Goyrand had told them at dinner.

"This is not about vengeance or revenge. Vengeance poisons the mind. It dulls your thoughts." He spoke like her father, crisp, no mincing words or parables. She felt in the end she had known him all her life.

"This fight concerns the rights of man," he said. "Your rights and mine too, never mind the colour of my skin."

Madlienne pondered on his words all night as she lay awake under the stars nursing her grief still fresh as the dew on her mind. She felt his words, their meaning deep inside, but did not understand. A new world was opening its doors and there was so much to learn. The pain of her loss weighed heavily on her chest. She could not blot it out. It made her angry. Her only solace being those thoughts of revenge that were alive like visions when alone. Nothing would make her happier than to drive a bayonet to the hilt into those vigilantes who had murdered her father without allowing them time to defend themselves. Her joy would come in hearing them squeal like wild boars after she had dealt the fatal blow with her knife, after her bullet had slowed their flight through the thick undergrowth in the forest. To hear them groan while the gurgle of life seeped through their nostrils, this would bring her peace. Vengeance was her only resolve. She knew she would never be in total agreement with Citoyen Goyrand on this issue. She needed vengeance to poison the mind until it became the incentive to kill.

CHAPTER THREE

Madlienne was on her feet before the rest of the camp. She followed the narrow footpath to the river and walked along the smooth stones until she came to a secluded spot where she took off her clothes and jumped into the water. It was cold but soothing. It assuaged the pain throbbing in her head, the aftermath of fatigue with little or no sleep. She heard the bugler sound the reveille, although she did not know what it was; she surmised it was some sort of signal. She dressed hurriedly and rushed back to the camp, feeling the early morning breeze drizzling lightly against her skin. Dawn had already filled the sky with its light, a faint shade of lilac, which paled even the darkest complexion, its colour clinging to things. The slow moving clouds assumed its hue. The male members had mustered in the centre court where she had met Citoyen Goyrand, sleep reddening their eyes. She spotted Theodule's tall frame towering above the others in the front row, with Constantin at his side.

Ti Frère, Argos and Jean were in the second row. She walked up casually and took her place next to Constantin. Citoyen Goyrand was about to address the men, he did not seem pleased having to wait for her to find her place in the ranks. It was a daily ritual and she would soon learn its significance. No one laughed.

"I will not ask you where you've been," Citoyen Goyrand said sternly; "I can surmise from the looks of your hair. Just remember, neither time nor I have time to waste waiting."

With these few words she was quickly forgotten as he turned to the rest of the contingent haranguing them on their state of preparedness. This meant little to Madlienne although she pretended to listen attentively, distracted by the large red, white and blue flag flapping on its bamboo pole. In the course of her first day, Madlienne discovered that there were fourteen other women besides her in the camp. They did not bear arms. They had followed their men, to cook and wash for them. To provide a moment's pleasure between the fighting and foraging, spontaneously like the weather and proved more formidable than the enemy in their devices.

The weather had reduced their advances to a crawl as they sought shelter from the rain's bite. The surge of water pouring down the hillsides had transformed their secret tracks into riverbeds. The men remained huddled with their women under protection of their tents. Madlienne experienced a strange sensation, pity, for the women in camp. To her they were no more than beasts of burden, at the pleasure of their men. It was a passive existence, definately not her lot, one she could not understand, or fulfill. She was determined to be a fighting woman. Her body would cease to function rather than submit to servitude. It had become for her a solemn duty to attend the camp of instructions. Learn the drills; the art of unarmed combat; weaponry; signaling; intrigue; above all else, the discipline of the game called war. In those early days it was routine to be jeered by comrades. Those same men who preached equality and brotherhood like it was a cure for the malaria that often attacked their ranks thought she would fare better as a wife and they all harboured dreams of her in their bed. They had conveniently forgotten the little episode on her first evening in camp. Those who remembered equated it to luck. Her deft determination, indomitable will, and keen brain mobilized into a unit of strength, soon placed her ahead of her class. Slowly, with acts that displayed subtly, superhuman courage, she won the respect of her peers. In demonstrations, her instructors called on her to illustrate examples that required peak fitness, secretly hoping she would wear under strain, flaking to fragments in their arms, moistening their shoulders with her tears. But their schemes only helped to strengthen her resolve, converting the last dregs of frailty, in her, into a steam-driven fighting machine. After three grueling months she learnt to execute the most taxing manoeuvres with the precision of a seasoned campaigner without a grunt of pain, becoming the envy of those who jeered, now seeking to emulate her prowess with an honour in their eyes that resembled adulation.

It was during this period in her life she met Louise . . . "Louise, Louise!" The name creased like a crumpled cotton sheet in a smile across her lips, strumming her heartstrings with a melody that had survived through the years. It sang its sad tune inside her; an unrequited dream with its meaning never to be revealed, nor fully understood. Through memory's telescope, she glimpsed Louise traipsing down the narrow footpath to the river with her gourd in hand and a bundle of dirty clothes balanced on her head, swaying as she trod barefooted over the pebbles. Instinctively she had followed those hips, lithesome like bamboo caught in the wind. Her lips moved, but Madlienne was too far away to hear the song. Only that her brown skin laughing in the morning sun brought back childhood memories of goat pelts that were warm, particularly on cold nights. Until that moment, they had never met. Louise was new in camp. She had barely noticed her squatting on a log outside one of the tents in the faint glow of twilight the evening before, darning a shirt. She was young and in many ways appeared different to the other women in the camp. Her body was plump, not drained and haggard from frequent child bearing like the others; her figure bore the oval shape of women she had glimpsed in paintings in some drawing rooms of the great houses her father had sacked . . . A sharp piercing scream envelops her mind. It comes from the river. She runs towards the sound, her heart pounds.

Through the thicket, she sees Louise lying on her back on the ground, her skirt pulled over her chest covering her face. A recruit, whom Madlienne recognizes instantly as one of her colleagues from the class of instruction has already discarded his pants and is climbing on top of her. Louise is thrashing out with her hands, in a losing battle to protect her innocence. He is hell bent on his mission; he does not observe another presence. Madlienne charges forward like a wild boar ramming her head into his chest, knocking him off his feet, into the water. She draws a hunting knife from her waist, the one she had found months before in the cave, now cleaned and sharpened into a killing instrument, she was now trained to use effectively. She stands crouched over the prostrate form of Louise, her body itching for a fight. The recruit, dazed by the element of surprise, offers no resistance. He lifts his hands high above his head to signal surrender, picks up his pants and runs into the bushes like a whipped mongrel, cowering with fright. Madlienne fills the gourd, then pours some water over Louise's head. She untangles the skirt wrapped around her neck and covers her nakedness, ironing the creases in the calico with her hands. Louise opens her eyes; she is still bewildered from shock. Madlienne gives her a drink of clear water holding the gourd to her lips.

"You are new in camp," Madlienne said. "You should not come down to the river alone."

"I come to stay with my father. My mother die last week," Louise replied, a slight tremor in her voice.

"You lucky. I have no mother, no father," Madlienne said. "No brother or sister either. Maybe, you can be my little sister?" They laughed, Louise slowly regaining her composure. Almost to the instant, a deep affection towards each other was born, forged by chance, in loneliness and the memory of deep personal loss . . .

Madlienne stayed by the river, whetting the blade of her hunting knife on a smooth piece of sandstone to while away the time, until Louise had finished her washing. She helped her haul the wet clothes back to camp to dry on the frail lines of plaited lianas she had hastily strung up outside her father's tent. It was a civilized and domesticated beginning for the two women, who from that day would become inseparable. An evening seldom passed unless they were seen together. By innuendoes and acts of veiled persuasion—art forms at which Madlienne was a past master, some she had successfully practiced on the boys when she wanted them to do her bidding, she inveigled Louise to repent her daily household chores and enlist as a soldier, much to the chagrin of her father who did not approve, as like most men, he felt it was not in a woman's character to bear anything other than children. Madlienne supervised her training and defended her honour against the jibes of her male companions whenever they out-stepped her self-imposed bounds of tolerance. Their minds rooted in the tradition of their forefathers could not accept a woman entering this manly reserve and capable of serving with the same honour and distinction as they.

"God help us when she hear them big guns and she think is thunder." Or, "Wait till cockroach climb up her thigh," they'd say. Nothing was new. They were the same taunts levelled at Madlienne, which only pricked her earlobes but never reached her mind.

"It's a male world," she'd say to Louise, to comfort her. "They don't want us to share in it—but we'll show them."

Madlienne became big sister, although there was little difference between them in age. Perhaps it was the hard carapace, like a tortoise, covering her external appearance that made her seem older, or the brazen will etched into the creases on her face when she frowned. No one will ever know. These memories were painful. The sores refused to heal. They aired and festered whenever she remembered the brutal massacre of her people in the daylight's glare: They stung the corners of her eyes and swamped her brain like a deluge, until a tender corner in her heart released its tears. She could not openly admit. She and Louise were opposites. The femininity in Louise was unmistakable, even when she bore arms and charged the enemy alongside the men. The provocative twirl in her hips, the sensual pout on her lips, her hair in curls under her bonnet rouge, her eyes perpetually smiling as though her thoughts were lost in another world where pain and suffering had succumbed to the charms of joy. It reflected her contented soul in a world she could never be part. She was a victim of circumstance who found recreation, communing with her spirit. Madlienne, although blest with the lithesome figure of a heron, sleek and rounded in the right parts that bore the mark of many sons, exuded a masculine charm. It was her line of defense against the men who surrounded her daily, her tortoise shell. It insulated her from their natural urges and helped to protect Louise when that ageless fever transformed them into somnambulists in the dead of the night and their bodies ached for a warm pair of thighs to seed their sorrows.

Drums . . . they were pounding her head, again. They had grown faint, but never stopped. Now they returned with intensity, like hurricanes. The kettledrums of the Northumberland fusiliers, their tone refined, foreign to her ears, rivaled note for note the harsh incessant beats of the *tambour*, the ram's hide, drawn tight against the mouth of a hogshead cut in half, the only drums she knew before confronting the enemy. All night long they rolled, mingling with the delirium that swelled her head, while cannons raged. Those kettling beats, persistent, with the urgency of gentlemen calling; hands groping her breasts under fire, battling those other wild beats which kept pace with her heart, struggling to unnerve the anchors of her soul that rooted her in the earth and would not yield an inch of ground. Impounding her within a fortress, whose walls encircled her being, driving her to the brink of madness. It was not her kind of battle. She preferred the open field where she could face the enemy, eyeball to eyeball, gun to gun. It offered a choice—to run or stay. But this was war. It followed you even in your sleep. She had been trained to defend a cause called freedom which she did not understand completely, but liked the sound of it—with the one life that was no longer her own, but belonged to a whole nation, without a flag. No symbols, not even an anthem, except for the Ca Ira, which she knew only the tune. Those who had been disenfranchised because of the pigment of their skin had no choice but to ape the antics of the revolutionaries whose paths of glory swayed along parallel tracks, but never merged. She had learnt to stoke the howitzer blindfolded with her musket slung over her shoulder ready to greet the red tunics as they popped up like flares over the ramparts. Darkness, the colour of her skin, was a friend. She saw with her ears and heard with her nostrils. The pounding of cannons shook the ground under her feet severing the sharp divisions of day from night. The air coddled with sulphur, thick as rain clouds, her eyes burned red answering shell with shell. Through the singed light that peeped on her with the suddenness of dawn, she saw the wall of dead towering like a mountain above her. They outnumbered the living. The cannons kept on pounding until their noise became a dry hacked cough, spluttering, then fading to whispers. There were no shells left; her powder horn dry; no musket balls left in her bosom; no sleep. It was time for surrender. She stood to attention with her band while the British general, strutting like a crayfish on the bottom of a river basin, hoisted his colours on the same pole where the tricolour, a tattered rag, had not deserted its post. There were no victors, no vanquished. Those faces swollen with the pall of death had won the moment. Redcoat and bareback warrior entangled in a mass of human debris that only time would extricate. They shouldered their arms and filed out of the fort, four abreast, the unwilling survivors. They had been accorded the honours of war as a gallant foe whose exploits would be remembered in history as the ragged band that twisted the lion's tail and bloodied his nose. Madlienne marched at the head of her platoon; too dizzy from the shock of defeat to look back on the carnage she left behind . . .

These indifferent moments scratched on tattered sheets of parchment was all that was left on her mind. It intoxicated the childless serenity of old age when ague rattled her bones with the afternoon's chill. Her hands encircled a teacup of leaves, thumbing its warmth to evade the numbness in her fingertips. She sips. A youthful vigour warms her spine. With it enters Louise. She had spent a lifetime remembering, never wanting to forget. She had been her shadow through all the early battles, her body, both shield and foil against the odds that entered that sacred space where Louise lived and breathed, until she acquired the stomach to kill with the same unscrupulous ease as Madlienne, without whimpering from pangs of remorse. It was a friendship which engendered the subconscious urge of motherhood, built on their loneliness and grief, which as women they suffered in silence among their peers. The purity of this friendship harboured no shame.

A jealous fit fired through her body when Theodule suddenly turned his affections from her to Louise. It brought out a hostility in her that was bestial and savage as lust; it could not be quelled even after jostling with the enemy. She hated the giggles that Theodule drew from Louise at the mere sight of him. She could have killed them both when those fits knotted her bowels and griped like menstrual cramp. Had it not been for the cause and the vengeance she had sworn to reap in the sacred name of her father, she would have strangled them barehanded. Hatred, bottled inside her, unleashed its fury on the enemy. She raged and bellowed across the battlefields oblivious of caution, dispensing death with every forward stride. Jealousy had driven her mad. It flared on the first night of every full moon with vivid realism, echoing the night she accidentally stumbled on them together. She had felt the slight rustle of the flannel blanket against her feet when Louise woke, a bare hint, betrayed by a whisper of cold air. There was a sinister tone in the movement. She felt it in her bones but elected to remain still, feigning sleep. Then her mind chose to dismiss it as call of nature — the normal kind. She followed Louise's shadow until it disappeared between the tents, where the men slept, waiting for it to materialize on her return to the warm spot beside her, but when she saw the tall figure of Theodule emerge from his tent, her mind clicked. She heard him whisper, inaudibly, it was too dark to read his lips. Then Louise reappeared, Theodule took her by the hand and they strolled away from the tent together, in the direction of the bushes. Full moon was piercing through the thicket. The shadow of the trees concealed their shape as they strolled under the canopy of leaves, ignoring the beams of light spurting through the branches.

Madlienne shot up spurred by a compulsion outside herself which came spontaneously with the wind. Barefooted, with the inborn stealth of a cat, her feet immune to blisters, she inched forward into the shadows, towards the spot where the couple had vanished and felt the dirt track under her feet, its grit gathering between her toes. She had only travelled a short distance, when she heard a sigh. It was Louise. She knew. It was not long before she spotted the clear outlines of their silhouette. Moonlight was streaming through the branches and the darkness at close range, was not dark enough to hide them, not through her eyes. She saw the tall figure of Theodule, his hands embracing the body she knew was Louise; his mouth on her mouth as they slid to the ground in unison. A guilty feeling came over her. It questioned her rage. She had never experienced this feeling before, eavesdropping on their moment of intimacy. She felt her own breasts. The nipples had become firm. A sudden restlessness had taken hold of her body, shaking in a frenzy. She wanted to scream, but no sound reached her throat. She felt short spasms of air rush through her lungs to be expelled as swiftly as they entered. She was so close she could have touched them. The air around her suddenly became clammy and humid. Her clothes stuck to her body, particularly between the inner folds of her thighs. The wind blew cold against her skin but did not refresh her. Mist, as she had known it, thick across the hills, crept across her mind forming a barrier to blot reality, as Louise began to murmur her music of joy.

"What do I want here?" She asked. Her mind refused to accept the moment's reality; the reason for her rage. Switching to the sound of kettle drums instead, the music of destruction; she braced herself to face the truth as if it were the foe. Her lips trembled—the bitter bile of betrayal splashed in her face. The dull spark of the firefly lit up her eyes. She hung her head, ashamed of her own feelings and slouched back to her blanket under the stars, folding it around her like a long lost lover, found, and cried. Her tears were not for Theodule, although in some remote corner of the mind her body craved for his hands and that part of him that once angered her in the river, when she felt it squirming between her thighs. It was for Louise and the loss of innocence that would alter forever those changeling feelings hidden under her skin, crudely surfacing at various intervals, particularly when she felt alone. Although they were unnatural, they controlled her will.

It was a loss as final as death that left its bilious remnants in her mouth long after the past had mellowed into history. Theodule had stolen the only thing sacred to her in this world. He had defiled it with hands that had once held her. These complexities would never be part of her understanding although their dosage paralyzed her limbs and brought its season of tears. She awoke with dawn, the events of the night lodged in memory's bank to be recalled when the future allowed. Louise was nuzzling against her on the grass. A smile of contentment framed her lips. She stroked her hair, got up and trudged towards the old brass bugle pegged to its post near the weapons rack in the centre of the field. She brushed the night's dust from its mouthpiece, raised it to her lips and sounded the reveille.

In war life is measured in teaspoons. A day in battle is equal to a hundred years. Time often outruns its clock. At Rabot, the testimony of battle was brittle shards of bone, wet and red, where the flesh still clung. Fear was an unwelcome ally, screaming like a sick child without its voice all night long, longing to be nursed. The fighting was fierce, the enemy pouring lead down their throats through the barrels of their muskets. Twice they were beaten back into the bushes and twice they regrouped and repulsed the attack. Losses were heavy on both sides. In the final onslaught Madlienne, aided by her contingent in a surge of superhuman effort, probably sensing that elusive dream called freedom slipping from their grasp drove the British back to the sea to the refuge of their ships. When the dead were sifted from the wounded, Theodule was among them. He had stopped a bullet with his chest, a tiny wound no larger than a thumbprint, marked a spot leveled with his heart. Death had come to him like sleep, unaccompanied by its agonizing companion, pain. A few spurts of blood marked the point of impact; Madlienne wiped it away with her skirt before shutting his eyes and prising the smile from his lips with her thumbs when she closed his mouth. Louise could not control the river that flowed freely down her cheeks, accumulating like sweat in tiny crystal beads on Madlienne's shoulders. There was no one else she could turn to for solace, least of all her father. His advice would be, "Get another good man fast and forget the dead." These were heartless times. Grief was an emotion misunderstood and often considered a form of madness.

They made a rough hammock from the remnants of the Tricolour they had taken with them into battle, stained with the blood of both friend and foe, they slung it through a stout bamboo pole, freshly cut from a nearby thicket. The men took turns carrying the body across the ridge back to their camp, with Constantin refusing to yield his place for the entire six mile journey, racing through bush and thorns, while the pole slid from shoulder to shoulder behind him. Madlienne remained calm throughout. She had seen too many deaths to become distraught. Besides, she knew she was the crutch on which Jean, Argos, and Ti Frère would lean when they saw Theodule's body. They had remained in camp, on Madlienne's orders—perhaps it was premonition. She never understood why she had not picked them to accompany her on this sortie after receiving the call from La Croix, the great brigand chief, saying that the British had landed in full force off La Convention and had established a beach-head. Years later she would sit for many days in the solitude of her self—imposed seclusion, pondering on this decision. An arm of hers had been severed. Its phantom would twitch as long as memory survived.

They buried Theodule at the base of the flagpole where the Tricolour had flapped in the breeze and Madlienne first saw it in the heart of Citoyen Goyrand's camp. A bugler blew the last post, skipping the notes to wipe his tears. For Louise, nothing would comfort her other than Theodule's presence, alive, as she would always remember him. He was her first and only love. In his arms she had become a woman, a part of his ribs. Part of her was now rotting in the earth, like a seed lost in an intractable sleep, failing to respond to the resuscitating charms of air, warmth and moisture. She withdrew from the world, to her other heaven, the one that leaked through her smiles in the heat of a battle deep within herself, there Theodule still lived and breathed, only now she could not touch him. She could no longer feel the warmth in his arms, or his hot breath pouring down the nape of her neck. The joyful soul shattered like a porcelain vase, into a million tiny shards, irreparable, losing forever the smile and the gurgle of laughter that once frothed around her lips liked the river, when it surged.

CHAPTER FOUR

Fighting patterns changed. Engaging the enemy in open combat had proven costly. It had decimated their ranks. Many a seasoned veteran was among the dead. They could not match—not even with their courage—the accuracy of musket fire from the guns of those venerable campaigners who lived and breathed the ancient game called war, since the days of Crecy and Agincourt. Those whose tenacity had been exemplary, whose resolve was only to be remembered in the annals of history, remained indefatigable: No sooner a line fell under a hail of bullets, another would rise like weeds to take its place continuing to inflict with deadly authority, severe losses among the ranks of the Army in the Woods. They were as lethal with the musket as their forefathers with the longbow. Secretly, Madlienne admired their bravery and fighting skills, their morbid dance to the kettledrums, actions tuned to every beat. Her side was no match for that rigid discipline born at Hastings, fostered at Crecy and Agincourt and finally executed at Blenheim. The Republicans had taught them well, but that could not offset the inevitable. They sensed defeat. To win they would have to embrace the element of surprise and make it an ally. Inhabit the mountainous terrain which straddled the island like a back bone, with its impenetrable rainforest and transform them into battlegrounds.

They broke into small bands under the cloak of night, no more than twelve, moving with the speed of the light through the undergrowth; through enemy lines, imitating the cunning of the mongoose to carve a trail of insalubrious slaughter in their wake. La Croix himself disclosed the plan at Caille Parque during the council held with all his chiefs. Madlienne represented her group. The message was drummed weeks in advance, to every corner of the land. She traveled alone on foot arriving at Caille Parque after a journey lasting two days and two nights, which included getting lost on countless occasions in the unmarked jungle, in parts where no living thing had ever crossed. Citoyen Goyrand had done his work. The Army in the Woods had been honed into a fighting unit with its several branches stretching from coast to coast in frequent contact with each other through the drums. Their sound was the compass, which steered her safely through the undergrowth until she heard the echo from other cutlasses hacking their way towards her.

"Goyrand can afford to gloat on his success," she thought. "This army is now a whole damn nation in the woods."

She felt proud. It had taken a little more than a year to build. He had returned to his commission in Guadeloupe marvelling at his accomplishments. His agent was Marin Padre, a businessman in Castries, continued to procure arms for the Army in the Woods. He also furnished them with bandages, medicine, and food. Through his own personal contingent of runners, he was in constant contact with all the camps and with his principals at the revolutionary council in Guadeloupe. He also had direct access to Victor Hughes, the undisputed chief of all chiefs, who paid the bills.

Madlienne returned to base, much wiser than when she had left. Her knowledge broadened through conversations with the other chiefs present. The events that were unfolding became clearer and her perspective of this war for freedom, narrowed to a single word—survival. The journey through the impenetrable forest, with additional scratches and scars all over her body, was rewarding. From then on, her interest would be the lives under her command, for only the survivors would reap the harvest when peacetime came. Maturity beyond her years had covered her shoulders with its cloak. Her natural leadership instincts and maternal thoughts merged. She would stay close to her own until it was over before venturing out on her mission; vengeance would wait, but would not mellow with age.

Madlienne had left camp at sunset on the third day after her return, with a small band of warriors. Their target was the Des Marinières estate in Praslin, where the drums had told her, the British General Sir John Moore had pitched camp for the night. This General had been a scourge to the army in the woods. He had duplicated their fighting habits and had taken the war to them deep in the bosom of their forest. His craft was stealth and had enlisted a band of Black Rangers, whose savagery was not learnt in the sacred colleges of war that nurtured the white regulars, but hinged on a promise of freedom, for they were not freemen. Moore had been successful. Entire camps were surrounded, surprised in their sleep, killed or taken prisoner. He had to be stopped before the wave of panic creeping through their ranks turned to hysteria. If anyone could match his guile, it was Madlienne. La Croix had hand-picked her for the job. The General was to be taken prisoner and used as hostage to secure the release of their men. Madlienne and her group circled the estate memorizing the position of every hut, but there was no sign of the soldiers. Intuitively, it smelt like a trap. Taking Argos and Constantin with her, they entered the smallest house after darkness—which came quickly and was as thick as treacle—had settled over the land to seek information. The rest of her party remained under the bush listening for the sharp click of a trigger or the snort from a horse, grown restless waiting. Inside Madlienne met a middle-aged couple. The woman was plucking grey hairs from the man's head while he reviewed her handiwork through a piece of mirror, which he held, with a trembling hand, between her and the oil lamp. They were not startled by the intrusion. There was no privacy in their lives.

"We are friends," Madlienne said, "we are looking for the soldiers!"

"They are not in here," the woman replied, "they gone. They stop to water their horses and they go before it get dark," the old man looked up at Madlienne and grinned.

"What road they take?" Madlienne asked.

"Everywhere," the woman replied. "Some go to Lombard; some leave for Troumassee; some I see going up Raillon." They had split into groups and were searching for camps. Madlienne knew that she would have to be cautious on the way back to her own camp. She would have to avoid the Chemin Royal like the plague and return via the long circuitous route through Mahaut, where the bush, their traditional ally, would provide cover.

Madlienne and her band returned to base in a drizzle of morning showers without sighting the enemy. Her hair wet, sweat and rain water, cold against her skin. She was curious rather than surprised to observe a small crowd gathered at the entrance to her tent. She jostled through intent on discovering the source that had stirred their curiosity. They yielded as she pressed forward with Argos and Constantin close behind. Jean and Ti Frère were there, straining to prevent the more adventurous ones from entering. Ti Frère hooked his arms around her shoulder;

"Don't go inside, *Sais*!" He said, pleading; "Don't go!"

From where she stood, her eyes had already swept over his shoulder. She saw Louise lying naked on the ground in a pool of blood. A rage, more brutal, more intense than the fit that consumed her when she saw Louise and Theodule together, swelled through her body, her muscles twitched like a horse whipped from a mild canter into a gallop. He could not hold her back. The ball had chewed the left side of her face leaving the other half intact, sufficient to recognize her. The light brown skin and soft curves lying face downward, the musket Madlienne had taught her to grease, held firmly in her left hand. Her brain matted with bits of skull and hair was plastered about the tent—on the blanket where she had slept; on the pole that held the tent in place; utensils; everywhere. In that one enduring second, that seemed longer than an hour, Madlienne surveyed the scene, squeezing a pair of tiny teardrops through the corners of her eyes, hoping secretly that no one saw. She wanted to be assured, without prompting that Louise had held the musket to her head and had pulled the trigger herself.

"Let me go!" she said softly, to Ti Frère, whispering in his ear as she entered the tent. It was a cruel end to a life in the full bloom; a life that had responded to the murmur of one voice only, Theodule's and wanted no other. Grief had dulled its teeth around the figure that once swayed in the wind, the light-brown complexion that once laughed with the sun. Theodule's death could never be recompensed in the arms of another. Her hatred for the world boiled inward until its steam blew off her head.

The sudden passing of Louise resurrected those passions in Madlienne that had slept inside her, until then. Those twisted thoughts of torture and revenge were coming back to her in dreams. She had never forgiven the men who had killed her father. She longed to know their names. The rage she had cleverly harnessed within was bristling its mane. The only comfort was to see her knife entering their stomachs. They deserved no more than animals. This would purge the restlessness and those unpleasant memories, which clogged her thoughts before she could grow to understand the meaning of all the new things she had learnt. Loneliness was an unwanted companion sauntering by her side. Fate had been unkind. She would have to sever herself from Argos, Jean, Ti Frère and Constantin, before they too became victims of life's conspiracy, whose plans it seemed was to denude her of everything she cherished. She was not sure what fate was, but she was certain that she needed to make a sudden turn in her life, if she hoped to save the rest of her tribe. The vengeance buried deep in her heart had been exhumed. Her father's death and the death of her people would be avenged. War had not healed the wound, only tempered its jabs of pain.

She smiled through the few loose teeth left dancing in her gums, mirroring the years saddened with regret. Pangs of guilt had eaten away at her flesh for many a night with unrequited dreams of a lost youth. The torment was at times unbearable. She had done what had to be done and was at peace with herself. However, there was one regret; she hoped that God would pardon her for it when her turn came although she would not repent. In her heart, she felt it was not a sin. It returned to haunt her every year in lent, when the immortelle's blood-red blossoms flared from the surrounding hills; when the itch of age resurrected pains from the wounds of her past. They returned as vivid as the daylight to haunt her. Names flowed from the pages of memory; some, mere acquaintances, those who had become her friends and even her enemies. They merged to become companions, along with Clarrisia whom she acquired after selling M. De Brette's old grey, and with whom she shared her secrets, knowing they were safe. Towering above them was the flame, the blood red immortelle, consuming the chambers of her heart. The one name above all others that made her blush—Louise. Age had not quelled that fire. It was the secret returning to haunt her with its visions of a face disfigured in death; a face plastered across the hills of mornings when she opened her windows to greet the dawn. Her gaze blinded by various shades of green, shaking off the blue of night. These shades mingled with crimson flashes splashed like blood when the sun's first rays bled with the immortelle in the wind, in lent. Her feelings seethed with rage seeing those annual blossoms on the eve of Easter, in a month of repentance and forgiveness. There was no one with the level of compassion to understand her needs, assuage her fears and make her whole again. No priest could expunge the memory of a love for which there was no substitute. Torment flared and waned like a malady in her bones for which there was no cure. It took root in her very soul.

The Brigands' War ended without truce, haphazardly as it begun. Ten years of fighting left its mark on the most seasoned warrior. Tension and fatigue devoured the mind. Survival was the only code the Army in the Woods absorbed. General Moore had taken the battle to their sanctuary, in the heart of their country. He had mastered their art of surprise and had infused it with his own ingenuity. They were falling like flies into his traps. Marin was arrested in Castries and their supply lines were cut. No ammunition, no food, no medicine. Moore, they nicknamed *Le Fleuve*, for he had wreaked havoc on their numbers to rival the malaria that thinned their ranks during the rainy season. The drums spoke. La Croix had been captured. Madlienne knew in time her number would call. Though their tracks had never crossed, she knew *Le Fleuve* was on her tail, for her group was the only surviving band in the South that were yet to come face to face with his Black Rangers. She summoned the four survivors from her father's clan. They had been loyal to her throughout.

"I must leave," she said, "I must go to Xenon."

"We don't understand," Argos said. The past for them was dead. They had found a new life in this camp.

"I remember clearly the words of Citoyen Goyrand—we are fighting for the rights of man," Jean said.

"What rights! What man!" Madlienne exclaimed. "My father was a man. He had rights—the right to live. I have been fighting for ten years and I have not avenged his death."

"We will come with you!" Constantin said.

"I lost my father too, and all my brothers," Ti Frère chipped in.

"No!" Madlienne replied, "There are some things I can best do alone."

"It is our fight," Constantin said, "all of us."

"I'll do what I have to do alone for all of us," Madlienne said firmly. "*Le Fleuve* is closing in on us. We have no powder left, only enough to hunt for food," she explained. "I will break camp. Every man for himself! To live we must separate. Please don't follow me. A group is easy for *Le Fleuve* to find. Alone we can melt in the woods."

She opened her arms and embraced them. Ti Frère cried. Madlienne mustered the remainder of the men and women. She had become their commandant after the veterans withdrew to form smaller groups in order to survive. She had held them together and had won their respect, a tribute to her exemplary courage under fire.

"I cannot stay here and watch you suffer," she said. "No medicine for your children; no bandages for your wounds and no ammunition to attack the enemy. I cannot ask you to surrender either. To live, we still have one chance, and that is every man for himself! We must separate. For me there is something I have to do. I must go and find the men who killed my father before they die from old age in their beds."

The Army in the Woods understood. Survivors from the days when they ridiculed her with their jibes, during her early months of training, now stood with heavy eyes as she milled though their ranks bidding farewell. They were hardened men with hearts stouter than their local timber. They moved hills, when she asked. She had become more than their companion in arms; she had become their valiant leader. They would never forget her. Their hearts weighed with sadness, as she embraced them one by one with a parting word for each individual. She knew them by their nick-names, even the ones they hated. They were bursting at their seams to withhold tears. They knew their fighting days were over. The cause was lost. Argos, Ti Frère, Jean and Constantin walked with her to the edge of the forest, for a final embrace. They watched until the hems of her skirt merged with the trees and the wind ceased blowing dust in her wake.

She followed the footsteps drawn on the hillsides by the Cibonaes centuries before her when they fled from the coastal plains in a vain attempt to avoid their traditional enemy, the Caribs. She had mapped them in her mind. After ten years she knew where each one led through the rainforest, along the steep ledges and perilous gorges—harsh slashes in the clayey loam, which nursed the mahogany, *bois d'amman, laurier cannelles* and *acajou*. Alone, in their shade, which protected her from the sun, she steered towards her destination. Birds chirped high above her head in their branches, soothing the sadness that walked with her thoughts. The occasional hiss of a fer-de-lance from the undergrowth reminded her of danger as she brushed past, but her mind was bent on one resolve, one that she had postponed, but had not forgotten. To her it was more than duty. It was her pact with destiny, she would not rest until it was fulfilled; nothing would stop her, not even the demons of the forest that were so fearsome in her childhood. Late in the afternoon, she crossed the outer pickets that marked the boundaries of the Xenon plantation. The labourers were returning to their huts after a hot day in the cane field, the tools of their trade slung over their shoulders like muskets. They were the armies of the aged and the lame, with no place else to go. They had stayed behind while the younger ones—their children and grandchildren—fled from a life of drudgery to follow the armies of liberation swarming in the woods. They had listened to messages of Brotherhood and Equality from the lips of Citoyen La Crosse, the young revolutionary from Guadeloupe. He had visited them with the promise of freedom to every man who bore arms against the oppressor, and they were initiated into the new order. They also knew their enemies. The planters, who refused to submit to the edicts of *La Declaration des Droits les Hommes et des Citoyen*, were singled out as the main culprits. Yet by a generous stroke of providence they were allowed to remain unmolested. But there were those who continued to swear allegiance to the House of Bourbon; those aristocrats, who openly ridiculed the revolution in public, calling it the action of criminals, yet were unwilling to spill a pinprick of blood in defense of their cause. They were singled out as the real traitors of the revolution and were sent to the guillotine without the luxury of a trial.

La Crosse had swelled the ranks of the Army in the Woods with every able-bodied man, regardless of age. They waited until the lights in the great houses went out. Slave, ex-slave, maroon, *affranchi*, and mulatto came, regardless of their status, oblivious to colour of skin. The planter had fallen asleep. He too had supported the cause hoping to get a better price for his sugar when the fighting was over. They turned their backs to allow their servants to flee in droves, leaving the children and those that were too old and accustomed not to bother about change to manage the labour on the plantations. On the estates, La Crosse had established an army of contacts known only to a chosen few. They were scattered throughout the island. They were the old trusted house-servants whose duty it was to listen to the gossip in the households and report all they had heard to the drummers. The drummers were everywhere. Sometimes they were the trusted servants themselves. At Xenon, Madlienne's contact was Tergis. He was her father's friend. She had seen him come to their camp, at the base of Morne Gimee, before his head had turned into a gray woolsack. He had grown up together with Desolee, but a slight limp caused by a wound he received as a boy, in his right leg, prevented him from running away. It also prevented him from working in the fields and from very young he had been groomed for the position of butler. A kind master had taught him his language, and he spoke it with a distinctive lisp, that was not apparent when he spoke in his local dialect. Tergis was also a drummer. He played the drums at *belle aires*, for the *piquant*, and *deux bottes*. He also knew the larger drums, the ones that spoke. His grandfather had taught him their alphabet. No one bothered him. He moved about the estate as he pleased on his old mule, which had been given to him by the master's son as a foal. Tergis was an aged icon, revered not only by the master and his family, but also by his own people. He never complained, or showed signs of remorse, even when chided like a child for being mischievous, a condition he never understood despite serving under several masters with varying degrees of ethics. He accepted his estate and bore the pangs of his condition inwardly with dignity. On moonlight nights, when the full moon decided it could rival the sun, he rode alone deep into the forest, where he hid the talking drum to beat out troop movements in his locality, together with rumours of unrest and the latest news from France as they unfolded from the master's lips at dinner. His messages reverberated against the dark hills, until they caught the ears of other drummers hiding there. He would listen until he heard the repeat, a dull distant echo of the sounds he had made. Others farther away in the bush would again relay that echo, until it reached the ears of the Army in the Woods. Tergis was old, but age was not an impediment, for his ears were sharp.

The drums had borne the message ahead of her. He knew she was on her way before she left, the daughter of his friend. She was a child when he last saw her, sitting on her father's knee, fielding the words as they spoke. It was a sign of wisdom. Tergis knew that even at her young age her talents were extraordinary, more so for a woman. He would not recognize her. Many a moon had set since he had taken that excursion into the forest to warn Desolee that someone had squealed. The planters were planning to ambush him and his men. For five years Desolee spared the western plantations and turned his attention south, where the spoils were leaner. It was during this period that he tried to grow his own food. She waited until the noises of the night were hollering at the top of their voices, crickets in the coconut trees, bats in the orange groves and frogs, croaking in the ponds. She saw the lights in the great house grow dim. An old man with a limp came out on the front porch, down the steps and shuffled across the lawn to his cabin. She waited until he lit the lamp inside. After she carefully surveying her surroundings to ensure no one had followed him, she crept like a child 'on all fours,' which made the night seem darker as she was closer to the earth. She rapped on the cabin door, using a prearranged signal to identify her presence. Four knocks followed by four more in rapid succession. The drums had told him to expect her.

"Who knocking my door?" The voice inside inquired, "If it is the devil I not there!"

"It is not the devil," Madlienne replied, "It is his wife. The woman with three breasts."

It was the code. The drums had accurately delivered their message.

He unlatched the door, standing between the lamp and the doorway, to block the light so that no one would see her enter. It was a trick he had learnt from a young master when he visited the cabin rooms after madam had fallen asleep in her bed upstairs, sloshed on a mixture of claret and gin. Madlienne moved swiftly to a corner where the lamp would not enlarge her shadow in the window blinds.

"This is not the usual mission," she said, "that is why I come myself."

"You are Solitaire's child," he said as he examined her features. "But you look more like your father. You must be very lucky."

Madlienne smiled. She felt a bit uneasy under the old man's meticulous glare. She was not fond of endearments. They had no place in her psyche.

She had worn the hard caste of a soldier over her skin for ten long years. It would not crack easily.

"I come to settle with the men who killed my father." She spoke softly, without a gram of emotion in her voice. "You know them?" She asked, knowing that Tergis was the depository of all the information her band received and he was never wrong.

"The men who killed my friend?" Tergis inquired, wanting reassurance. Madlienne became pensive as he moved to a chair close to his bed and slumped into it.

"Yes!"

"Every little child here at Xenon know them," Tergis said.

"I want their names," Madlienne said.

"All of them? I don't know all," Tergis replied with a grin, "they had more than twenty of them that ride that day. I don't know where all is now. That was a long time pass." His face pained from loss of memory.

"What you going to do?" He asked Madlienne.

"Revenge!" She replied.

"Some are big men here in Soufrière." He referred to the district by its old name before the revolution. "They ride from here. Their leader was a man they call Gimat. He was *colom* on this estate."

"Gimat!" The name curled off her tongue like shaving from a joiner's board. "Gimat," she repeated it; a name she must never forget.

"He go back to France to make his fortune. He couldn't make it here." "Gone back to France?" Madlienne exclaimed, as though it was impossible.

"It have more than ten years. A lot of people die these last ten years. Even if you find them, which magistrate will hear your case?"

Tergis had learnt to leave things in the order they were discovered. To stir old wounds was dangerous. He had underestimated her tenacity.

"I will find the men who kill my father even if they are rotting in hell. I will dig up their bodies and kill them again."

Anger swelled in her neck. It made her stutter. "If you know them, give me their names. That's all I want."

"It was still dark when they left. When they get back it was night." "But you know them!" Madlienne's patience was fraying like a tether. Any moment it would snap.

"Only the big boys. The rest was little mulattoes trying to play big, to please the boss."

"Give me the *Gros Pichards*, I'll find the rest."

"They have things, you better leave alone," Tergis warned, but Madlienne was not convinced.

"My father was your friend. You want me to tell you how he died?"

"No!" Replied Tergis; "All I want is for you to live."

In the lamplight his eyes turned red. Madlienne always hated having to watch a grown man cry. She considered it a sign of weakness. She never saw the other side. The compassion; the anger brought on by the inability to strike back.

"There was Theobald and Clercien from Diamant, Nervais from Ventine. They plan the whole thing here on this estate. With Gimat giving the orders in place of the big chief. They swear to stop the stealing once and for all. I did not know what they were going to do until they came back in the night drunk and singing. The chief pay them a hundred *livres* when they get back. They take it and ride back straight into town."

"Which chief, he don't have name?" Madlienne inquired.

"Baron d'Minvielle," replied Tergis. "But you cannot find that one. He under the coffee trees," pointing outside. "The men you want, all fight on your side."

"I have no side," Madlienne retorted.

The flame of revenge seared from her eyes, she was a woman possessed. It was burning inside her.

"If they catch you, it will be the guillotine. If you go outside Soufrière, the English will hang you."

"I am not stupid," Madlienne said with a finality that indicated to Tergis that she had carefully planned her mission. She would not alter her path. He recited to her a list of names adding and deleting as his memory allowed. There were twelve names of which he was certain—the four ringleaders and eight of their followers. The other names did not stick in his head although he swore he would remember them by face. All except the ringleaders were mulattoes.

"Men without a race," Tergis said.

"I don't care. I want to know all of them." There was a stubborn streak in Madlienne. There would be no compromise. Tergis spotted this instantly. "You so much like your father. From the minute he make up his mind to runaway that was all he talk about, until he did."

"If God will allow, none will escape." She repeated the names Tergis had given to her, over and over, until like leeches they stuck to the film of memory. She had no other means of remembering. She could neither read nor write.

The British had occupied most of the colony except for La Convention. Perhaps they still remembered the thrashing they had received from the revolutionary army and had steered clear from the district. The republican flag flew proudly from the main flagpole on the Diamant estate. She had spied it in the distance from Xenon. To Madlienne, it was a sign—she was welcome there. Tergis had told her; Madame Dupiny was in dire need of a housemaid, a donkey to ride around the great house, tailored to her peculiar comforts. She had had a constant flow of maids since the death of her trusted servant Berthilde.

"Berthilde did not die, she just faded away." Tergis said. Overworked and fatigued, Berthilde's body could no longer respond to the constant stream of commands framed at a moment's fancy from a sofa in some dark corner of the drawing room where Madame Dupiny lay all day crippled with rheumatism. In the morning, Madlienne was on her front steps in search of work. The overseer eyed her suspiciously. At first he thought she was a runaway from another district. It would be the last thing he wished. The penalties for harbouring runaways were too severe—sometimes it meant death.

He inspected her closely, as though he was contemplating the purchase of a thoroughbred mare. His eyes stuck to her cleavage. He had acquired a taste for black women and many little mulatto heads were to be seen playing about the yard.

"You say you're an *affranchi*, but you have no papers." He looked askance at the statuesque woman standing a clear foot above his head. He knew on this subject, he had to be firm.

"I lose them when town burn," Madlienne spoke with an air of humility; it added feeling to her story.

"That was years ago," he remarked. "Where you been hiding all this time?" "In the woods," she replied, bowing her head as if she was ashamed to admit.

"With the soldiers?" He smiled. "So you are on my side."

"I am tired of fighting I want something else to do." Clercien's eyes pierced through her clothes feasting on the contours of her body. She was aware, but remained unperturbed. His questions shifted from the objective to the intimate and he asked them with a casual air of authority like it was a divine right. To Madlienne they seemed trivial.

"You slept with the soldiers?"

"Yes, I was a soldier too," Madlienne replied.

Clercien laughed. "Nobody works here unless they sleep with me," he said matter-of-factly. Madlienne pretended to blush when she heard his remarks. At a time when *Egalité, Fraternité* and *Liberté* had been seasoned on everyone's lips, she was surprised by his rashness. Obviously, he did not know the person to whom he was speaking. He was not desirable by any stroke of the imagination, a stark contrast to Theodule on every count. He was short, with a paunch that bulged like a pumpkin in front of him, a pair of hairy hands, close to the ground, resembling a crab. He walked with the bowlegged gait of a rider that was comfortable only on his horse. His face had the perpetual sad look of a clown. It cracked and pained him when he spoke. Madlienne chuckled to herself, gripping her bundle tightly under her arm.

"You'll take me to your master, or I must find him myself?" She struggled to be polite.

"I am in charge here," he said, bellowing with the seal of petty authority.

"If you in charge, I have a job or not? Tell me if I must stay or go."

"Come," he said, "I will take you to madam."

CHAPTER FIVE

Madame Dupiny was old, but very alert. Age had curved her spine and she moved about balancing on a walking stick, wincing with each stride. Her body smelt of a curious mixture of stale sweat and *eau de bain*. She glanced at Clercien as he entered the grand room, hobbling towards her sofa with some difficulty, sipping her morning coffee from a *petite tasse*. "Where did you find that one?" she asked, without raising her head from the teacup. "She looks like a man."

"She is the new housemaid, Madame."

"I can still manage by myself. I don't need your help."

"But Madame . . . ."

"Don't but me!" Madame exploded—there was plenty of fire left in that frail body. "I asked you to get me a maid, not a manservant."

Clercien did not like being humiliated and was furious as he paced aimlessly up and down the room, refusing to make human contact with his eyes. Madlienne surmised that he had gone through that ritual before. She was curious to find out how he would handle it. She had seen glimpses of his arrogance, outside.

"She is nothing like Berthilde—poor Berthilde. She died you know." Madame looked up at them from her coffee, speaking to no one in particular. There was a hint of pity in her eyes. A wry sadness, which she seemed to summon at will. Madlienne thoughts turned briefly to Louise. She too knew how painful it was to lose a friend.

"Can you wash, clean?" She asked suddenly, changing the subject.

"Yes," replied Madlienne.

"Yes who!" Madame Dupiny was becoming hostile again. "In this house you answer, yes madam, or no madam."

"Yes madam!" Madlienne replied, sniggering. The new order had done nothing to change Madame Dupiny's ingrained habits.

"You will have to wash, sew, cook, take me up and down the stairs, and put me in my bath. You understand all that."

"Yes, madam," Madlienne replied.

"I don't have time for people who can't work. Show her to her cabin," she addressed Clercien. "Give her the one where Berthilde used to sleep. She looks like a good girl. A little coarse but she will manage. She's strong." As they turned to leave, she shouted to Madlienne.

"Don't take all day. Just put down your things and come back. There's plenty to do around here."

"Yes Madam." Madlienne replied, mincing the words like a private responding to an order from a superior.

Clercien led her to one of the cabins at the back of the house, surrounded by cacao trees. She noticed the surroundings had been kept clean. There were no leaves on the ground. The cabin had not seen a human face in years. Inside, cobwebs dangled from the ceiling and dust had settled inches deep on everything, particularly the floor. The room also reeked of an odour like musk, the fermented mixture of human sweat and mould.

"I must leave you," Clercien said. "I have work to do in the fields. But I will come back tonight."

"Wait!" Madlienne said, "I don't know your name."

"Clercien," he said forcing a smile through his gums as he hurried to find his horse. The name lit a sore nerve.

'Clercien! Clercien from Diamant?' He was one of the conspirators, a priority on her wanted list. Fate had smiled on her. She found an old *latanier* broom curled in a corner by the broken-down bed. The furniture in the room was sparse. There was a small table with a carafe for drinking water, which smelt like the room, an armchair with a busted seat, sorely in need of recaning, two chairs that did not sit squarely on the floor and a broken-down bed with a coconut fibre mattress pockmarked with fungus. Mildew had lodged in the linens and had replaced the varnish on the old bedposts. The condition of the room made her forget Madame Dupiny's instructions, albeit momentarily. She had to tidy the place first if it was going to be her new home. She had never done that kind of work in her life before, but her feminine intuition came forward. She took up the broom and began pulling down the cobwebs. She hauled the mattress out on the steps and swept up a dust storm that tickled her throat until she coughed. She found a straw mat curled under the bed, which she unrolled at the entrance after purging it of its share of dust. It took a better part of the morning to resuscitate the place. When she returned to the great house, Madame was snoring on her sofa.

The day's drudgery was a mild indicator to the night's entrapment. She did not know when Clercien would return from the fields. She had not seen him for the rest of the day. He had been far away from her mind as she tried to cope with the new routine of housework and the constant flow of commands from Madame Dupiny, especially to replenish her teacup. She had become addicted to coffee, which she gulped like medicine. It frayed her nerves and made her fretful. Madlienne discovered the liquor cupboard in the dining room with an assortment of crystal decanters, which contained brandy, whisky, rum, gin, and every conceivable brand of liqueur, some seemingly untouched for ages. She learnt to lace the coffee with ample shots of gin to silence Madame Dupiny until the lamps were lit and it was time to carry her upstairs.

Madlienne was trying to induce sleep under her grey blanket wrapped around her naked body. The chill from the night air was working miracles on her sore muscles. Her cabin door flew open in a rush of wind that slapped her face causing her to sit upright on the bed. Freed servant or slave had no right to privacy in their quarters. In the dark, she saw the squat outlines of Clercien in the doorway. She was trained to expect the unexpected. She flexed her muscles, stretching out her arms to their full length over her head.

"What you want?" She asked, not in the least annoyed by the sudden intrusion on her privacy.

"I come for you," he replied walking towards the bed. He had been drinking. She could tell from the slur in his speech and the uncertainty in his footsteps as he crossed the floor. He sat beside her on the bed, his breath crisp, pungent with the stench of raw cane liquor.

"Every woman wants Clercien's seeds," he said, draping his hands around her as his mouth searched, uncertain of the location of her lips.

"I come to give them to you."

His hands felt heavy, on her breasts, pawing with an awkward grace, unsteady, giving further notice of his condition. His lips made a strange hissing sound on the nape of her neck; she made no attempt to stop him. His actions were clumsy for a man of the world. She was too tired to laugh. She allowed his hands to wander along the contours of her body, while she remained still, almost lifeless, it was too soon to register her hate. She remembered Maitre Charle's story about the spider, luring the fly into its web. It would be unexpected when she struck. His rough palms clawed the inner path between her thighs leading to her soft grassy mound. He touched it and his body went wild, quivering. Overcome by a sudden attack of ague, his teeth clattered between the gums. His tongue came down on her nipples, first the left, then the right, then both. A slight shiver shot through her spine. A mild reminder of Theodule in the river—but here, she was in control. He did not bother to undress. He fumbled with his pantaloons, his mind wrapped in a haze of uncertainty induced by cane liquor that was also the source of his courage. Unsure of the exact location of the buttons that held his pantaloons in place, he tugged and pulled until it fell below his knees. He climbed on top of her like a swimmer struggling against the tide. She parted her thighs to receive him. A searing pain shot through her body. It felt like a dagger stabbing deep into her innards. It shook every inch of her bowels. She cringed, tensing her muscles. Gradually, her mind relaxed. She remained silent, not offering any form of resistance. Clercien grunted the foulest obscenities and rode with the same carefree abandon, believing he was bareback on his horse. His fingernails dug into her buttocks, spittle on his rum breath, lathered her face. His mind was in another dimension where he felt strong—in an open field where the wind was belting the canes. He rode until his body surged on a wave of excitement, leaping into the air, howling at the top of his voice. With the same sudden thrust that he began, he stopped. Cursing softly as he slumped across her; his energy, sapped, his head between her breasts. Soon he started to snore.

Madlienne eased her body from under him. She cleaned herself with her blanket, at the same time examining her body with her fingers, to assess the extent of the damage he had wrought on her tissues which burned like a fresh wound, making her irritable. She remembered the hunting knife in her little bundle below the bed. She bent over and took it out of its sheath and placed it under her pillow. He was one of the men responsible for the death of her father. She could kill him as he lay speechless beside her if she wished, but that would be painless. She would not deprive herself the joy of hearing him whimper like a rat when the poison hardens in its bowels. She wanted him to beg on his knees for his life. Her joy would come in denying him that favour. The thought assuaged her pains. Stretching to her full length—like a corpse on the coconut fibre mattress still reeking of must—beside him, she too fell asleep.

Close to dawn, the cocks were crowing in the yard from their perch in the cacao trees, their noise coming through the roof. She felt Clercien shaking her by the shoulders, but was content to remain in the haze between consciousness and sleep. Her head was spinning and the bed under her moving like an earthquake. He stopped when she opened her eyes. Although the sun had not come up over the hills, the fore-day morning light was bright. She could see through the cracks in the timber of the cabin. Clercien had slept in his field clothes never bothering to remove his boots. He had recovered from his stupor and was sprightly crowing like one of the cocks:

"Why you didn't tell me you was a virgin?" At first Madlienne pretended not to hear, but he was persistent. She looked across at him under her eyelids, with a wry smile.

"That what you waking me for?" She replied with a question. She turned away from him abruptly, her face towards the wooden partition. She felt his hand stroke the ridge along her back, coarse, but soothing. She broke the silence,

"You know Monsieur Gimat?" she asked quietly, replicating the same mood he had invoked. She felt his hands stiffen.

"Why?" Clercien stammered.

"I don't know," Madlienne replied, "I just ask." Clercien paused. She heard him sit up at the edge of the bed.

"He was my boss, before he went to France. I work with him both here and at Xenon."

"He will comeback?" Madlienne enquired.

"If the guillotine doesn't get him first—he will." Clercien's curiosity was aroused. She felt the bed boards rattle as he lunged towards her.

"Gimat was your man?" He asked, as he fondled her breasts. She swerved away from his reach.

The years came stinging back with a light drizzle tapping the shingles on the roof of the cabin. Clercien did not pursue her. He got up and folded his hands behind his head perhaps contemplating on the day's work ahead. In the silence that separated them, Madlienne withdrew with her thoughts, to a spot deep inside where memories peep from every dusty corner. From the shining blade of the hunting knife she whetted every night on a tattered leather throp salvaged from an enemy knapsack on the battlefield, to a white throat slit above the Adam's apple, images floated before her. They were all dead; the camp, her father, Maitre Charle, Theodule, Louise, yet they were the cause for which she lived. Her mind would sometimes focus on the hunting knife. She could not remember after which battle she found it. She confused the knife with the one she found in the cave years before. Secretly, she wished she had known its original owner, however, for what purpose, she did not know—she surmised he was French, from the *fleur-de-lis* carved into the bone handle. These tranquil interludes did not erase, from memory, the four names she undoubtedly memorized and would never forget: Theobald, Nervais, Gimat and the one who defiled her temple of innocence—Clercien. His days were going to be short, that was certain. She would choose the right moment.

She could not focus on the precise moment when she decided to concentrate on the leaders and forget the followers. The followers were merely boys. They could not have acted alone. They were cajoled by the ringleaders in exchange for favours—puppets manipulated by minds other than their own. They were bought. They knew that they would never be accepted as equals on their fathers' side, but the white half that oozed through their pores pained for recognition. She had grown to understand the mulattoes. She had fought side by side with some of them and found them brave. She had seen too much suffering, too much pain. Killing them would avenge nothing; their mixed blood was sufficient pain. They were fatherless like her and had rejected the mother who succoured them. They were the products of a senseless age, where the colour of one's skin enslaved the soul and that was punishment enough.

Clercien's eyes turned white in his head like a pig when he felt blood gushing from his neck. He tossed from side to side, clutching his throat with both hands, hoping that a miracle would stem the warm flow staining the sheet. His voice had become a gurgle; his tongue stuck to his palate. She had slit his windpipe with her hunting knife. He had ravaged her body earlier as he had done repeatedly on nights when he returned drunk from the fields. She waited for that precise moment when he was neither drunk nor sober; when he would wake from his stupor and pause to gloat over his new found conquest. She had memorized his habits. His hands would begin to paw her body, his organ swelling with an unholy passion which made her feel unclean. She was swift, like a fer-de-lance. She spat and stung, her father's name ringing in her ears. She dragged his body to a safe spot under the cocoa trees, away from the cabins, where they found him, white like a sheet, with his tongue hanging out, in the dirt, swollen, and covered with ants.

On the Diamant estate Madlienne served Madame Dupiny dutifully, with her daily teacups of coffee laced with gin, until she grew too frail to venture beyond the confines of her room, bed-bound, collecting bedsores. The loss of movement in her limbs did not restrict the constant stream of orders—It was impossible to break a lifelong habit. However they were seldom observed for she could not remember beyond the last minute. Before she died, her son, Raymond Dupiny, returned from France with his young wife and assumed his father's seat.

Theobald was easy prey. Madlienne had met him during her frequent visits to the cane field. It was crop-time. His responsibilities were endless, more so on account of the demise of Clercien. They seldom allowed him to leave his station. He occupied a small corner at the sugar factory, which was run in partnership with the owners of Xenon. He pitched his hammock on evenings and fell asleep listening to the vats boil. His skills lay in transforming cane into sugar. Madlienne waited until the season was at its full height, when everyone would be too tired at night to visit friends and family, scattered across the four corners of the plantation and its environs. After she had given Madame Dupiny her nightly rub and powdered her bedsores and tucked her in for the night, she stopped by briefly at her cabin to collect her small bundle. It contained among other items, her hunting knife.

He knelt on the hard concrete factory floor begging her forgiveness. The whip that he had driven into the backs of old men stoking the fires, coiled round his neck like a snake.

"Remember my father?" She asked. The words hissed through her teeth. "Desolee!" He showed no sign of recollection. Fear filled his eyes. He died before the cold iron blade snipped past his ribs. Madlienne felt a mild perversity in silencing cowards. To her, it was a deliberate duty, a favour to mankind. There was no place for them under the sun—not in her sphere of thought—those who thrived by knifing their victims in their sleep, knowing they could not strike back. But even as she was convinced of the justification for her actions, she remained plagued by a dilemma; to kill them, or to let them suffer slowly alive. In dying, death was an easy end. Alive, fear swelled in their heads, until it made them mad. First, they had to know she stalked their shadow, keeping her identity anonymous as the night. They would never see her in any form or shape, only a phantom somewhere in the dark, waiting to pounce. A creature of their own fragility, armed with supernatural powers. They would know that Clercien and Theobald had died, but the motive for death, was still a mystery. This had to be established. The world must know. The idea of carving a cross on their bodies came to her when she had finished Theobald. Seeing him lying on the factory floor, like a carcass about to be stripped of its hide, caused her to think. He had offered no resistance except snivelling. He had involuntarily drained his body of all its fluids—urine, sweat and faeces. When she coiled his whip around his neck, from the first lash, all that was left was to drain his blood. She regretted the one-sided contest. She wanted him to be like a man, not a cowardly animal, too timid to watch his own blood spill. It was more difficult to kill him in his sleep.

'Only cowards do that.' She thought and she was not one. Watching him die offering no resistance made her feel guilty, although his death was not a callous act of murder. She rehearsed the scenes from the past in her mind: her father, Maitre Charle, The Camp. Then Theodule, Louise . . . They demanded vengeance. With a firm hand she sliced across his chest from shoulder to shoulder, then from neck to gut. It was her mark of revenge. It reminded her of her father and the crosses he had drawn with his machete on the lawns, at the great houses he had sacked. She wanted the world to know that his death was being avenged. The war of attrition was over; the battle with her conscience was beginning. Gimat, their leader was safe, for the time being in France, but she was willing to wait a lifetime—if she must—until he returned. There was the small matter of Nervais still to be attended. It would be handled in her own good time, again, she would wait.

The Army in the Woods had been disbanded. They were now a conquered people, disillusioned and dispossessed. They roamed through the towns and villages seeking shelter in any crab hole they found untenanted, fearing reprisals from the same Republicans they had so valiantly defended. The promise of freedom that was used as inducement to bear arms against their oppressors remained only a promise. In peacetime it was no longer possible to separate comrade from oppressor; they hid under the same white skin and no one bothered to make the distinction. In many ways their living conditions for these former warriors had become far worse than slavery. In the old days there was plenty to eat and a roof over their heads. The hard work on the plantations and the whip across their backs were their only complaints. They were prepared to forgive the several acts of cruelty leveled by sadistic owners and return to the fields rather than hovel under verandahs after nightfall to shelter from the weather. Or, to congregate in the burnt-out shell of houses, digging like crabs under the foundations in search of warmth, when dampness tickled old wounds. They fought each other for scraps foraged from refuse heaps to stave off hunger and raided their own for rations, especially clothes, which were in scarce supply. All the venom pent up inside, reserved for the enemy was being vented on each other. When peace was finally restored, the

British rode into the town of La Convention, hoisted their standard and left. A treaty signed in Paris, gave in part, full pardon to all those who had fought in the wars regardless of colour. This was a small emancipation. It gave the Army in the Woods a new lease on life. It allowed them to return to their former masters without fear of being punished as runaways once they resumed their stations, without acrimony. Those who had been free men returned to their former trades. Madlienne ventured to enquire from comrades she knew about Argos, Jean, Ti Frère and Constantin, but no one knew of their whereabouts, not even those who had been together with them in camp until the end. They had vanished before the army had been formally disbanded, not deserters, because the fighting had ceased, but like a thousand others, they had blended into their surroundings and had become it. She felt an overbearing urge to go and find them. Her mind wrestled with it. Her mission would not wait. Not a day passed without them visiting her thoughts. She knew they were alive and they would find her when they needed help.

The young mistress of Diamant had been accustomed to tending the needs of her husband and with the passing of Madame Dupiny, Madlienne was no longer required on the estate. She returned to the Xenon plantation, to Tergis and his little cabin to wait there for Argos, Jean, Ti Frère and Constantine and to plan her next move. Very pleasant memories of those tranquil years remained with her for the rest of her life. They brought with them an inner peace. Only the thirst for news of Gimat remained a blemish on that period. Tergis had learnt from listening to the gossips around the dinner table that Gimat had become a landlord in France, he owned a vineyard. He had also purchased an abandoned estate in the north of the colony. Details of the transaction were not quite clear. Nothing was clear in the life of that man. He was himself an enigma. No two persons described him alike and he seemed to be everywhere except in the colony where he was a wanted man. Madlienne gathered every bit of information and stored it for the future, building from the fragments a picture she could recognize, whenever he reappeared.

Peace had returned. The mills were grinding the island back to a state of prosperity. The fighting had ceased. It was several years before anyone realized that the ships with their cargoes of human degradation no longer called at the ports. The auction blocks in the town squares where human life was bartered and sold like cattle had become termite havens, beaten by the sun and rain; rotting unprotected in all kinds of weather. Some were dismantled and committed to ovens as fuel for the brown loaf. Fear, which drove some of overseers to the brink of madness, retreated like a soldier crab, back into its shell. It no longer hung heavy in the air. They were up and strutting again through the fields with their whips, mustering courage from the backs of the aged and infirmed, too lame to hit back. The mulattoes, who during the early years of crisis had remained invisible, obeying orders and making sure that they were on the right side of the fence, becoming in time the most vociferous supporters of the Revolution, quick to denounce impostors and prescribe novel forms of punishment for them, were at their old tricks again. With the Revolution a thing of the past and the new order slowly clearing the mud from its toes, they were reclaiming their status as the island's second strata of nobility, after the planter and his sons. Their voices were turned inward, among themselves, seeking to build walls of security that would isolate them from the labourers who were principally black. They were clamouring for a separate class of citizen. Any act of aggression on their numbers was actively denounced as persecution (by a favoured kind).

Stories of Desolee's murder a long time ago had been resurrected and were making the rounds in all the taverns in town. It gave fillip to their ego and the feeling of superiority they needed to survive. Those who had once claimed to be unwilling conspirators and had only accompanied the ringleaders under duress were boasting in public about the gory details of their deeds after consuming more than their normal quota of rum. Divisions among the classes were clearly delineated by the colour of skin. The mulattoes belonged to neither class and were despised by both. The news reached Madlienne's ears through the combined efforts of former colleagues and friends. Out of these idle boastings, details of the slaughter became clearer. They were from the lips of eye-witnesses. They had arrived at Desolee's camp well before noon on that fateful day and waited until it was time for the siesta. They knew that Desolee and his men were creatures of the night and would retire when the sun would be at its zenith in the sky in order to conserve their energies for their nocturnal activities. They waited until the last of the group disappeared into their huts, until they heard the flies buzz over the garbage pits where remnants were thrown to rot. Though their numbers were few, Gimat broke them up into groups and they attacked according to the four cardinal points on the compass, swift and furious like the wind.

One night, clothed in the darkness of her thoughts, Madlienne visited a tavern in Rue Zaborca, in the town of La Convention. The tavern was run by a former comrade who had sent for her to hear one Valentine, a mulatto, gloat on how he had nailed an old man to the walls of his hut on the point of his bayonet. He had repeated the story every night, word for word, when he got drunk. It was his only claim to fame. From an adjoining room, where the publican kept his stores, Madlienne remained unobserved, and listened. 'Maitre Charle! He is boasting how he killed Maitre Charle.' She remembered the body, skewered to his cabin wall; the old man who had held her on his knees many times as a child telling stories. He loved to tell her about a far country across the water, further than France, or England, on the other side of the world, where the grass was a man's height and the animals were larger than houses. He told her about his journey in the bowels of a ship, laying prostrate for four complete weeks like a man in his coffin and chained to others like him. There was little room for him to move. The cramps that seized his body made him wish he were dead. She was battling the urge to rush out from her hiding place and rip Valentine's tongue from his head. While it would not have served any useful purpose, the consolation of reducing him to matter before his friends was indeed tempting, but then, the punishment. His mulatto friends would hang her without trial and in time, Valentine would assume the dimensions of legend; he would become the hero and poor Maitre Charle, the fabled villain. She followed him out into the night at a safe distance, until he staggered into a dark alley where the shadows of the houses on either side added to the sombre blackness. There, under a dark verandah, with no light coming from either above or within, she confronted him.

Surprise had a sobering effect. It rendered him speechless. She scalped the clothes from his body with her blade without touching his skin. He knelt naked at her feet blocking his vitals with one hand—out of an innate sense of modesty—even in the dark—while attempting to field the swishes from her blade with the other. He was like a caged animal, snarling and grunting at the flashes of silver that streaked all around him as Madlienne toyed with his body. She enjoyed every minute of it. Despite his fear, he mustered courage and tried to defend himself. The sharp blade sliced across his chest, shoulder to shoulder and again along the sternum, down to the top of his stomach. Modesty fled. His hands gripped his chest, squeezing the raw flesh as his blood flowed. Like a streak of lightening, as suddenly as she struck, Madlienne became one with the dark, leaving Valentine to grope for the remnants of his clothes peeled slowly from his skin and run as fast as his rubbery legs could bear his weight, all the way to his lodgings. This closed the curtains temporarily on an episode that was becoming a drama of epic proportions. It silenced the mulattoes. Terror, which was never too far away from their shadows, had returned.

A veil of mist enveloped the town, its vapours reeking of sulphur. Mild tremors shook the earth day and night. Rumours that the end of the world had come was spreading about town and people flocked to their God to beg forgiveness for the slightest sin. So intense was their fear, no one dared to brave the street at night. With superstitions unchained, the devil roamed the streets accompanied by one of his handmaidens. They were afraid that this evil pair would permeate through the haze, thick like a pigeon pea soup, to carve the sign of the cross on their bodies. It was divine irony, the devil marking a sign of the cross on his victims' bodies. It sounded so palatable, everyone believed.

"Valentine meet a *Diablesse*," they would say, when they recounted the tale. "He mark himself to save his life. He come too close to the devil."

Nervais, more than anyone else knew the significance of the sign of the cross on the bodies of Theobald and Valentine. He knew it was connected to the mark Desolee left on the lawns of the great houses many years before, after a raid. His role in the cold-blooded slaughter that *sextidi*, in the month of the *Floréal*, many moons ago, came vividly back to his mind. His fears convinced him that he was next. Unable to face the streets, he collected a few possessions and fled, leaving a wife and five young children behind to fend for themselves. Nervais' disappearance became the focal point of interest in every conversation. Speculation was rife. He could write, but he left no note behind. Every god-fearing person firmly believed that he had made a pact with the devil, who came to claim him in the noonday heat. The fact that he had taken along a few articles of clothing and food did not alter their thinking. His disappearance was ripe material for the gossip flaring around town; particularly the taverns and they embellished it as it made the rounds. His whereabouts unknown was all that mattered. It was about two years after he had vanished from Ventine, a group of hunters returning from the chase found a body hanging from a *chapote* tree on the edge of the forest along a frequently used path. It hung there, swinging in a light breeze as if wanting to be discovered. They had not seen it in the early morning light when they passed, it was not there. The body was still warm when they cut it down. Rigor mortis had not set in, but life had fled. At a glance, they identified it as Nervais, although he had aged considerably over the two years of absence. The body was gnarled and twisted like a baobab tree and the flesh had melted between the bones. Only a tight skin held his parts together. Apart from some red blotches on his cheeks, his complexion had whitened to the shade of cassava starch. The length of his hair and the ribbons that were his clothes suggested that he had lived like a hermit. He may have been hiding in one of the many caves in the hills, dug by the Arawaks generations before, to protect their families from the savagery of the Caribs, from which they surfaced only at night in search of food. The same caves that Madlienne had commandeered and used effectively in her fight for freedom.

Three of the ringleaders who masterminded the massacre of her people were now one with history. That casual smile, not always casual, but came from deep within to warm her lips, when the smell of victory filled the air, creased her face when Madlienne heard the news. He was a victim of his own hands, a testimony to the power of subterfuge. He could not live with his guilt. It eventually consumed him. Fear would hound them all. Their days and nights would be filled with it, looking over their shoulders in every dark corner; walking in groups, afraid of being alone, afraid that she would suddenly appear, the tall *La Diablesse*, to drain the blood from their bodies with her fangs. Before life fled she would carve a sign of the cross across their chests, leaving them to drown in pools of their own blood. She knew the power of fear, the web it spun over the minds of men, entangling them in its threads; strangling them, until they could no longer breathe. She had used it as a weapon. It was a formidable force. She convinced herself sparing the lives of the others was now necessary. They would live to die a thousand deaths before nature claimed its dues. However, there was one who could not be allowed this leisure, the one who had become for her the embodiment of their guilt. One lifetime would be too short for him to suffer. If she should go before him, she would find a way to return. She would not allow nature to bestow her kindness on him: to allow him to fade away in bed surrounded by grieving relatives. If this were to happen, the thin layers of faith that were slowly mustering around her soul would dissipate. Whatever smattering of hope that she had gathered from prayer would become a mockery of everything that she had learnt to respect as sacred. He was the ringleader—Gimat, the most important cog in the wheel. His name had become a receptacle for her hate. By piecing together the quilt of many colours that was his guise, the several varied anecdotes without a common pattern; she knew it would take more than the fear of death to rattle his nerves. It would require her presence.

She sat in her rocking chair and pondered. The grey in her hair itched and she scratched until the blood crawled like a crab under her scalp down to her cheeks making her lips tremble for a moment. They trembled whenever she felt powerless. Time was ticking fast, old age could not wait. Her patience was thinning like her blood.

'Forty years is a long time to wait. I don't know how long I got.'

Notwithstanding the power of her resolve, she knew that she was powerless in some matters. She felt helpless determining the length of her days. Once strength allowed her raise her hand, she would complete her mission, even if she must crawl on bended knees. There had been too many deaths in her life to believe she could gamble with immortality and win. Many terrible things had happened, some more crippling than old age. This would be the crutch on which to lean and hope. She had outlived many storms. It was the way of the world. She had come through. She had survived; her only wish was to endure until Gimat's return . . .

CHAPTER SIX

She remembered the year when she moved from the *Quartier de la Convention* to *Ville de la Félicite*. By that time, their old names had been restored. La Convention was again known as La Soufrière and Félicite as Castries. She preferred the revolutionary names, being a revolutionary at heart who could never be converted to convention. She accepted, however, change was inevitable although she was powerless to fashion it to her way of thought. She never understood the politics of the day and never attempted. She was at home with French and British. Each honoured her with respect. To the French she was a soldier who fought with distinction under their banner. The British called her the honourable foe and extended their subtle courtesies. She had come to Castries to reside with Monsieur De Brettes as his housekeeper. Monsieur De Brettes was old, bordering on senility. She had met him through Clercien when she worked at Diamant, on her first visit to town to collect provisions. She found him quaint, a bit eccentric, with his hunchback, bald head and spectacles—thick like vermouth bottle glass—perpetually pinned to his nose. He wobbled behind the counter with the speed of a tortoise, repeating each item in a feeble voice that acted as a mirror to his short-term memory. Items which were too heavy for him to lift, like the hogsheads of flour and bully beef he would point out among the disorganized mass of inventory, with the tip of his quill. There was always a quill in his hand no matter what time of day she came to the shop. He would record each item on a sheet of wrapping paper as it crossed his counter, carefully blotting each word he wrote, dipping the pen in a jar of ink, anticipating the next item of purchase. He would gaze in awe at Madlienne as she swooped down like a frigate bird on a barrel of codfish, dumbfounded as she rolled it leisurely towards the cart outside. He had told her repeatedly that she reminded him of an aunt on his mother's side of the family, who his mother said, should have been born a man, but changed her mind minutes before birth. He had repeated this so often that Madlienne imagined a huge buxom woman with the De Brettes' face peeping over his shoulder at her from a safe distance behind the counter. Clercien told her that De Brettes was a real Count.

"The blood in his veins blue, not red."

From then, Madlienne developed a curious interest in his hands and neck where the vessels protruded above the skin. For a while she believed Clercien, until she became aware that Madame Dupiny's veins were the same shade as De Brette's.

"If he is a real Count, what is he doing in this part of the world?" She asked Clercien. "He should be in France counting his gold and silver."

"He is a poor Count," Clercien replied, pretending to offer an excuse. "From the day he landed he has been at his trade. Maybe his family was glad to see him leave."

De Brettes had started his trade under the flamboyant tree by the pier the moment his feet touched land. He began humbly, selling beads and trinkets he had brought with him from France. The labourers and the *affranchi* patronized him, for these items were cheap, well within their meagre means and they adorned their arms and necks with them, particularly on Sundays. Gradually as his business grew, going through the cycles of change from hawker to vendor, grocer to haberdasher, his stature followed in stride. He rose to the rank of full-scale merchant with his own utility store across the street a few yards away from the spot where he began, within the span of five quick years. He eventually purchased the building from his debt ridden landlord and refitted it to suit his purpose.

Monsieur De Brettes was a bachelor of modest tastes and a small bed-sitter on the mezzanine floor more than adequately served as his private quarters. He closed his store religiously at noon for lunch and did not reopen until well past two in the afternoon. He had no fixed hours for closing and only did so when fatigue seized his limbs, by which time all the other shops were securely fastened for the night. Madlienne felt an instant fondness towards this quaint old man, who was a friend to all his customers, in particular, children. They swamped his shop for liquorice sticks, which he gave to them without worrying about cost. He was a generous soul. Madlienne often brought him sugar-cakes, a mixture of coconut meal, grated fine from fresh dried nuts, and stewed in syrup until it hardened like bonbons. In turn he always found a stray end of cloth for a bodice or a skirt to give her. Through these exchanges, their friendship grew. He decided it was time to retire when his memory began to fail. Tergis had died. It was not sudden. He had been complaining about a sharp pain in his legs from the time Madlienne came to Xenon and then his eyes grew dim. Unable to walk made him bitter, often morose, but blindness broke his spirit. Gradually, he lost control. Madlienne cared for him like a surrogate daughter providing his meals and keeping him clean, throughout the period he remained incapacitated. This was feeble consolation. He spoke of dying and welcomed it like an ally. He went to bed one night after a heavy meal of tapioca and did not wake up in the morning.

When Monsieur De Brettes asked her in his gentle tone to join him as his housekeeper in Castries, she jumped at the opportunity, without considering pay. It was a means of relieving boredom while she waited for Gimat's return. De Brettes was the consummate French gentleman and she knew she would be happy. He had acquired a small cottage at Trois Piton in the district of Castries, within sight of the fort at Morne Fortune and the valleys of Cul-de-Sac to the south and La Carenage to the north. He had purchased it during the years of turmoil, as a resting place when he visited Castries on business and it was too late in the evening to travel. During the Brigands War, a self imposed curfew committed everyone indoors as soon as the sun set. Although the journey from Castries to Soufriere at that time was by boat, it was not entirely safe. Bands of privateers roamed the water in canoes, outracing the coastal brigs. They often attacked for money, stores, ammunition and firearms, cautious not to kill or maim their victims as any such act was sure to incur the wrath of the British or French navies that were never too far away. The journey by land was virtually impossible and could only be undertaken in convoy, with mule packs and a pig-iron constitution. After leaving Anse La Raye, the road tapered to a track that veered through jungle and virgin forest, where the fer-de-lance was king. It took two full days traveling by land to reach the town of Soufrière, after resting the first night at Canaries estate, if fortunate to get that far without being attacked by man or beast. It was a playground for highwaymen who could blend with the dark undergrowth and set their traps to capture the unwitting traveler.

The cottage was small but comfortable with two bedrooms located on the eastern side, the smaller of which was occupied by Madlienne. The drawing room occupied the other half of the house. Conveniences were located to the back and detached, together with a small kitchen, large enough to take a dining table and four chairs. The stables were located to the west under a *mammey-apple* tree, where Monsieur De Brettes kept his buckboard and his grey. The rooms were sparsely furnished, puritan to be exact, with only the essential bits and pieces. They drew curious glances whenever they ventured into town, the old man and the black woman seated besides him. Castries was already the capital of the colony and attracted a mixed haversack of inhabitants. French and English worked side by side, oblivious of each other. The French were principally the plantocracy and the English, merchants. In between were the mulattoes who had gravitated to overseers and estate owners, although none of their holdings exceeded five *carres*. The *affranchis* were principally tradesmen—coopers, cobblers, masons, carpenters and blacksmiths. There were also the labourers who worked on the estates threshing the cane into sugar and in the homes of the French and English, tending their needs. Nearly all labourers were slaves, whether in the households or in the fields, for very few freemen elected to remain in bondage after they had purchased the right to be themselves. The slaves were seldom allowed out alone in the streets, not even on errands.

During her early years in Castries, those weekly excursions into town churned out the usual suspects. Every short middle-age Frenchman she met was a potential candidate. She eyed them askance from head to toe looking for a vague resemblance of the man they called Gimat. He had become more than an obsession; he had become unshakable like a dogma. He had surrendered his right to life and liberty. He had withdrawn his right to the pursuit of happiness when he directed the slaughter of her people. Nothing could save him from her wrath. Not the miles that divided them, or the sea. She had forgiven the mulattoes. They were merely mimics—after three deaths had generated fear within their ranks, they were absorbing their own self-inflicted punishment. Fear that had driven them to seek refuge in liquor; fear had grounded them as prisoners in their homes at night; fear would eventually consume them—one by one—when they could no longer withstand its embrace. They would survive long enough in a state of drunken stupor, to repent their sins, always shadowed by the might of that unseen hand ready to mark their breasts with a sign of the cross. Fear would addle their blood until it congealed and refused to flow. Suicide would be their only release. That was enough for her.

Monsieur De Brettes had sold his building in Soufrière along with the entire inventory in the shop to a young entrepreneur, fresh from France, who, like him, had come to the Islands to seek his fortune. As part of the agreement, he retained a share in the business, which provided him with a small pension that would take care of his needs for the rest of his life. Madlienne tidied around the cottage, weeding and building a series of footpaths using flagstones she had found in the neighbourhood, along the banks of a small stream that trickled in wet months through a gully at the back of the cottage. She collected plants of every description and transplanted them, creating a flower garden like the ones she memorized from paintings in the drawing rooms at Xenon and Diamant—her only points of reference. The property had a few fruit trees already bearing, in particular mango. She planted sour-sop and sugar-apple from seed, plums from broken stalks she smuggled from the neighbours. On Thursdays, she hitched the buckboard to the grey and helped Monsieur De Brettes to dress for town. He had bought the buckboard mainly to go to church on Sundays but never found the time. He was agile despite his increasing years, however, his short-term memory was beyond repair. She had to constantly remind him of the days of the week and the time for each meal. Together they were a team. Madlienne cooked his meals and washed his clothes, while he did his utmost to teach her to read and write on evenings after dinner, before retiring for the night in brief interludes when lucidity prevailed. Throughout these exercises that seldom lasted an hour, before sleep claimed him, her interest was concentrated on France.

"How far away is it? Does black people live there? They say it very cold—even during the day—is that true?"

"With your height, in France you'd be a dancer," Monsieur De Brettes told her. The idea was flattering. That night she dreamt that she had gone to France and was dancing in the streets, although she had never learnt to dance. The next day she asked Monsieur De Brettes to teach her to dance. He promised, but frailty militated against it.

She never passed up an opportunity to prod him about Gimat. He had known Gimat's mother. For many years she was counted among his best customers. She was always at the store in search of thread to match a particular cloth. Sometimes, being the eldest, Gimat accompanied her and drove the wagon. When he became manager at Xenon they grew closer. Gimat had acquired an insatiable appetite for money which Monsieur De Brettes lent to close acquaintances with modest interest. Alexandre Gimat was a product of the islands. He was born in Martinique where his father had owned a sugar plantation. He was forced to sell it to repay his gambling debts—a habit that was hereditary and which the son, in turn, acquired, much to the chagrin of his mother. Bankrupt and reduced in status, the family moved to St. Lucie, where Gimat Senior found employment. Gimat grew up on the Ruby Estate near Xenon, where his father was placed in charge of the sugar mills, which ground the cane into *muscovado*. His skills carried a premium as the sugar he made was crisp and light and needed very little refinement. It was consumed locally and always in demand. Unfortunately, he was a hard drinker and was unable to assume higher responsibility as he always needed direct supervision. He was a wreck functioning only by habit. He died before the boy was old enough to understand his father's plight. Gimat, the son, became a citizen of the estates—there were no boundaries—along with the mulatto children who roamed half-naked through the pastures pursuing mischief. He was a wild child. His mother was a *cabresse*, the daughter of a mulatto woman and a planter. Except for the charcoal specks that were her eyes, no one could guess that she had a black grandmother. Her skills as a dressmaker were legendary among the planters' wives and their concubines. By these humble means Madame Gimat tended her five children. Alexandre was the eldest by four years from the second. After twelve years of plodding with needle and thread, she surrendered to the charms of a retired army colonel about twice her age, married him, and followed him to France with her four younger siblings.

Alexandre Gimat was by then learning the craft of manipulating souls from seasoned overseers with more than twenty years experience and on the point of retiring. He had acquired a penchant for the whip and was allowed to assist whenever there were floggings to be administered. In his formative years, his mother was bent on sending him to school, which was held on the Diamant Estate in an abandoned building that had outlived its usefulness as a warehouse. She worked assiduously to earn the coppers to ensure that he did. The school teacher was a spinsterish lady, an elder sister of Madame Dupiny, who felt it her god given right to educate the planters' children in the art of reading and writing the French language and in arithmetic. She never charged for teaching, but insisted that parents purchased all the implements necessary for their children's' education, including black-board, chalk, slate and texts. The young Gimat displayed no claims to brilliance. From an early age it was certain that his interest lay elsewhere. In crop season he would play truant to wander through the cane fields, needling the workers, who already had grown to despise his presence. He drew the overseers' attention to those who were either lame or sick and were lagging behind with their tasks. An impish grin cracked across his face when the whip leveled across those unfortunate backs. There was a sadistic streak in his mind; he would not allow a moment's respite on mischief. He reveled at the sight of people in pain and inflicting it was a pastime he enjoyed.

At school, Gimat was a renowned prankster, creating situations to relieve boredom in class; a cheap laugh, drawing all the attention to him. His favourite prank was to stretch forward on the bench to the row in front, while Miss Lartigue was busy concocting a problem on the blackboard. He would gingerly loosen the hair ribbons of the girls who religiously sat there, directly in front him. He would then tie them together so that the girl in the middle would be joined to the two girls sitting on either side. Not to be contented with this sleight of hand, he would call one by name and remain nonplussed as they tugged and pulled each other about till their necks sprained in the process, while his cohorts roared. He never feared the rod; a switch cut from a tamarind tree, which made welts on his back, when Miss Lartigue's vain attempts to arouse the goodness in him fell short of patience. The rod was incapable of curing his insatiable appetite for mischief. By all indications in later life, Miss Lartigue failed miserably. Although he learnt to read and write and work his sums, the frequent floggings only served to instill a bitterness in him that reeked of perversion and cruelty.

"Monsieur Gimat is your good friend, you say, how come he doesn't write you?" Madlienne asked to steer the conversation in her direction.

"The least he could do is send you a message to say he's alive. That is what friends do. Where in France he is?" She would continue hoping to lurch his memory.

"France is a big country . . . I don't remember where." She could feel him searching his mind.

"St. Etienne," she would prompt. He had mentioned that name to her many times before although never directly linking it with Gimat.

"Yes, St. Etienne. How did you know?" He would ask with a chuckle.

"He was a good man, before he burnt himself out," Monsieur De Brettes would say, sometimes confusing father with son in the confusion that was left of his brain. A slight tug on the strings of his memory opened its doors. Father and son intermingled in his speech, but Madlienne was capable of prying them apart.

"He always spoke about his wife and children when he was drunk. He wanted to take them to France, but didn't have the money. He gambled, you know, like his father. But France without a King is not a safe place to be."

"Now that there's peace in France, do you think Gimat will come back?" Madlienne asked, attempting to focus his attention on the son. She had no interest in the father; he could not return.

"There's nothing to do in France. Why do you think I came here?" Monsieur De Brettes was always guarded about his political leanings, but it was clear to Madlienne that he was a monarchist at heart. A large print of Louis the Fourteenth, the Sun King, adorned his drawing room.

"Things would have been much better if we had a strong king," he mused on the prospects of a united France, where the king controlled the assembly with good reason and sound judgment. Thoughts of Gimat's likely return fired her spirits.

"You really love this man eh?" Monsieur De Brettes would ask with a footnote of regret, perhaps feeling the pangs from some deep affection rumbling inside towards her, one he could not adequately express. There was no remorse, just a murmur from the heart of an old man.

"I did not know him," she would reply. "But he knew my father."

She would stop to give him his bowl of soup and sat quietly watching the spoonfuls disappear into his mouth. Before he could finish eating, he would begin to nod.

Monsieur De Brettes was consistent in his description of Gimat when able to separate the elder from his son. His long-term memory was irreproachable. It returned to him in spurts, coloured with details and events. He remembered Gimat as a short burly man who did not care too much about his manner of dress. He wore a stringy red beard, which remained uncombed and knotted in wild clumps around his chin for days. He was bald in the middle of his head and the hair thinned out to the sides in unruly waves—a sallow sunset over a placid sea.

"He resembled a pirate without a ship. He had a strong smell of sweat in his clothes. He was very strict," Monsieur De Brettes would say. "He punished his workers for the slightest offence. He told me so."

"He hated thieves." Madlienne would add, to prod his memory.

"Stealing is the worst crime man could ever invent." Monsieur De Brettes would say, thinking of the losses he suffered through larceny on his premises before and during the wars.

"He hated us," Madlienne would say, pretending to be close to tears, to reassure herself of the hatred she bore for this man she had never seen. Madlienne would retire for the night with pictures in her mind, each snippet replacing a blank space in the huge tapestry she weaved; a tapestry she could never complete because there were many missing chapters. He was a man known only on the surface. Underneath was blank. The anecdotes followed the same nightly pattern, revealing no more than Monsieur De Brettes remembered, but she kept on prodding nevertheless. Monsieur De Brettes eventually succeeded in teaching her to write her name, ending in a flourish with a tail on the last alphabet. He made his will, leaving everything he owned to her. He clung to life for a long while after, although obviously sinking as the days sped by. Finally, his memory faded and could not respond to his name. In the last days he experienced a second childhood, messing himself and cooing like a dove when he did it. Madlienne nursed him like an infant. For old age, there was no cure.

She assumed total control of the *ménage,* executing her daily chores with the same zeal and indifference as when he directed her. Her thoughts often strayed during that period to the four survivors from her tribe. She knew they were strong and had survived the season of adjustment after the wars although she had not heard from them: Argos, Jean, Ti Frère and Constantin. They were the only remaining fragments from her youth. It had always been mystifying why they did not try to reach her after the Army in the Woods had been disbanded; she was not far away. The thought that they might have been captured and sold again into slavery in one of the neighbouring islands often crossed her mind. It made her sad. Her obsession with vengeance, however, made her selfish. It sometimes blocked her ears to the groans of Monsieur De Brettes, in his room begging for a spoonful of water to quench his thirst. She missed her blood links to the past; she should have gone in search of them when they did not appear. Maybe she would have rescued them if they were prisoners. At least the doubt that often clouded reason would have been put to rest. Emotion, like a flame, flickered until she learnt to be at peace with herself. There would always be doubt, but her mission was outside its sphere.

Monsieur De Brettes chose an Easter Sunday to say goodbye to the world. He woke up that morning feeling sprightly and gurgling in the gibberish that was left of his speech. Madlienne fed him a light pap; a mixture of cow's milk and cassava bread, then sponged his body with a basin of lukewarm water and red lavender, to suppress the odour of illness that clogged his pores. Seeing that he was in such good spirits she carried him to the small porch and placed him in his rocker. From there, the road was in full view and he saw the faces as they passed, although his mind could not register events nor recognize people. She turned in to attend to her cooking, a chore from which she derived much pleasure but was not proficient. She returned later to check the direction of the sun on his face; it had started to turn warm close to noon, the stew was simmering on a slow coal fire, and the house was filled with its smell. She found him, resting peacefully in his chair, eyes closed. He was no longer among the living. Death had wrapped him in its sheet and had already skirted away with his soul. He had fallen into that everlasting sleep, from which no one awakens, a welcome smile stuck to his face. It seemed he had just met a long lost friend. Madlienne did not experience any deep feeling of loss, although she missed his companionship. She always knew he did not have much longer to go, after his mind had shut its doors on the world. She counted the minutes from day to day, but could not predict the hour to expect the unexpected; one regret which hounded her for the rest of her years was not having learnt to read when M. De Brettes attempted to teach her. She had seen him drool over the alphabets in the books he kept around the house, adjusting his spectacles to draw words from the pages into his mind. She marveled at the pleasure he derived in doing so, when the house was quiet and the light, bright enough for him to see. She wished she had been more attentive.

The neighbours came to her assistance during the period of bereavement. They helped bathe the corpse in a mixture of strong rum and bay leaves. Afterwards, they dressed him in his white drill suit, which he had never worn while he was alive—he had it made to go to church but never found time to go—and placed him in his coffin. They brought a young priest to the house to read the last rites over the body and then they laid Count De Brettes to rest in his yard, serene in death in his plain board coffin, which they had nailed together from bits of local lumber. All this they did in one night and a day. They came every night for the first week to keep vigil, to ensure that his soul did not return to haunt the house. They came with their incense and herbs; ground coffee and several demi-johns of cane syrup and strong rum. This was only Madlienne's second encounter with death in a domesticated environment—first with Tergis, which was simple. The estate gave him a Christian burial and an overseer read the last rites. Everything she experienced at Count De Brettes' place was too complicated for her to understand in a flash. It woulf take some time to absorb. She could not fathom the customs of those who were of her own shade and colour. They rejoiced in death. For them the soul had become a free spirit and would roam the earth as it pleased, contrary to birth, when the soul enters the world in chains and will be bound for an entire lifetime. This made her feel sad. The fact that she was a bound spirit that would only be released at death filled her with a certain unpleasantness. She would not return to normal until they were all gone. At the end of the seventh night, after they had consumed every drop of liquor and eaten all the stores in the house, they left. Madlienne tended his grave as though he was alive under the mound of earth, daily uprooting the stray weeds as they sprung between the white roses she had planted, always whispering to him as she worked. This became a course of habit, first thing on mornings, just as the sun came up over the hills, after she had warmed her innards with a fresh pot of coffee.

The impediments of old age clung like baggage to her waist. They wore her down. The last thing she wanted was to be seen with a walking stick. It would injure her pride. She deplored the thought. After Monsieur De Brettes died the small stipend from the business in Soufrière stopped. She had to fend for herself. First she started a kitchen garden on a nearby plot, which she gradually extended in tomatoes, cabbage, yams and other small items, for sale. Whenever she reaped she took the produce on her weekly visits to town and sold them to the shopkeepers and their assistants, who had befriended her. To supplement her meagre returns she began raising pigs, only to discover they were very intelligent creatures, who answered to their names, and nuzzled against her, when she stroked their coarse bristles, particularly the sows, which she reared mainly for their litter and never had the heart to slaughter them. Life was calm, not like earlier years when she answered the call to arms and her body was perpetually warped in a state of siege. She encountered new friends and cemented new relationships. They were shopkeepers with whom Monsieur De Brettes traded during his lifetime. The households around town, who had heard of her prowess, stood in awe whenever she walked under their windows. The tradesmen who were grateful that their weekly quota of vegetables could be delivered at their workshops paid her handsomely. They knew of her role in the Brigands War and bowed with immaculate reverence whenever she entered their shops, as a mark of respect. They had long ceased to observe her complexion, only her stately bearing mattered. She carried it with the hallmark of nobility. Her name had already become synonymous with legend and Frenchmen told stories to their children about the living reincarnation of Jeanne d'Arc, the maid of Orleans, in their very midst. They removed their hats in her presence as though they were in the company of divinity. They ran to their friends breathlessly, to relate how they had met and spoken to this great French warrior that had routed the British at Rabot, Praslin and Cul-de-Sac. Who carried the colours shoulder high at Morne Fortune, even in the face of defeat. It was sacrilegious to mention her by name, only a chosen few were permitted this luxury, but not without a nod of disapproval from discerning fanatics.

By a curious combination of luck and her own ruthless ingenuity, Madlienne became acquainted with Raphael. Raphael was a mulatto, who managed an estate in the north of the colony on behalf of an absentee landlord, whom she learnt, had never seen it. Moulin-a-Vent had been abandoned and had only started producing sugar again after thirty years of inactivity. The landlord had purchased it as his retirement home for he intended to return to the colony when his body could no longer withstand the cold French winters. The news stimulated her sixth sense. Raphael was young and very talkative. They met at the same shops every Thursday. Raphael had a son; his name was Phillipe and was no more than seven years old when she first got to know him. He was battling with asthma, withdrawn, pale and sickly. His condition forced Raphael to take him along wherever he went in order to care for him when the attacks came, without warning. He fed him liquorice sticks to ease the constriction in his chest and his lips were permanently stained with their characteristic dark brown colour. Madlienne became attracted to the boy. His father being a congenial sort allowed him to play with her whenever they met. He knew who she was and was pleased that she had chosen to befriend them. Madlienne the master prodder had gathered from Raphael, very quickly, his wife had died in childbirth and there was no one at the house to be trusted with the welfare of this sickly child. Not the old midwife, on the plantation, who had delivered him and had a reservoir of experience concocting cures for a variety of ailments. He probably still remembered his wife who had died in her care, despite her wealth of knowledge. Besides, Phillipe was frail with a sallow complexion and part of the cure was plenty of sunlight. The boy was not a burden, he followed his father everywhere. On days when he was allowed relief, he appeared as lively as the next child who did not have his affliction. His father was grooming him early, for a profession he would quite likely follow; to succeed him on the estate.

Madlienne knew the herbs that could alleviate the condition in the child, and offered her help. Every Thursday, she brought a bundle and gave detailed instructions to Raphael on its preparation. The medication was slow in getting to the root of the child's ailment. It took more than a month before Raphael began seeing signs of change in Phillipe's condition. He first observed that the attacks were coming less frequently, only on damp nights when cold winds blew in from the sea. Then there was a general change in

Phillipe's composure, he slept soundly and was sprightly throughout the day. Somewhere in the convalescent stage Phillipe developed a dry cough, which made a distinctive whooping sound and came from the depths of his chest. It frightened Raphael, who in his ignorance thought that the sickness had become ingrained in his lungs and was beyond cure. Madlienne prepared a bottle of syrup, using a select mixture of herbs:

"If the cough don't go before this is finished don't call me by my name again," she said.

The Sunday afternoon, following the Thursday she had given the elixir to Raphael, Madlienne was about to retire for her usual afternoon nap, to wake up before the crickets began to blare from their lofty perch in the coconut trees, when she heard a wagon draw up outside her cottage. She heard the snorting of horses and peeped through the jalousies. Raphael was helping Phillipe to the ground. As she came out to greet them, Raphael shouted:

"I come to call you by your name! The medicine work!" They were still clad in their Sunday fineries and had travelled to her house from church. The child seemed unusually frisky. Colour had returned to his cheeks. Seeing him run around her little cottage, like boys his age, gave her the greatest pleasure. Raphael was sitting on the pinnacle of joy.

"If you ever need my help," he said, "don't hesitate to call me."

Madlienne smiled, it was a loaded grin, filled with malice. The moment to pose her questions had finally come.

"You making a profit now, I hope?" It was a veiled gambit and Raphael being talkative by nature swallowed it.

"I don't know. This is only my third season. Monsieur Cartier keeps the books. I don't own the estate. I manage it."

"I always thought that you was the owner, the way you buy things and fight for the last price." She had lied, deliberately to steer Raphael's mind away from her real purpose.

"The owner is in France," he said, with a note of resignation.

"Some people in this world are lucky," she skillfully injected.

"How a man can stay in France and expect you to make money for him here, on the other side of the world?"

"All of them do it—sometimes," Raphael replied.

"The owner must be very rich," Madlienne commented, concealing her eagerness to push the conversation further.

"They tell me he was a manager himself once, at Xenon, in Soufrière," Raphael announced, proud to impart his knowledge. Madlienne's lips began trembling. The hate bottled inside her was rearing its ugly head. She was afraid she would not be able to frame the next question. She paused, clearing her throat of the phlegm rising to stifle her thoughts. She had to press on. She was close. She could feel it. The years had not dulled her instincts.

"You know his name? I from Xenon too."

"Monsieur Cartier says he does write pages and pages of instructions to him. Every time he write, he wants to come back to live here, but can't make up his mind."

Madlienne wondered whether he had heard the question, or was he evading it. A caution born from natural feminine intuition always guarded her moves.

"What's his name?" She asked directly, without betraying the singular interest which masterminded the conversation.

"Monsieur Gimat. Monsieur Alexandre Gimat—You know him?"

Madlienne shook her head. It was a negative response, an affirmation to confirm her fears. She had gambled on a hunch and the odds ruled in her favour.

"All his children big. Monsieur Cartier tell me his wife die."

This was good news. At last, there was another frame for her tapestry. She would spend the night weaving it in; filling fresh details in corners that have been vacant for years. Gimat the widower, somewhere, exiled in France, still dreaming of the day he would return to this island; to the sugar estate his funds had restored to full production. She could see him in her mind's eye, cringing in the tentacles of a cold winter, homesick for the islands. From then on, every Thursday when they met, their conversation acquired a new slant:

"When is your boss coming?" Madlienne would shout, to which Raphael would reply:

"When I see him I'll send to call you."

The friendship between Madlienne and Raphael blossomed. The old woman, well past middle age, but agile like a cat and the young man who was sufficiently fair to pass for white, despite the crop of wool on his head that substituted for hair. She adored Phillipe and brought him presents every Thursday; a ripe papaw from her garden—a melon, a mango, or a young piglet. She would select them from the evening before and always checked the wagon before leaving next morning, to ensure, whatever it was that she had chosen was aboard. Though not often, Raphael continued to visit her, bringing along Phillipe. After innumerable promises, Madlienne finally mustered the courage to visit them. It was a strenuous journey, which started at dawn and ended on the stroke of noon. It was one of those bright Sundays in early August, the air humid and the body responding in rivers of sweat. Sunday was the only day in the week reserved for leisure, the other days were crammed with activity, from planting to housecleaning, harvesting, haggling, and shopping. Notwithstanding, on the estates, during crop season, even Sundays were workdays, particularly when the canes were late and every available second mattered.

Moulin-a-Vent was miles away from the highroad that led from Castries to the northernmost town of Gros Islet. She had never ventured in that direction before although she knew comrades who during the Brigands War had roamed the area and had taken part in the burning of Dauphin. Her progress was hampered by frequent stops along the route, asking for directions. There were several by-roads, leading to other estates, which made the journey confusing. She was fortunate always to meet someone willing to help. She had sold Monsieur De Brettes' old grey, before it became lame, and had purchased a strong mule. The distance from where she lived to Moulin-a-Vent was more than ten miles and the young spirited mule guaranteed a safe return.

Little Phillipe ran out ahead of his father to greet her. They were both surprised. They had given up hope on her countless promises. Raphael was convinced notwithstanding the blue skies her visit would bring lightening, thunder and rain. All the canes had been harvested. Madlienne's eyes swept down the valley from the hill where Raphael's house stood, following the fallow fields that curved towards the coast; in the distance, she saw the sea.

"This year you'll make a fat profit," she remarked, thinking about the broken backs and sore hands that harvested the crop.

"Maybe, for the boss, but really, I don't know," he seemed a bit sad. It was unusual.

"You sick?" She asked, feeling concerned for his health. She knew only too well the hard work in growing cane and then converting it to sugar. She had not done the work herself, but the island was spotted with cane fields from its northernmost extremity to the south. She had heard the complaints of both planter and worker, long enough to know.

"I'm not sick," Raphael replied, "it's the labour. I can't get people to cut the canes. Can't find people to work now-a-days."

"You did well," she said, pointing to the fields where nothing stood between the breeze and the dust floating towards the skies with every gust.

"It take from February till now to get it done. I don't know what to do next year, when crop-time come."

"God on your side," she said, "you're a good man."

"Monsieur Cartier will not listen when I tell him I need more money to run this place. He say the boss will get vex. He send and ask if I want him to come to show me how to run the estate. They say I have to use the whip if I want to get anything done. I rather go. I never had to beat nobody, not because they black I must beat them to work. We have too much land and not enough people to do the work." His frustrations brought him close to tears.

"You have a clean heart, a clear conscience; you must not be afraid," Madlienne said, as they went into the house where the food was waiting. They ate, drank and spoke for the rest of the day, resurrecting bits and pieces of trivia to pass the time. She was particular in not broaching the subject of Gimat, though it was foremost on her mind. Raphael's housekeeper, Josette, was old, but was adept at preparing his meals and making a mild *mauby* draught, that only had a hint of the bitterness of the bark and a generous smattering of aniseed. When evening came they were sad to see Madlienne leave. Weeks would pass by before Raphael met her in town again.

She no longer kept the regular Thursday schedule. She had begun slaughtering her pigs and was making a spicy sausage, *boudin noir,* which could only be sold on Saturdays, when the taverns overflowed with drinkers in the afternoon. It was not only a tradition, but drinkers believed that the *boudin noir* absorbed the alcohol in their stomachs and prepared them for further consumption. She stayed in town late, until everything was sold, before taking the trek back to her little cottage at Trois Piton, to sleep all Sunday before beginning her chores for the new week. When she met Raphael again, some six weeks had elapsed. He was bright and cheerful, his usual self. The estate had made a huge profit from the sale of sugar and he was to receive a five pounds bonus for his pains. He was alone; Phillipe had not accompanied him. He was at school in Gros Islet. The wheezing had disappeared along with all the other symptoms and he was by all accounts cured. Although she missed him, Madlienne was overjoyed at the news. Her medicines had worked. Raphael was also celebrating the reconciliatory feelings of Monsieur Cartier. He had invested in six strong young men to help Raphael replant and to work the next year's crop. Raphael was in good spirits. She did not inquire about the boss, out of respect for his feelings. She did not want the exuberance to melt from his face. She had mastered the art of patience and was prepared to wait. They exchanged their usual pleasantries and disappeared to attend to the chores, among which was the traditional haggling with shopkeepers over the latest prices.

Madlienne contemplated returning to Soufrière to search for Argos, Jean, Constantin and Ti Frère, but her obsession with Gimat had the better of her thoughts. She felt that she was getting closer to him and could not give up the chase. She did not want to become entangled in a long drawn-out search that would take years to resolve. There were no clues or any definite point to start. If they were still alive they should have found her. They were not daft. Everyone in the town knew she left with Monsieur De Brettes for Castries. She was reasonably certain that the rumours about the men with the sign of cross, carved on their chests, would have reached their ears. It was Desolee's mark of vengeance, endemic to the tribe. They knew its meaning and her solemn vow. They would have known she was alive and pursuing her mission. During the several years she had spent in Soufriere before going to Castries, she was unable to locate anyone who could tell her anything definite concerning their whereabouts, so why now? Old age for good reason brings with it a certain degree of cynicism. Clarity develops beyond reproach. She would always harbour fond memories for the last of her tribe, but travelling back to Soufrière to find them, was a bit too much to ask.

CHAPTER SEVEN

A rumour had taken wings. It hovered over a town far removed from secrecy like heaven from hell. It was whispered in the taverns, between shopkeepers and their gossip-prone assistants; in the workshops and in dark corners under the stairs, in the homes Madlienne visited with her produce. Soon, it reached her ears. She was bewildered. She accepted the system despite its obvious faults and would not envisage how any new order could work effectively to preserve the peace.

'If all the labourers in the colony were made free men with one swoop of the pen, how could the planter survive?' She thought. 'Freedom can only be won in battle, by force.'

She could not conceive it any other way. Being an *affranchi* who had never experienced slavery, she was at pains to understand the domesticity of the mind and body suffered in that condition. She was aware of the cruelty, which she attributed to bad masters. After all, she had fought for their extinction, but no sooner the war was over they regrouped and reconvened their evil practices. She also accepted there were good masters and the good outnumbered the bad.

'When these men cannot get people to cut the cane and grind their mills, they will turn their rage on us.'

In her fight for freedom, the concept was, with victory the status quo would be reversed and the 'weak would inherit the earth.' She had been told this happened in St. Dominique: a New nation was born, but the country had lost the peace.

The island was enjoying an era of prosperity beyond the imagination and nothing that would disrupt this change in fortune should be contemplated. She remembered being a victim of Clercien, despite her status and freeman or slave had little meaning in the eyes of a starving planter. Armed with this thought, it was impossible to imagine how emancipation would improve the lot of the labourer.

'Who would care for him, when he was free.' She was never pleased to learn that one of her people had been ill-treated. Yet, some things were impervious to change. At the end of the war of liberation she was appalled by the misery and suffering her people had inflicted on themselves. Some who had fought by her side in the name of freedom were scavenging like rats under the cover of darkness. They shunned the daylight, fighting each other for scraps and a corner post against which to rest their head. Before the final battle was fought and won they had enslaved themselves again in choosing the most abject method of survival by returning in droves to the estates and the masters from whom they had fled to join the Army in the Woods: a domestication of mind and spirit that no free born soul ever understood.

The politics of the world did not matter unless it affected Madlienne directly. Change was its most disrupting element and she learnt to accept it as inevitable. Her vision of life had changed from that of a girl up-rooted from the serenity of an idyllic childhood to adulthood among a horde of vicious killers with varied philosophies, which more than often was contradictory. One could never correctly assess her thoughts, nor anticipate her reactions. Sometimes blood poured in her dreams, on other occasions she walked among clouds. She could not remember the faces she had killed in battle, or the numbers felled at her command. She longed to forget that era in her life, but it would not fade. She had killed in the name of *Egalité*, *Fraternité* and *Liberté*, yet in the end nothing was equal. The brotherhood was divided, and liberty lay with the slain. The futility of her efforts was easily assessed by the many times she was rebuked by her own people for her deportment. They thought she was haughty; conceited; fighting class; struggling to be white. She read it in their eyes and in her heart these insults bled. The frequent interrogations by a drunken overseer, who thought she was a runaway slave—one of Clercien's minor crimes—made her wretch uncontrollably. The paradox of existence, rebuke and rejection from your own kind as well as from others, made civilization a misnomer, remembering the smiles and feigned courtesies on the lips of those would not accept her status. The colour of her skin had created a wedge. Pride was the domain of the elite. When she first came to town, the shopkeepers' clerks were always too busy to serve her and went to elaborate lengths to blindfold the proprietors from the little chicaneries conducted right under their nostrils. Although it hurt inside, she was above such trifles. She was not unduly perturbed by events. To protect herself, however, she had Monsieur De Brettes concoct some false papers, in particular, a certificate of manumission, which officially registered her freedom. She kept it in her bosom wherever she went. While she was accepted in her own right as a member of the community a bit of protection was far better than finding a cure in those early years.

She had grown into a living relic from the Brigand's war, looming in the eyes of men too young to know its scourge and thought only of its glory. It was a gradual transition from the perceived slave of M. De Brettes to a reincarnation of the Maid of Orleans. The English families in their typical businesslike fashion dealt with her fairly. They did not, however, go beyond the normal courtesies extended to one another. Their eyes betrayed a distant feeling, a vague contempt that dared not venture beyond a stare, yet spoke volumes. The system had its checks and balances.

'How long would this last,' Madlienne asked herself, 'if the new order made them all poor?'

When the rumours about emancipation were confirmed through proclamations in the streets by the official town crier and by parish priests in all the pulpits around the island, a cloud of restlessness mushroomed over the colony, enveloping the estates under its umbrella. Sporadic outbursts of violence broke out on several estates among people who had become restless from years of unfulfilled promises and bondage. At Roseau, a large sugar estate on the West Coast, the slaves mutinied. They held the white planter and his family hostage and kept them for several days in the heights, surrendering only after their camp had been surrounded by a volunteer force, mustered in Castries on short notice to quell the revolt. Their manner of execution, stealth; silent in the dead of night, was identical to another campaign from a distant past. Whoever planned it, knew the details of Desolee's artistry. By some strange miracle of fate, no one was killed. The British commander at Fort Charlotte on Morne Fortune, visited Madlienne one evening, while she was lighting her lamps, with a small contingent. The commander was a tall double-barrel man who filled her small drawing room with his girth. It was unusual for Madlienne to find herself looking up into a man's eyes. She felt uneasy, almost dominated by his presence. He was huge, a giant almost, who with outstretched hands could easily touch the rafters if he tried. He was not a man to mince words either. Armed with the brusque precision of his race, he approached her directly.

"Madlienne Des Voeux! You have heard of the petty insurrections plaguing the colony of late. I have in my possession certain information, which leads me to believe that they are being fomented by certain unsavory elements in our society. I am here to solicit your help."

English was a language harsh to her ears. No matter how smoothly it was spoken, rolling like velvet over the tongue, to her it was coarse. She picked her way through the sentences, a few words here and there and imagined the rest.

From his opening statement she deduced the purpose of his visit, although unable to interpret everything he said, even after running it through again and again, in Creole, in her head.

"You asking me to be a spy?" She intimated, tactfully.

The commander smiled; the interrogator's cunning gleam frothed around his lips. "No," he replied; "I am here for information—soldier to soldier."

"I finish fighting forty years now. That's more than your age." She lowered her eyes to his chin searching for sprouts of gray. He was clean shaven with hair clipped short and sleek around the temples like an extension of his uniform.

"These little skirmishes have the appearances of an orchestrated plot to destabilize the peace."

Madlienne listened attentively; slight tremors were quaking through her body.

"We believe that certain trained insurgents have been smuggled into the colony to spur these revolts. There are not too many of you around with that skill, which gives me reason to believe that you have certain knowledge which you may wish to impart." His voice was crisp and firm. Madlienne remained quiet, undaunted by his colossal stature. He looked down at her with eyes that bore the green reflection she sometimes saw in the sea. "Are you willing to talk?"

Madlienne challenged his gaze and his eyes returned her stare. It was from the start a battle of wits. She was not sure who would be the winner. It was years since she had played that game; however, she recalled all the stops. She began, searching his face for a mark of sincerity that would encourage her to speak, which had nothing to do with his persistence, but her own eagerness to flush the grief that had been buried inside her for so long.

"I was a young woman when I go to war. It was the right thing to do. I spend ten years fighting for a cause I never understand. When the war end I put down my weapons and walk away in peace. I don't know nothing about what you asking me and I don't want to know."

"Keep your ears to the ground, they will come to you," he said, "When they do, you will report to me." He turned, pretending to leave, but hesitated holding on to the brass handle of her door. He toyed with it between his fingers then looked straight at her from under the bushy furrows of his eyebrows.

"Do you know one Constantin?" he asked, measuring her face, as he spoke, for change; for the slightest sign of surprise. Madlienne's heart stopped. 'It cannot be; it cannot be,' she repeated to herself without moving her lips. It had been forty years since she had heard that name.

"I fight side by side with him, in the war." she replied. The training she had received from Citoyen Goyrand was only a reflex action away,

'Never give more information than is necessary to give,' a small voice piped in her throat.

"He says you are his big sister," he prompted.

She knew there was more to be said to be said. She was a veteran at that game; she played it well and had never lost.

"It is a different time to now," she said. "He lose his family in the war. He was lonely. I was a sister to him."

"We are about to pop his neck," the commander said, with an air of finality. He had without doubt established the motive for his visit.

"What Constantin do for him to hang?" Madlienne asked; "hanging is the worst kind of punishment."

It was the end reserved for common criminals. When shorn of dignity and every form of self-respect, their necks would be wrung on the gallows till their tongues turned blue and dangled out of their mouths. It was a death also reserved for traitors. She had seen many in her time. Thoughts scrambled through her mind.

"We caught him at Cannelles training persons in weaponry."

"That is not a crime!" Madlienne blurted, the tremors rising to her lips.

"I too have my orders. Treason against the crown is punishable by death. Hanging to be precise," the commander said.

She watched him pensively, standing in the doorway, while his men who were patiently waiting outside began mounting their steeds, thinking he was about to leave. Madlienne made a faint gesture with her hand, he signalled them to wait.

"He is a prisoner at the fort, you want to see him?" Madlienne did not reply with words but nodded in the affirmative.

"He gives no information except to gargle in that untranslatable language of his, that he is a soldier of the revolution and has nothing more to say. He keeps repeating himself."

Madlienne suppressed a smile. She knew he would learn nothing from Constantin. No torture would loosen his tongue.

"I will come tomorrow," Madlienne said.

"I knew you would volunteer your help. He pretends he is mad. But he did call for you through our interpreter."

Madlienne could no longer hold back the smile. The faith of the tribe in her had been preserved. She would go to Constantin.

"It will be early in the morning," she told the commander.

"I knew you would co-operate," he said, extending both hands to her. She shook them. To the Englishman, it was the birth of an alliance. To Madlienne it was a glimpse of her cunning.

"Go to the postern gate, the one facing the sea. Give your name to the guard. I will arrange safe passage." He clicked his heels and walked into the twilight towards his horse. As he mounted he called out to her.

"Please come unarmed. You will be searched." They exchanged glances; long dark looks that did not need words to form their meaning. Madlienne stood in the doorway watching them ride back to the fort, their red tunics fading through the vines that overhung the road. They were no more than twelve, with the commander leading the group two lengths ahead. She continued to watch them until they merged with dusk.

Argos, Jean, Ti Frère and Constantin had returned to her life just as she was beginning to accept the dictates of her mind, convinced that they had succumbed to a fate more hideous than death. They did not reach her after the war, nor did they send a message via one of their comrades returning from the field. They had vanished from the face of the earth without trace. In this small corner of the world, it was not possible. Everyone knew each other and was either related by blood or marriage, or a combination of both. Marriage, not necessarily in the conventional sense, but through concubinage carried the same weight. The thought that they were alive somewhere, surmounted all other thoughts. They were a part of her, each inextricably bound by a bond deeper than friendship, firmer than the camaraderie born under fire with trust more sanguine than blood. She was their leader. Their fealty was for no other. A crude tribal instinct fashioned her thinking in such matters.

It was her duty to protect them no matter the cost. Constantin would open to her. He would tell her the truth and she could not betray him. It was a dangerous mission. The commander was eager for blood. He would have it with or without the information he was relying on her to extract. The agility that once coursed through her muscles was priming through like a rusty spring in an old musket. It would be foolish for her to think that she could capture the fort single-handed, even if she were to succeed, what next? She had to survive. Her real mission was far from complete.

Before the night had rolled its sleeves and bolted with the dark, Madlienne was in her yard hitching Clarissia, her old mule, to the cart. She had put on her old black dress, the one that had been given to her by Monsieur De Brettes from his unsold stock as a Christmas present, after the fashion had passed. She had last worn it on the day of his burial. She steered Clarissia by the bridle into the narrow dirt road. She had planned to leave before the neighbours got up and began inquiring about her movements. She knew they had seen the soldiers and would be curious about the nature of their business. Madlienne had always been a private person and would not submit to excursions on her privacy, no matter how slight. She mounted the buckboard with panache, flexing to crack a slight twitch of the whip across Clarissia's back as she clipped gingerly away.

Dawn broke while she was crossing the ridge, with the small town of Castries trapped between its toes. Its light swept across the eastern hills stirring the mist that rose slowly to greet the rolling clouds, moving swiftly, pushed by a westerly wind, out to sea. A man-o-war was anchored in the bay; she saw the white ensign unfurl from its mizzenmast. As she approached the compound that housed the fort she heard the reveille sound. She remembered the drills, the muster rolls; sleep draining from the eyes of the soldier as he hitches his trousers to find his musket . . . The sun broke through a cloud to leapfrog over the town. There it was, calmly on her back with morning smoke from the ovens curling upward to embrace the hills. The early morning air soaked through her clothes with a slow drizzle. Madlienne dismounted and climbed the stone steps that led to the postern gate. Its features had remained acutely familiar. She had climbed those steps before, in another age, as a combatant answering the call of duty. It was the same walls she had stoutly defended, with musket ball and the cannon, firing blindly into the dark at an unseen enemy, until there was nothing left to fire. Sculpted from the sedimentary rocks that littered the hill, buttressing above the natural contours of the land, which curved and sloped like the work of an uneven hand, the old fort stood solid in the morning light. The breaches in her walls long since repaired and blended with the original structure, weathered by sun, wind and rain. The cold stones under her feet came alive with memories of the familiar.

'The ways of this world is strange,' she mused. She knocked at the gate. A guard with the comical features of a marmoset framed in a peephole, peered myopically into the light.

"My name is Madlienne Des Voeux, I came to see my brother," she repeated calmly. The guard pulled back his face and closed the peephole. She heard the bolts that sealed the main door retract, into their clamps. The hinges yawned and the door limped open.

The guard clicked his heels. "To the main barracks, Ma'am, the captain's waiting for you."

He pointed to an old stone building, grey like the clouds and overrun with coralita vine. She entered the building virtually unnoticed, the main door ajar, leading to the drill room. She moved forward slowly, admiring the display of arms and banners that hung from the walls. At the end of the hall, two sentries were posted outside a red door above which hung the coat of arms of England: three lions carved on a wooden plaque and coated with an ample application of varnish, which reflected the furniture in the hall like a mirror. The sentries clicked their heels in unison as she approached and presented arms. One of the sentries opened the door; the commander was seated behind his desk. Madlienne bowed to the sentries and walked past. The commander rose jubilantly to greet her. He was filled with the exhilaration of meeting a long lost friend after years of absence.

"You see, the soldiers respect your rank," he said, in that cheerful drawl, that made him human under the uniform, although toiling under the obvious strain of dispatches piled on his desk. Madlienne knew it was all an act:

"I come to see my brother," she said, her face blank, showing no outward signs of emotion, although her heart was throbbing like the drums.

"I know you are a woman of your word—a soldier's honour."

Caged in by her own defensive silence, Madlienne stood before the white commander, neither smiling nor serious. She watched him gather the papers from his desk and place them in a heap to the side, under a brass paperweight.

"I will take you to your brother. He is in one of the cells below," he grinned. They descended a narrow flight of stairs, which led to another landing that was level with the parade ground outside. They walked a short distance until they came to a set of spiral stairs, leading to a subterranean passage below ground level. It was dark and damp and lit by tallow lamps at intervals along the walls. At the end of the passage, they came to four heavy armour-plated doors less than eight feet apart. Each one had a peephole large enough for a man's head and grilled with cast iron bars. Madlienne recognized the cells. An armed guard patrolled the narrow passage, listing like a ship from side to side. As they approached, he clicked his heels to attention, tensing his muscles. A short fat soldier came rolling like a barrel down the corridor with an assortment of keys chained to his waist. They made a jingling sound with each stride. This and the curious creaking from his new pair of boots betrayed his presence anywhere. He was the gaoler and a living image of the job. He fidgeted with the bunch of keys hooked to his heavy leather belt, uncertain, until he finds the right one to open the door to the middle cell. Madlienne was convinced he was alone in the loneliest job in the world; befriended by neither friend nor foe. She bowed, slightly tilting her head to thank him

And he smiled back in recognition.

The commander entered the cell and asked Madlienne to follow. The gaoler closed the door behind them, turning the key with clinical precision. A faint ray of sunlight reflecting from some distant object shined through another iron bar grill, blocking a small opening inside the great stone wall. Its purpose was uncertain as there were no other exits than the door they had entered. Madlienne did not know what lay behind the walls, but she remembered her experiences in the cave many years before. She knew light could stream through the smallest crevice in a rock. The fort was built on the crest of Morne Fortune in the full glare of the morning sun. It struck its ramparts—first thing on mornings—like flares fired from a thousand cannons all at once. The light could have come from any source, deflected from a shiny doorknob, a mirror, or even a pool of water. In the right hand corner of the hall, facing Madlienne, the stooped shadow of a man, crouched against the wall, caught her eye. His head was bowed and his hands folded around his knees, perhaps in the same posture he had slept. The rest of his body escaped the splutter of light virtually shining from nowhere. Madlienne squinted to adjust to the mass of grey wool directly in front of her;

"Your brother, Madame!" The commander said pointing to the emanciated figure huddled in the corner, doubling to keep warm.

"He may be old, but it took ten men to take him with the help of a snare."

"A snare?" Madlienne frowned.

"Yes, a net. He's a big fish. We wanted him alive."

Madlienne spoke, forcing a sly smile whilst staring at the motionless body in the corner: "If he is my brother, I will know—leave us."

The commander hesitated a moment, Madlienne gently raised her hand, indicating to him, to go. He understood. He knew his presence would not produce results. He rapped on the cell door three times with the hilt of his sword. The gaoler opened. Leaving them alone was a difficult decision. He now had to trust her and hoped she would speak the truth when debriefed. Constantin would not speak freely in his presence, even if it were in that garbled tongue he could not understand despite years spent fiddling with French. He was anxious for results. Whatever Constantin would say to Madlienne could save lives, his men and his own; nothing was more strategic.

"If you need help, shout! I'll not be too far away." He closed the door behind him and the goaler turned the key. He was quite pleased with himself. The little he knew of intrigue, he was putting to good use.

Madlienne moved closer to the figure crouched in the corner, cautiously at first, straining for a sign in the gloom. His clothes were shredded and spotted with bloodstains. They hung like buntings from his body. As she drew closer, Madlienne observed a jagged gash on his thigh. It was not deep, made either by a whip or some blunt weapon. She surmised he might have received it during the struggle resulting in his capture. The wound was clean. Seeing it raw and undressed made her nauseous. She had seen many wounds, some fatal with the lifeblood pulsing in spurts, some barely oozing before the heart stopped pumping. For a moment she forgot the purpose of her visit, motionless and unable to speak. A change had occurred in her body. She was conscious of it. She could no longer stand the sight of blood.

By then, Madlienne had wished, with all her heart that the figure in the corner was Constantin. If he really was, she would soon know. In the forest as children, they were never used their right names. The elders feared the children could be confronted by one of the many malevolent spirits, hovering over the trees, using human voices to whisper names in the wind. These spirits, they were taught, would then lure them to a secluded spot in the innermost recesses of the woods where no human form had even dared to wander. There to be skinned and eaten alive, with hearts intact still beating in their carcasses. As they pranced through the underbrush under the shade of the *Acajou,* Mahogany and *Laurier,* forming a gigantic arch over their heads, they called one another by other names, confusing the spirits, reducing their powers to a feeble state of impotence. Names they had never heard before, concocted on a whim, infused with the ingenuity of childhood. They listened as their echoes reverberated through the vast expanse of trees, growing loud and distant. Sometimes, they shook with fright hearing their voices vibrate against the barrier of mountains and could only console each other after they had fled back to safety of camp . . . These nicknames, or *nom savane*, were later assimilated into codes and hammered into the night when the drums chanted their solemn liturgies to the Army in the Woods.

Madlienne bent forward and raised his head. His eyes were wide open, looking through her as though she was invisible.

"Ti Toe!" She whispered. His earlobes shifted slightly, erect, gathering the sound.

"Ti Toe!" Madlienne repeated the name he was given to protect him from evil in the forest many moons ago. A name hammered out on the drums when he disappeared on his many missions. His body twitched. Light came slowly to his eyes.

"*Sais!*" She heard his deep voice call.

"Sais, is you?" He had remembered the code. It was Constantin. He had called her by her *nom savane*.

He had aged gracefully. Apart from the drizzle of grey in his hair, his body was lean and firm. Her emotions ran wild. She did not know whether to hug or give him a good tongue lashing for not finding her sooner.

"The eyes not good. I didn't see was you standing there." He got up, opened his arms and swallowed her into his chest. As he held her, her mind rolled back to that morning in camp when they said their last good-byes.

"Where Argos? Jean? Where Ti Frère?" She spoke in their local creole, itching for news, hurrying for replies before the words came out of her mouth.

"Guadeloupe," he replied sadly.

The brief spasm of joy drained from his cheeks as a cloud came over his face. His eyes reddened into a firestorm and he began to sob.

"We lose! We lose!" Repeating the words over and over again. "Shuuush!" Madlienne said, placing a finger to her lips, "You don't want the English to hear. They outside," pointing to the door.

Madlienne took out a large multicoloured cotton handkerchief which she used both as a headscarf against the rain, and a *serviette* to mop her face when the sun made her sweat. He slumped on the edge of the canvass cot wedged to the stone wall of his cell; it was his bed. He had not slept in it as she suspected, it showed in his eyes.

"We lose!" He repeated again. "It not like the old days—too many traitors." Madlienne pretended to understand.

She remained standing, her back to the door, blocking Constantin from clear view, in case anyone was peeping through a secret peephole. Constantin warbled to himself. Not everything he said was intelligible, but as he spoke of the demise of himself, Argos, Jean and Ti Frère, Madlienne felt the pain in his voice and was most attentive.

"When we was losing the war, a boat come in at Dauphin and take Citoyen La Crosse and the other *blancs* that was chiefs in the revolution. They take us with them to Guadeloupe. They let us come ashore with our guns and make us march though Point-a-Pitre to a camp outside the town. They keep us there for a week, with others like us, they had no food. When we couldn't take it again, we complain, but they did not listen to us. As soon as La Crosse reach they throw him in jail. The new leaders didn't want to hear nothing about the revolution. They say we have to see for ourselves. We raid a few estates because we was hungry; a few *blancs* die; they catch us; put us in chains and sell us like horse. Argos, Jean and Ti Frère stay, they say they tired fighting. Not me! I run away in the hills where I meet *Negre Maron* that living there long before the French come. They never catch me. I use to come down from the hills every Sunday to see Argos, Jean and Ti Frère. They stay at the same plantation they went to after they break camp, a place call Colombette, it far from town. They tell me the French was looking for men to come to St. Lucie and Dominique to show people how to use guns. I take a chance an give up myself. I couldn't take sleeping in the bush anymore. I getting old. They didn't ask me questions, they give me a full pardon an take me to Martinique. In Martinique they test me in everything: with gun, with knife, cannon, powder, everything. I show them everything I know. One night, no moon, they take ten of us in a small boat from Diamant and put us ashore at Gros Islet. At Gros Islet some French planters come to meet us on the beach and take us to a camp they make for us at Barre de L'Isle. They tell us they going to help us make the army in the woods ride again. I was glad. They even give us a flag. But things not like the old days. You can't trust nobody, people carry news."

She absorbed his words with mixed feelings. She was glad to learn that Argos, Jean and Ti Frère were alive. However she was hurting inside to learn that their free spirit was broken by the chain after having fought so valiantly in the name of the revolution for the rights of man; for the cannons of liberty and the pursuit of freedom. To be sold into slavery at the end of it all, equated to another great betrayal which she had heard of from the lips of Monsieur De Brettes, the defilement of the Prince of Peace by his own disciple, for thirty pieces of silver. The bitterness within her rose like a fever souring her mouth. Her temples throbbed. The Judas kiss felt warm on her cheeks reminding her, she had no country, no flag. Her only allegiance was to her tribe, what was left of it.

"We had to show the people how to fight, all they getting was promises, nothing after that." Constantin continued. "They tell us the English want a new kind of Slavery."

"And you believe them after what they do to you?" Madlienne injected, but he was not listening.

"They tell us, that all poor people will have to go back to work the cane: *affranchi*, mulatto, *petits blancs*, everybody. Whether they want or not. They promise to hang anybody that didn't want to work. They say the English will close all church and they will put the priest in jail."

"The French did that one, in the name of Revolution. Now they want to fool us again," Madlienne said, visibly annoyed.

"I was tired of the bush, *Sais*; I can't go on living like a animal all my life," Constantin said. "All the French trying to do is to use us to get back what they loose. They want to line their pockets with gold, from your sweat. You forget already what happen when we give them St. Lucie on a plate. You forget they had promise us that nobody would wear chains again. An you remember what they do?"

"The English want me to tell them everything you say," Madlienne said. She wanted him to be apprised of the real purpose of her visit.

"*Pauvre Diable*! They don't know the power of blood. What they think you'll tell them?" Constantin said, sniggering, knowing he was not alone in the world.

"The English will hang you whether you speak or not—you know that," Madlienne said. Constantin looked up at her, his eyes beaming. The strange gleam on his face was neither fear nor chivalry. To an astute warrior, the English plan was clear. They were not being kind. The plot was to get him to speak, fair or foul and Madlienne was the bait. What he first thought was a simple matter of granting his last request had become subterfuge. He was confused. His mind clogged. He never understood intrigue, war was a simple matter, kill or be killed, it was not hard to understand. In dying, lips remained sealed.

Going to the grave with your secret was an honourable thing, not prattling like an old woman who had seen the devil on her last day and was hastily repenting her sins to the world, hoping that at the last minute she would be reprieved from another eternity in hell.

"I will not see you again," Madlienne said, "I will remember you when I pray, which is not often," she added.

She knew their conversation had come to an abrupt end. He would say nothing more. Not that he thought she would betray him, nor that whatever he said could be extracted from her under torture. The regimen of years of training ingrained in his blood had clamped his mouth shut. He said no more than what should be said. There were no exceptions, not even for a close relative. They embraced for the last time. Madlienne turned towards the door and rapped hard, while Constantin slumped lifeless in his corner and folded his arms between his legs.

The commander was ecstatic. "You spent a long time in there," he said.

"I never see the inside of a prison before," Madlienne replied.

"He was your brother?" The commander inquired, the tone of his voice confided a childlike eagerness for knowledge.

"He is," Madlienne replied, implying he was still alive.

"You understand I will need every bit of information if I am to quell these pockets of rebellion plaguing the countryside."

"He said nothing you don't know already," Madlienne replied.

"Like what?" he enquired.

"He tell me how he was captured and brought here to hang."

There was an edge of anger in her voice, a bottled rage that imploded as she looked at the commander in the eye.

"That is all!" He exclaimed.

"He doesn't trust me," she said, "he trust nobody." She would not betray Constantin. Whatever was spoken between them would go down to the grave with her. There was a plot to sink the island again in a sea of chaos. The commander's informants were right, nevertheless, she would not be the one to confirm his fears. Whether he believed her or not, the commander was quite pleasant as he escorted her back to the postern gate. Madlienne felt the wind ruffling through her clothes as she descended the stone steps to find Clarissia's head buried in a tuft of grass nibbling away.

The burial detail was hastily recruited from the back streets of town and unceremoniously carted to the fort. There had not been an execution on the premises since the wars. They had forgotten how to hang. The excitement was driving them into frenzy. Like crows they hovered around the pasture, silhouetted against the morning sky that had lowered its flag of cloud as a mark of respect for the man about to die. They trudged across the open *savane*, driven by the slow lethargic rhythm of a dead march towards the fort, then up the steps to disappear through the postern gate.

They reappeared within a matter of minutes wheeling out the body on a handcart under the watchful eye of a handful of soldiers. Outside, in the open field, they swooped like scavengers on the body, stripping off the remnants of clothes then placed it in a wooden box one of them had brought out of the fort, balanced on his head. They lowered the coffin in a freshly dug hole. The earth was soft, moistened by morning rains. The dirt rested lightly on him. They left, under the same cloud of silence as they came: an orderly had given them each a tanner. By evening they would be drunk in the taverns about town, recounting the morning's event. Naked, like the morning he was born, Constantin was delivered to his maker. At last, for him there was peace.

For Madlienne, it had been a sleepless night; her mind boiling like the ravine behind her cottage in rainy season, growing restless as the hours raced towards dawn. Thought after thought exercised her brain, but could not crystallize. She knew she was powerless to help Constantine and hated the feeling. It made her sick. Argos, Jean and Ti Frere were beyond her reach. Gimat, the man she held responsible for the annihilation of her tribe, was very far away. Her muscles ached as her body belched its paroxysms of hate. She could not decide which crime weighed heaviest on her conscience—her inability to lift a finger to save Constantine from a shameful felon's end, or, to stretch beyond the barriers of the sea and dig her fingers into the soft cartilage of Gimat's throat. She tossed and turned on the bed, wrestling with her pillow. Sometimes it is far better to let old wounds fester, dry and then become forgotten. Tickle them, they hurt. She stayed on her back looking up at the ceiling while her world shrunk to the size of a plum inside her with her heart outracing its pulse. Rage was her fuel; it fired her brain beyond the point of fevers. Gradually it settled on that solitary act she had to pursue. The sooner it was accomplished, the sooner she would be at peace with herself. A thick haze, like early morning mist on the hills, settled on her mind. Slowly, very slowly, sleep came. It was close to dawn.

CHAPTER EIGHT

It was a dry, hot year. June had come and gone and still the rains had not come. The ripe canes shriveling in the noonday heat split and burst into flames before they could be cut. Cane fires swept through the profits on all the small estates and dented returns from larger ones. Rivers; Cannelles, Roseau and Castries, were reduced to trickles. Added to this catastrophe, an outbreak of swine fever raged throughout the length and breadth of the colony. Madlienne did not escape unscathed. She suffered a total loss of her swineherd. Consequently, she was forced to return full time to her kitchen garden which she fostered with pails of water painstakingly fetched from the stream behind her cottage. Miraculously, it still flowed. Manure from Clarissia's dried dung, enriched the soil and hastened maturity.

Phillipe had grown into a fine young man, drawing blushes from the young ladies whenever he came to town on Thursdays, in place of his father. He had finished his schooling in Gros Islet and was helping to run the estate. Raphael did not have the means to send him to France for further studies as was the custom, but was quite willing to show him the details of his trade, knowing that one day Phillipe would succeed him. Phillipe was contented with his post, which had no real office. The variety of chores he performed under the direct supervision of his father gave semblance to a position of responsibility and not an apprentice. Madlienne, delighted by Phillipe's rapid strides towards full manhood, became impatient on Thursday mornings during a lull in activity whenever Clarissia paused for a call of nature. She looked on him as a godson, although she had none, nor had she ever been asked to sponsor a child. She had returned to her usual habit of visiting town on Thursday's again, being entirely immersed in her small vegetable and ground provision business. She had organized a system of pre-selling her produce one week ahead and parceled each order in tiny heaps tied with lianas; delivering as soon as she arrived. No sooner this was done; she sought confirmation for the next week's supplies. She relied on a combination of habit and memory to service her customers, collecting her hard-earned coppers on delivery.

The Thursday morning routine acquired the semblance of a drill, between deliveries, payment and purchase. Madlienne was usually early, well ahead of the traffic that arrived as the town opened for business. She could be seen darting to and fro, between the tethering posts, outside the several shops on Rue Pont, the town's main street, making her deliveries before Phillipe arrived. Phillipe gave her an incentive to complete her task swiftly so as to spend time chatting with him. From him she gathered news about Moulin-a-Vent, from important snippets down to morsels of trivia. For her everything about that place was important, even the colour of the sky. Raphael, on one of his rare visits told her he was building a house for his boss. Monsieur Cartier had given him *carte blanche* to credit lumber from the three leading business houses in town. He had come solely to introduce his son to the proprietors to facilitate deliveries in his absence. His presence on the estate was imperative. The building in progress and the impending harvest absorbed his undivided attention beyond exhaustion. Madlienne's interest focused on all activities related to construction; it served as an indication of Gimat's return. Her adrenalin flowed in expectation of the affirmative whenever she slipped the obvious question, which was too skillfully crafted for Phillipe's juvenile senses to grasp:

"When is the boss coming?" She asked, pretending no particular interest in his response.

"Next year perhaps," Phillip would reply.

"After he see his profits?" She often inquired with a grin, after teasing him on his prowess with the girls. Sometimes she would rephrase, avoiding suspicion, by making a joke.

"Boss still coming, or he change his mind again?"

"Monsieur Cartier say he coming. We have to finish the house before he reach."

Their conversations were animated with gestures that appeared unreal to a chance observer. Yet to them, it was an extension of themselves, reaching out to each other, bridging a gap, generations apart, conversing fully on topics real or imagined. Madlienne's thoughts, however, were always geared towards positioning herself to strike. She had to be in place on Gimat's arrival; before he could settle and rebuild his coterie of friends. Alone he was vulnerable. Her friendship with Raphael and Phillipe would provide the opportunity.

It was a bad year for sugar, although Raphael said that they had recovered the money spent on labour and food. He had repaid the notes at the lumberyards and the house was shaping into a habitable structure. Emancipation had come and gone, not that this produced much enthusiasm or motivation among the workers; some were now paid a pittance for their labour, but they went about their tasks at a pace slower than snails. It was the period of apprenticeship and they were told that they were to serve their former masters for seven years in exchange for food and lodging before they were declared absolutely free. To them nothing had changed, only the whip had been removed. At Moulin-a-vent estate the situation was slightly different; because in the old days Raphael had never resorted to floggings even after he had been chided by Monsieur Cartier for being behind schedule; the people never forgot him for this. It was the only estate to register a full turnout the year following Emancipation on the first day of the cutting season. Raphael was loved by all. This love transcended the colour bar because he had a soft heart. Monsieur Cartier made no mention of profits but when Raphael asked about his bonus, because by June the cane had been cut and the mill had already produced forty tons of sugar, Monsieur Cartier told him discreetly,

"We need all the money we can find this year to finish the house."

He made it seem like Raphael's fault that the house was costing a small fortune to complete. What began as an ordinary bungalow, had sprawled into a mansion. It had been under construction for eighteen months with frequent stoppages on account of specific supplies required for finishing that never seemed available on island when required. Monsieur Cartier's frequent visits further aggravated the situation. Every time he came, he demanded changes. Rooms had to be enlarged; additions to a structure that was already too big to house one man were hastily decided in the heat of discussion, to suit the taste of someone they had never met. Monsieur Cartier revealed the fussy side of his character, always bickering about some feature or other that did not meet his expectations. He relished the knack of making Raphael seem like an imbecile in the presence of the builders. He claimed that Raphael could do nothing right without a lecture. It was an exasperating experience; it almost sent him mad. Phillipe communicated all this to Madlienne when they met. His father had told him how Madlienne had saved his life with her medicines. He had grown to love her like the mother he never knew and confided even his personal secrets. He had inherited his father's talkative disposition and held nothing back. The Thursday after the building was finally completed,

Phillipe hailed her as he entered Delieu's small grocery shop on Rue Laborie, where they often met while purchasing provisions.

"The house finish at last," he shouted, his voice quavering with excitement. "The only thing missing now is the furniture and the boss."

Madlienne's face lit up in surprise,

"At last!" She exclaimed, shaking hands vigorously as though they were the ones who had completed the task. The moment that she had lived and waited for was fast approaching. Soon, she expected to hear of Gimat's arrival.

She needed to lobby for a position at Moulin-a Vent to be close to Gimat. Phillipe and Raphael would help her. All she had to do was frame her ruse. "When the boss come, you don't think I can find something to do for him at the house?" Madlienne lowered her voice wanting to be private. She did not like the assistant's eavesdropping, but Phillipe continued at the top of his voice:

"Yes! I will tell my father." The idea of having Madlienne close where he could bother her with his trifles excited him. He would no longer have to wait a whole week before they met. In his eyes she was not the battle-scarred veteran from a war no one remembered, though they bestowed on her a hero's honour, but the manifestation of the benign figure of a saint, sent by heaven to direct his adolescent fears along the right road to manhood.

"I tired of this hard work," Madlienne said.

"I will get my father to talk to Monsieur Cartier. He might let you start before the boss come."

Having persevered all these years she was about to reap dividends. Madlienne allowed two consecutive Thursdays to pass by without broaching the subject again. She had allotted reasonable time for Raphael to contact Monsieur Cartier. On the third Thursday she spotted Raphael and Phillipe at a distance going into Monsieur Delieu's grocery shop. It was easy to way—lay them, they never altered their habits. She had almost completed her rounds. The urge to accost them was strong, but a small voice inside held her back. She knew that they would likely be there for the better part of the hour so she continued down street until she had delivered the last of the greens and vegetables. When she returned she saw Raphael at the tethering posts. Two porters were helping Phillipe load the provisions on the cart. She rode up and drew her buckboard next to theirs. Raphael's horse was buried to the neck in a bucket of oats and he was running his fingers through its mane. Before Madlienne could dismount, Phillipe ran towards her, carelessly tossing the bag of potatoes he was carrying into the cart. "You got the job," he shouted;

intoxicated by the thought that he was the one to break the news. Raphael, on hearing her voice, looked up. He was a bit surprised, as she had just crossed his mind.

"I want to see you!" he said, as he walked towards her after patting his horse.

"Since last week I look for you. Monsieur Cartier thinks you are mulatto. But even then I had to argue hard to get four shillings plus food out of the old rat."

Madlienne sighed and made a sign of the cross. The stress of waiting for Monsieur Cartier's decisions dissipated with a lump in her throat. She was speechless.

"When can you start?" Raphael asked.

"As soon as you need me." Madlienne was unable to conceal her elation behind the grin that bared her teeth, still pearl white and intact. Her mission; its success had become her life's dream. Nothing could draw her away, not even the genuine affection she felt for Raphael and Phillipe. They were tools. She needed them to complete her task. They would lead her by the hand to Gimat. An introduction was all she required. She would choose her moment. The dilemma which plagued her after the visit to Constantin at the fort; the inevitable battle with conscience to choose between the abandonment of her lifelong project and going to Guadeloupe in search of Argos, Ti Frère and Jean was a thing of the past. She would act in their name as well as hers and when that final blow was dealt, she would surrender to fate.

She had been told that although the despicable trade had been abolished in St. Lucia and the other English colonies, it still flourished in the French and Spanish Islands. She became incensed knowing that the so-called masters were still trading openly in human misery within their boundaries. This knowledge did not increase her urge to rescue the sole survivors of her tribe, although it filled her with discomfort. There were other men like Gimat, indiscriminately cruel, whose only wish was to perpetuate the old order, to fuel their sadistic egos. Everything was linked, parts of the same chain: her brothers in slavery in Guadeloupe and men like Gimat at large, inflicting their brand of cruelty on souls that had grown impervious to it. She would never concede to oppression, although at times she wavered and tacitly accepted the condition for she knew no other. Age had woven a ribbon of gray through her hair; her spine had shrunk, causing her to walk with a slight stoop, yet her mind was alert. For her the battle about to be fought was one of wits, a vendetta that continued to gnaw inside; one of love and hate, which had to be put to rest before her eyes closed. She was now close to Gimat, she would never be able to forgive herself if she allowed him to escape. She consoled herself with thoughts that Argos, Jean, and Ti Frère were contented with their estate. Unlike Constantin, they never attempted to escape. She continued to lament the fact that they had never tried to contact her, to let her know they were alive and well. Her energies now concentrated on the plan she had drawn in her mind for forty years; its success was paramount in her sphere of things. Nothind was more important. All other matters would wait.

The date for Gimat's arrival in the colony had not been confirmed. He was expected before the last sugar exports sailed. Monsieur Cartier had become highly agitated each passing week as the packets from Europe drifted into port. He was becoming increasingly worried that his services would no longer be required, once Gimat settled at Moulin-a-Vent. He insisted that Raphael came to his office every Thursday to give him a full report on the events of the past week. He started a diary and recorded everything Raphael reported verbatim, in a tedious hand that distressed Raphael to the point of exhaustion. It was his intention to use the information to demonstrate to Monsieur Gimat his keen interest and maybe secure his post. Madlienne had taken up her job as caretaker at the house and had worked assiduously scrubbing every inch of floor, attacking the ever-encroaching phalanx of dust advancing with each gust of wind through the windows with a vigour that she had once reserved for the enemy. Two servant girls chosen among the relatives of those who worked on the estate were hand picked by Madlienne with Raphael's permission and a third, a young fair skinned girl, who dropped by casually one week later in search of work with a young child in her arms. They were to be her assistants, and to follow her instructions without questioning. Madlienne had not only assumed the management role at Monsieur Gimat's household; she was also running Raphael's as well. His house had survived without the presence of a woman for seventeen years, notwithstanding the efforts of his old housekeeper, Josette, who jealously guarded the kitchen as her mound of turf and dusted the few cobwebs from the corners when strength allowed. Raphael had not remarried after his wife died in childbirth and there was still an air of mourning about the house. The interior was dark with the few bits of furniture scattered loosely about. Madlienne marshalled the three young women through every corner, behind heavy mahogany pieces, clearing the dust that had heaped undisturbed; forming anthills in the comfort of dark crevices, where generations of spiders had bred and littered with their carcasses. The house breathed a new lease as sunlight floated through its inner portals, unchecked by the gloom that hovered like dusk through the rooms—ingrained in the wood—refusing to depart. Madlienne had the men to come and rearranged the furniture, erasing memories from the past, particularly the guilt that haunted Raphael every time he entered the house.

Both houses were now immaculate and functional, without a speck of dust on their floors. Madlienne looked back with pride at her achievements before concentrating outdoors. Landscaping at Gimat's new house came under her direction, whether Raphael had assigned this duty to her or not. The cane cutting season had come to an end and it was quite easy to commandeer workers found loitering outside the mill, shunting in turns to unload the last wagons coming from the fields. After some brief words of introduction, she could be seen trudging back to the house with two or three young men, to dig holes, carry stones and transplant trees hand-picked by her, to nurse that penchant for flowers and flower gardens she had acquired since she had seen prints of Versailles in the drawing rooms at Xenon and Diamant. The men worked willingly, without a grumble, sometimes late into the afternoon. She led by example. Almost tireless in her enthusiasm to complete the task she had set on the same day. Within a matter of weeks the transformation was complete. The narrow carriageway leading to the house from the main road was lined with pink oleander stalks, which Madlienne watered herself every morning from the cistern adjoining the house. Closer to the verandah she had planted canna from seeds and they were beginning to germinate. She covered them with coconut palms to shield their tender leaves from the noonday sun, removing the cover on evenings to absorb the dew. Bougainvilleas of every shade and variety found within walking distance had been planted close to the house so that they could trail along the trelliswork that decorated the porch. The ruins of an older house stood on the premises towards the rear of the new building; Madlienne had salvaged most of the round stones and the men borrowed from the mill had helped to arrange them around the flower beds planted in zinnias, sunflowers, and marigolds. A stand of Royal palms where blackbirds made their nest marked the boundaries of the back lawn: they had been planted there by a previous owner who had occupied the old building, now in ruins. Madlienne, in one of her curious moments, had asked Raphael about it:

"The ruins," he said, "they there since I was a boy." He had no idea that the place had been previously inhabited. It was only after he had began clearing the land, when various artifacts buried in the ground or weathering under the thick undergrowth began to surface:

"This estate has seen better times." He remarked.

He had unearthed a brace of rope miraculously spared the wrath of time, some rusted links of chain, then a cartwheel with its wooded sprockets intact. While excavating to lay the foundations for Gimat's house, he found a brace of shackles. The old midwife, Josette, had mentioned casually that the estate was once a stud farm, where the slaves were kept purely for breeding.

"It once supply the whole North with strong young men to work the cane." She had learnt her craft there, from older midwives, chosen for the task because they were considered unattactive. When the estate was finally abandoned because the master was too old to manage, she was granted her freedom and allowed to continue living in the broken down slave quarters where she still lived with two elderly women, too old to work. One of them had gone blind.

The grounds were properly manicured; the little flowering plants were sprouting from their beds under Madlienne's constant care. At last the long awaited letter arrived. Monsieur Cartier came himself on horseback to bring the news. Monsieur Gimat would be arriving in the colony on the second Friday in September. He was already in Martinique and was negotiating the purchase of a copper still from some old acquaintances that by chance, he discovered, were going out of business. The deep feeling of affection towards Phillipe and his father, which began soon after she had drawn out the malady from the child's body with her *tisanes* was becoming a hurdle in the subtle path of her plans. She had seen Phillipe grow into a young man and felt proud knowing that it was her skill that had carried him thus far. She knew whatever her plans she to ensure their safety beyond incrimination. This would be done even at the risk of capture. What was first conceived as an easy task was causing her to writhe in pain just thinking about it. She battled with her conscience to escape reality. She knew she should not bother about "the bridge" until it was about to be crossed, but those she had grown to love had become obstacles in her path. She spent long sleepless nights conspiring: anything she planned must exclude Raphael and Phillipe; they had to be far removed to avoid suspicion.

Days hung in the air with a lethargy that came with heat, lengthening as August dragged to a close. Nights were short, but anxiety drove away sleep. Evenings were pleasant, when it did not rain, dusk lingering in long streaks of amber that lined the western skies, holding the light until moonrise. Madlienne would sit under an old tamarind tree in the yard, surrounded by her three young helpers, spinning tales from her past, some real, some imaginary. She never spoke about the war, or the massacre of her tribe; just small insignificant anecdotes that would stimulate laughter, sometimes ending with a comic twist on a character that closely resembled her. The girls often quizzed her on marriage. It was beyond their imagination that she never bore a child. They were aware of her weakness for children by the manner she went out of her way to play with theirs. She would sit darning a skirt or some other garment, threading her needles without squinting—her hands steady. There were no signs of the tremors old age attracts, not even the slightest twitch. They had learnt about her from Raphael and Phillipe, most of which had been embellished by Phillipe, adding to her already superhuman stature to win their unreserved respect. They remained discreet, deliberately avoided asking questions (at first) about the war, although itching to hear her own version first hand. They had no reason to doubt either Phillipe or his father, but the aura that encircled them while sitting with a living piece of history pierced through the thin veneer masking their curious minds. The urge to hear these stories from Madlienne's own lips was overbearingly compulsive. One evening, Nickola, the fiery red head *shabeene* who had come with her child in her arms in search of work and whom Madlienne had hired out of compassion for the child, broke the uneasy silence with a direct question. She was a bit younger than the other two girls, and definitely more adventurous,

"They say you fight like a man in the war. Is that true?" To which Madlienne's response was equally clipped and evasive,

"If They say so, let They tell you." With this, she quickly switched to one of their favourite stories about a phantom that roamed the four roads at midnight, the height of six grown men, with a penis the size of a cannon . . . Everyone was in stitches, including Nickola. She never ventured to ask about the war again, at least, not from the old mongoose.

The day Monsieur Gimat arrived, it rained. It had been raining from the Sunday and never stopped until he set foot on his porch that Friday afternoon, shortly before Madlienne gave the order to light the lamps. Raphael and Phillipe had left for town at dawn, dressed in their best fineries. It seemed they were off to a wedding. Raphael wore his top-hat, which he kept in camphor balls for the greater part of the year, to protect it from the scourge of roaches. They were more common than rodents around the estate. Madlienne peeped through the curtain when she heard carriage wheels mincing along the driveway towards the house. She had been on edge all day, her heart beating faster when the wind raced through the trees and their branches swept across the roof. She ordered the girls about in an endless charade of dusting and cleaning until their faces reflected in every item around the house. The stress built from years of waiting turned to anxiety. No one challenged her caprices as the stream of conflicting orders flowed. They too were anxious to meet the man they were preparing to receive, the one they called boss, but had never seen. Drudgery faded from the repetitive nature of their chores, eyes screamed from their sockets as the day progressed, impatiently waiting . . .

CHAPTER NINE

It was beginning to get dark, but the light outside was strong enough to distinguish faces and objects. A slight drizzle welcomed the two carriages as they came to a halt in front the house. The one in front was driven by Monsieur Cartier's groom, whilst the other a few feet behind was under Raphael's care. Her body itched, goose pimples sprung like weeds all over her, in anticipation of a glimpse of the wanted man who had decimated her tribe, making her an orphan. The descriptions and anecdotes written on her mind, penciled in by those who knew him would at last be tested for accuracy. His forty-year absence coupled with his role in the massacre of her people was the only incontestable facts to which she was willing swear. He had been known to be devious; she could not trust the facts. She craved for a glimpse of that face . . .

The old man leapt gingerly out of Monsieur Cartier's carriage. The bulk and the brawn Madlienne imagined, had worn thin around the stature that lived in her dreams. He seemed old and frail, standing in the drizzle whilst Monsieur Cartier unraveled the contraption that was to shelter them from the rain; the parasol trembling in his hands as he fidgeted with the catch. Gimat was wearing a tall black hat that stuck in the air like a soot-blackened chimney from the stone ovens on the neck of town. He resembled a *bolom* from her stories she heard as a child, short, squat, his entire body close to the ground. The years had shriveled him; his clothes suspended like drapery from his shoulders, which flagged in the breeze as he walked. She recalled the funny little men, dwarfs that nosed about town on Saturday afternoons reading palms and telling futures, collecting their fees in advance, much to the changrin of their clients. She watched him evade the puddles in short precise steps as they made their way towards the porch, each footstep uncertain as to the firmness of the dirt under his feet. On reaching the front porch the rain stopped. Raphael followed them in, leaving Phillipe to organize the men to take the four heavy trunks stacked in Raphael's carriage, inside. Gimat entered the house looking up at the rafters. He seemed enthralled by what he had seen so far. Madlienne had taught the girls to curtsy and they genuflected at her command. Gimat clapped.

"This is your house, Sir," Monsieur Cartier said, making his simple statement seem like a profound declaration. "I hope you like it."

Gimat did not respond. Instead his eyes kept on roving. They swept across the ceiling, the partitions, the furniture, and the girls, scanning them from head to toe, finally settling on Nickola, who broke into smiles showing the gap between her teeth. Gimat nodded his approval. Madlienne was however uncertain; whether it was in appreciation for the work they had done or for was it for Nickola's fair-skinned beauty, who was unable to stay still, beaming blushes at every opportunity when her eyes met Gimat's. 'That old *dry ballahoo* still got fire in him,' Madlienne thought.

Raphael accompanied Monsieur Cartier and his boss around the house, strutting through the rooms, absorbing the various remarks. There were comments on the quality of workmanship, the finish in the furniture, the height of the ceiling, windows and doors. Even on the high degree of cleanliness.

"I have not observed a speck of dust anywhere," Monsieur Gimat said, aloud. Madlienne overheard, observing the gold flash from his capped molars.

Dinner was served in that time-honoured tradition, a la carte, beginning with hors d'oeuvres, marinated crayfish, which Madlienne had been told was his favourite dish. She watched from her subservient post, standing at a discreet distance from the table as he babbled and boiled with delight swallowing each morsel. The next course, tripe and pumpkin soup was served piping hot from a clay tureen, by Madlienne herself, with only a white napkin between the tureen and her hand. Gimat sipped cautiously, blowing the heat before the spoon reached his lips. He was truly a connoisseur like she was told. His nose like a hawk's bill, curved to absorb the aroma. His eyes moistening when the rich flavour registered on his palate: Madlienne had been wise to solicit Josette's expertise. Salad consisted of lettuce, tomatoes and carrots served raw, with boiled turnip and *cristophine* sliced and coated with a relish of olive oil, vinegar and salt. The main course was game, *ramier*, baked, decorated and served whole. Madlienne had suggested the menu to Raphael who became so neurotic about the idea that coerced Josette from her house across the hill to cook it.

"We must get things right on the first night." He told Madlienne.

Madlienne had not always trusted her informants, for once they were right. The abundance of his favourite dishes as Madlienne remembered them from the bits and pieces of information given to her over the years; overwhelmed Gimat. A smile curved her face as he cleared his plate. After port was served, Monsieur Gimat, Monsieur Cartier and Raphael retired to the porch to listen to the insects of evening; there all the species lost in their own peculiar discord struggled to outdo each other. Beetles clicked their mandibles; crickets blared, while grasshoppers whistled, altering the shade of their robes from green to black, in unison with night. Madlienne carried the tall oil lamp outside where they sat. It was heavy; the wind could not knock it down.

"My wife, God bless her soul, could not do better," Gimat told Madlienne, as she decanted another glass of port for Raphael, who was nursing his empty glass with obvious discomfort while the others sipped.

"Thank you," Madlienne replied, feigning reverence. "You are very kind." After Madlienne retired, Gimat looked across admiringly at Raphael and said,

"I can understand why you pay her four shillings a month. She is an excellent cook, better than the ones I left in France." Monsieur Cartier twiddled his moustache, while Raphael searched his mind for the right words that would not be a lie and at the same time assist in the enhancement of Madlienne's position at *Moulin-a-vent*. He could not frame a suitable response quickly and chose to remain silent. Personally he had feared the subject; it was he who had persuaded Monsieur Cartier to be generous. It was more than consolation to him that Madlienne's show of competence had pleased the boss and the teeth had been extracted from the issue.

Madlienne by nature had always been an early riser. The habit had been ingrained in her from early childhood, growing up with the birds and their shrill music piped through the leaves, shrouding the wilderness. She was already on her feet when morning curled across the hills listening to the sounds. At Moulin-a-Vent, this routine, at the start of the day had remained unchanged and unchallenged. She could be seen before first light as the sky began turning from black to grey—before a few crimson streaks coloured it in the east—hurrying towards the house, to open its portals to the cool morning air. She lived in a small wooden cabin Raphael had built for her, adjoining his place, from surplus lumber on completion of Gimat's house. He furnished it with an old bed and cotton mattress from his own meagre reserves. Madlienne only wanted a place to rest when night came. She had arranged to take the long trek home, to her cottage at Trois Piton fortnightly, where she would rest comfortably the whole Sunday to refresh her spirits for the grind of the two weeks ahead. Monsieur Gimat did not alter this arrangement. He only insisted that she seasoned the meats before she left on Saturday afternoons and to leave clear instructions for the girls to follow. He was very precise about his food. For Madlienne, this was a latent talent, which with Josette's help, unknown to Gimat, came to the fore. She had begun taking a serious interest in the kitchen when she assumed the role of general factotum for Madame Dupiny; she nurtured it during the years of caring for old Tergis and Monsieur De Brettes. They never raved about her culinary skills, which had remained undiscovered until Monsieur Gimat made it a point of issue at his house after he had sampled the meals. He always seemed to know the dishes she prepared herself and showered her with praises after belching the flavour over a glass of port. Despite those brief interludes when he displayed glimpses of a human soul underneath his skeletal frame, he always remained distant. Madlienne thought it sounded almost patronizing when he praised her, for clearly, he did not consider her to be of the same human race from which he descended. He remained aloof, with a cynical glint in his eyes which spelt cruelty, particularly when he was alone, following the girls as they moved through the house. All except Nickola, Madlienne observed.

During the early months after his arrival, he seldom spoke to her directly and gave his orders through Raphael as though he needed an interpreter to communicate. On one of her visits home she took out the old hunting knife, she had kept secure under her bed in a leather pouch. She whet the blade on the grinding stone in her yard used to sharpen her cutlasses for weeding, until the sliver of rust melted from the metal's surface and its cutting edge returned razor sharp. She spent most of the day nursing the point, until it was fine tipped like a bayonet. She had dented it on some hard object, she did not remember. Next morning, before setting out for Moulin-a-vent, she placed the knife among her little bundle of things, smiled and went out to hitch Clarissia to the cart in preparation for the journey back.

There was a vague sign of disillusionment in Gimat's eyes when he appeared at table for breakfast. Madlienne feared that he was reflecting the classic signs of boredom after two months and would soon pack his things and return to France. The long period of waiting was also beginning to take its toll on her. Her mind was playing with its little bag of tricks, feeding her wrong signals. Anxiety and impatience clasped hands over her head. Thoughts of failure depressed her. She was unprepared, the groundwork incomplete, Raphael and Phillipe, their safety foremost on her mind. She needed more time. Two weeks riding daily with Raphael around the estate, acquainting himself with his boundaries, meeting some of the workers who had lingered around after the reaping season to tend their plots on the fringes of his land—marked out by Raphael—he retired to his room on his return to the house where he remained for the rest of the day, surfacing only after lamps were lit for supper.

"He may be sick," Madlienne told Raphael.

"The change in climate perhaps," Raphael suggested, "The heat maybe too much for him."

Madlienne thought about it, but was not convinced.

"Something is wrong!" She insisted, pausing to think.

"Give him a hot bath and a long shot of rum and see if he wouldn't find himself," Raphael suggested. Madlienne mulled over this fresh piece of advice. It had some value. She had to get closer to him if her mission was to be successful. In her younger years this would not have been difficult, but with wrinkles grabbing at every fold in her body, she needed an ally. In two months, she was yet to spot a chink in his armour except for the manner he relished his meals. She thought of arsenic, but quickly discounted its use—'it would be criminal.' Her mission was to execute him and he must know why death came. He was a tough old soldier crab. He revealed nothing about himself, except for the first night when he could not take his eyes off the girls, particularly Nickola, whose innocent face had gripped his fancy.

An idea crossed Madlienne's mind, vaguely at first, but as the days sped by, it was giving her many a sleepless night. She was also becoming worried she had lost the nerve to kill. Many full moons had passed since she had last slit a throat. Watching the feeble old man sitting at table, lapping his soup like a harmless pup, evoked her pity. It was a dangerous sentiment, one that seldom appealed to her thinking—definitely not in her younger years. This strange compassion for a man she knew to be a heartless butcher, further slowed her plans as she deliberately concocted excuses to delay progress. Again that inherent caution, born from a primitive instinct for survival came to the fore.

'Whatever to be done must be done alone.' The memory of her father's death swelled in every part of her being. It had become a sombre rage. It gave her courage to persevere and yet the need to protect Raphael and Phillipe remained a serious issue that required careful planning. She could not neglect them; they had become her adopted family . . .

The cane fired by late November's rains grew tall, bending in the wind. Soon it would be Christmas and before long, crop season. The cycle would begin again. Gimat had been patient. He had not outpaced himself. He had rested his body in preparation for the great event: As an overseer, then as manager, the business of sugar was thick in his blood. It had plumbed a fresh vein of energy deep within him. Suddenly, he was alive to everything around him and rearing to go. He awoke while the house was still quiet, before Madlienne came to open the shutters and make up his bed. Fully dressed in a tight pair of riding britches, doublet and tall leather boots, she would find him pacing the porch, impatiently waiting for dawn to break. She would serve his coffee outside as he waited. He liked it strong and black with two teaspoons of *muscovado,* loosely heaped. He would gobble it down and as soon as the first crimson streaks appeared in the Dauphin sky, he would head out in the direction of the stables to saddle his horse. He acted as his own groom. Madlienne would listen for the sound of hooves at full gallop through the yard, following with her ears as the sound faded through the hilly, rock-strewn path, leading to Raphael's house. Until then their conversations had been little more than salutary with the occasional remark after a satisfying meal. They remained distant, never confiding the slightest inkling of trust to one another. He was obviously reluctant to draw a black woman into his confidences and make her his friend. She, not wanting to get too close so that when the time came for her to execute, her actions would not trouble her conscience, stood like a wedge between them. Gimat's attitude was not a matter she cared to discuss with Raphael or any of the girls, fearing the likelihood of drawing suspicions to her motives. The girls were inquisitive by nature. Raphael's penchant for small talk could set the rumour mills grinding until they reached Gimat's ears. She was his servant. He had accepted her to run his household and to supervise the affairs of his stomach. To be successful, she needed his trust. She had to be patient. Success depended heavily on his change of heart.

While the canes were being cut, Gimat would be away all day and did not return until the sun had sunk low in the sky and its light slinking behind the western hills ushered in a short twilight. Usually he came as the shadows lengthened across the yard with the last rays of sunlight behind the trees. There was no trace of wear in him as he enquired about dinner on his way to his bath, to rinse the day's sweat from his body. Madlienne laid out his dressing gown and drew his warm water with the assistance of Nickola, who kept the kettle boiling and took it to him whenever he shouted. Madlienne ensured it was Nickola who performed this task and no one else. She was contented to make his bed, tidy his dresser and remove the dirty linens from his room. She had hoped to discover a chink in his armour; one that made him vulnerable.

'What in that man that make him so cold?' she thought. 'I don't know what to do again to get close to him.' It bothered her. She knew she had to get to him fast. Gimat was a creature of habit, his daily routine, predictable. The slightest change would indicate deterioration in his health. Knowing that he died in his bed of natural causes was not a preposition Madlienne contemplated.

March came and the mill had started chewing cane stalks, spitting juice into the vats. The pan boilers, seasoned campaigners, knew the correct amount of firewood required for an even temperature. From field to mill, Gimat took charge of operations with the frenzy of a zealot. He rode with the wagons, ensuring that their pace improved with liberal use of the whip on the mules that never hurried before, until then. Raphael was left to supervise the cutting and stacking and the little hills of cane were mounting in the fields faster than could be transported to mill, owing to a shortage of carts. Gimat was everywhere. His mere presence was boosting efficiency to a new height never experienced before at Moulin-a-vent; engendered by fear enforced through a savage glint in his eyes as he rode by. Day stretched into the early night, but Gimat was unrelenting: he worked his men and animals beyond exhaustion, until the strain began to show on his face. One evening, at the height of the season, Madlienne's keen ears heard his horse cantering up the driveway, not at the full gallop to which she had grown accustomed. It was a change in habit; it seemed strange. She heard him struggle up the steps, his footsteps heavy, unhurried, crawling over the boards, she rushed out to find him in one of the wicker chairs grimacing in pain as he struggled with his boots.

"I can take them off if you want!" She said hesitantly, not wanting to appear intrusive.

"Get these damn boots off; they're killing me!" His words were crisp and he spoke through his teeth. "Then get me a drink!"

His tongue was heavy, pain seared through his eyes. Madlienne feared that it was apoplexy, a condition that was common to men his age, from which they seldom recovered. He was breathing heavily and his clothes smelt the musky odour of stale sweat. Madlienne knelt on one knee, yanking each boot by the heel like she did on the battlefield. The leather had swelled with his feet and tightened like a vise around his flesh. Both legs had turned blue where the veins protruded over the bone. Her moment had come.

"You killing yourself, working too hard," she said, "I will make a little medicine to put back the blood in your legs."

She rose, heading for her little bag of dried herbs, kept on a ledge over the grate in the kitchen, but as she darted towards the door, Gimat rasped, "You can do that, but first bring me a drink. My throat is sore."

She squeezed two limes in a pitcher of water, added a pinch of clove, a piece of cinnamon, over which she poured ample portions of red rum from a decanter that resided permanently in the kitchen reserved for the sole purpose of making these punches, which he relished. Sugar she added last—the brown *muscovado* which gave her rum punches their distinctive flavour. The slight swishing sound of her swizzle and the aroma of spices filtering through the house always served to ferret the girls from their nooks. They came to sample, swallowing ample portions long before it was ready to be served. Nickola who had been out in the yard lounging under the tamarind tree was the first to arrive sticking her fingers in the pitcher.

"You teaching us everything, but they have some things you not showing us," she said.

Madlienne did not answer. Instead, she poured the punch through a strainer into a tumbler; "Go, bring that for the boss!" She ordered, "He out on the porch."

She sifted through her collection of herbs, searching for the right leaves that would restore the circulation to his feet. Nickola placed the tumbler on a tray and vanished behind the curtains through the dining hall. Egyptienne and Marcelle came in from the rooms, where they had just completed closing the shutters for the night. A burning a mixture of *citronnelle*, incense and dried cow dung filtered through the house. They were performing their nightly routine, chasing mosquitoes. They usually completed this chore well before supper to allow M.Gimat to savor the night scents while he dined. Madlienne had Marcelle fetch a basin and an ewer, while Egyptienne lit a fire to boil the brew. Madlienne went about her task humming. She always hummed the same airless tune for which there were no words when she mixed her concoctions. It was part of the ritual. She was in particularly good spirits. This was an opportunity to be closer to Gimat; to look into his eyes and assess her strengths and his failings. She was busy preparing her mixture when Nickola returned.

"The boss say to hurry. His foot killing him," she was quite agitated. "He in a bad mood," she added.

"I'll soon take care of that," Madlienne said with a sombre inflection; her usual tone when she did not wish to be hurried or disturbed. She placed the dried leaves in a small mortar and sprinkled some salt over them. She added clear rain water from the cistern, pounding them to a pulp with her pestle. She continued humming the tune without words no one else knew, still pounding. She then poured the mixture into a pan Egyptienne had placed on the fire. It was warm and transformed the herbs into a green brew, which she stirred like soup before pouring it into the basin.

Madlienne returned to the porch with the basin, the girls followed her, Nickola carrying the ewer filled with cold water, Marcelle and Egyptienne each with a blanket. Gimat was nodding asleep in his chair. His half emptied glass was on the small coffee table. Madlienne placed the basin at his feet, the girls milled around eagerly awaiting instructions. She added cold water from the ewer, stirring it with her hands until she thought it was the right temperature. The strong smell of camphor stirred Gimat slightly when she planted his feet in the basin and the warm brew began seeping through his pores. He purred like a kitten as her fingers kneaded the muscles in his calves, manipulating tendon by tendon as she worked her way slowly down to the arches in his feet. Her fingers traveled nimbly over the swollen flesh from thigh to ankle, from ankle to toe. She laboured until tiny red streaks appeared in the veins. He never winced nor tensed while she massaged his limbs. He threw his head back in the chair and closed his eyes. His legs had gone numb on the surface, like the frostbite he had experienced in France. The pain he felt was from the bone. Her hands had reached the source of his pain, bringing relief. A soothing sensation filled his body, lowering his heartbeat; his pulse slowed as he fell into a deep sleep. Marcelle dried his feet, while Egyptienne, on Madlienne's instructions tore some strips from the blanket she carried into bandages. Madlienne made a poultice with the leaves and wrapped it around his legs, down to the toes. When she was finished, she lifted him like a baby and carried him through the house to bed: despite her years, her strength had never failed to respond to impulses. She could sling a hogshead of flour over her shoulder without clamouring for help, or lift a half bag of spuds from the storeroom to the kitchen without gasping for breath under the weight. She enjoyed displaying her strength. It ensured respect from the girls.

It was mid morning when Gimat appeared. Fatigue and the after-effects of Madlienne's rum punch had ringed his eyes. He entered the dining room still wrapped in his dressing gown with the bandages loose around his feet.

The swellings were gone. He strutted about like a loose ram in a field of ewes, without trace of the limp. He called for Madlienne: "Look!" He said, "the blood has returned to my feet! I can walk. The pain is gone."

"You not going out in the cane today?" Madlienne asked, unusually brusque. "You got to rest."

Gimat ignored the comment. He was elated like a child repeating his first few words of gibberish:

"Can't believe it! Can't believe it! I wish you were with me in France. In winter, my feet swell bigger than my head. The doctors say it's rheumatism, but they can't cure it. It's the blood that's not getting through to my feet." He was speaking extemporaneously with spit foaming at the corners of his mouth.

"You cured me with your native medicine. You got the blood flowing back to my feet. You can teach those doctors! With all their papers they are no use!" He was babbling like a ravine. He wanted the world to know that a miracle had occurred. Egyptienne and Marcelle interrupted their chores to follow him about the house, basking in Madlienne's glory despite their minor roles.

"I can rub you again tonight, if you want," Madlienne said, blushing.

"Yes! Yes!" he said, as he stretched his legs across a chair by the table for her to remove the bandages, twiddling his toes with joy. Madlienne had stumbled on the breach. She would work hard to widen the gap. She brought him his usual cup of coffee spiked with a dash of cognac. Its effects were further invigorating. She sent word via Nickola to Raphael that Monsieur Gimat would not come to the fields for the day, but required a full report in the evening on accomplishments. After a late breakfast, Gimat retired to his room. Madlienne's warning—to take the strain off his legs—had been heeded. She made several excursions with her basin and ewer to his room, alone, returning to report albeit briefly on developments to the girls. That evening, he did not appear for supper and was not to be disturbed. By the following morning he was bright and sprightly again; glad to be back in the saddle.

"You work magic with your hands," he told Madlienne as he left for the stable, and she believed him. With her herbs and concoctions she had inveigled herself behind his battlements, carving a tiny niche in some corner of his heart; worming through the stone core that protected his feelings to touch the soft tissue of his karma with her fingertips. Slowly, she was winning the battle; she knew—she was still a woman despite her age.

The pain in his legs did not vanish completely as he had hoped. It returned on evenings when he unsaddled his horse and walked across the lawn towards his house. Most times it was merely a slight zip; a tapping reminder. Sometimes, after a particularly strenuous day, it scorched like a bolt of lightening through the bone. He would hurry as fast as his legs allowed, straight to his room where Madlienne would join him with her carefully brewed concoctions—before he tidied himself for supper. Gimat told Raphael exactly how he felt; if there were any biases, he disguised them well:

"Without Madlienne's help, I would not be able to walk."

Raphael surmised Gimat probably would have sold the estate and returned to France and he would be looking for a job at his age, because he did not have enough money to buy, not with a cunning book keeper M. Cartier. Madlienne became the favourite of the household; the benign dowager, whose advice Gimat sought on any and every matter, whether clouded in doubt, or, requiring a second opinion. In addition to health matters, he consulted her on wages; on labour to harvest the canes before the rains came, even on financial matters relating to the estate. Whenever he ventured into town, to check his books in the able care of Monsieur Cartier, he always remembered to return with a small token to give to Madlienne after she had rubbed the life back to his feet. The other girls sensing that a relationship was developing under their nostrils became jealous, more so as Madlienne closer in age to Gimat and old enough to be their mother. Collectively, they felt that their status and that of their children would be advanced if the boss chose one of them instead as his favourite. They vented their envy using snide remarks, groveled under breath and moved about the house with lethargy charged with resentment whenever they spotted Madlienne. She had been at great pains to explain that there was nothing more than the relationship of master and servant. She knew her place. They did not believe her. They peeped through the blinds while she chatted with the boss; eavesdropped on every little conversation and followed her everywhere, if only with their eyes. They found excuses to enter the room while she was dressing Gimat's feet. They took turns bringing fresh linens, whether they were asked or not; a pitcher of water, or under the pretext of retrieving some obscure object they had forgotten. These untimely intrusions did not augur well for Madlienne. Guile and deception were the craft of her trade. She could not weave them confidently unless the centre of focus was shifted from her. She had seen Gimat feast his eyes on Nickola. He was old but French blood flowed in his veins. That night in her cabin she sat up in bed thinking, by morning she had a plan.

She waited until Gimat had gone into the fields and she was once again supreme commander at the house. She called the three girls into the kitchen.

She wanted it to appear displeased. Their behaviour had stretched beyond tolerance. Marcelle and Nickola had been insubordinate. They frowned as she spoke.

"I know the things you all been saying about me behind my back. The way you all come into the room when I'm there with Monsieur Gimat. I will not be here much longer to take your nonsense, so from tonight I will show Nickola how to mix the medicine and rub Monsieur Gimat foot."

There were instant disclaimers and petty squabbles between Nickola and Egyptienne. Also between Marcelle and Nickola, each claiming that it was the other who had brought false news to Madlienne. It ended with both Egyptienne and Marcelle stating categorically that they would have nothing further to say to Nickola, since they believed for varying undisclosed reasons; it was she who was the real culprit. They confessed to Madlienne how she had whispered to them and they believed her. They lied and she knew it.

"I tell you what I had to say. Now finish." Madlienne made her peace with all the girls at once, the squabbling ceased and she went about her chores with renewed vigour. Marcelle and Egyptienne stayed out of sight for a while in the other rooms feeling riddled with guilt.

Since it was Madlienne who had skillfully sowed the seeds of dissension within their ranks, causing minor conflicts between them daily, it was her duty to quell the outbursts between Marcelle and Egyptienne on one side and Nickola on the other. Their quarrels had deteriorated into raw personal abuse. She had allowed them the broadest latitude until they were about to exchange blows.

"Of course," she said, "None of you will want me to tell Monsieur Gimat what going on in his house behind his back." They froze.

This was a gamble none would take. Egyptienne pretended to storm out of the kitchen to sweep the house. She was the least guilty. The two other culprits hovered behind to plead their cases individually. Madlienne was not prepared to listen.

"Marcelle go make up the bed, I will to talk with Nickola," she said sternly.

After peeping through the curtains into the dining room to ensure none of the girls had hid within earshot, she surveyed Nickola from head to toe, her usual style before starting an interrogation, then, slowly she began: "Several time I see Monsieur Gimat look at you hard," she said, trying to be vague with her introduction, but hinting as she moved along.

"His wife die in France, you know, he hasn't got a woman since. You know what happen to a man when he stay that long without a woman?"

Nickola appeared too frightened to offer any response. She stood still cracking her fingers and giggling, all the while Madlienne spoke. Fighting to shrug off the paroxysms of fear which stupefied her, she ventured to mutter: "You know . . ."

"You know what?" Madlienne retorted angrily, before the words came out her mouth, clamping it tight. "What you want me to know?"

Nicola remained silent. Madlienne smiled, one of her cunning grins:

"Well if you don't know, you will find out."

Nickola was relieved to be dismissed surreptitiously, to return to her chores without much of a reprimand. As the day came to a close, she asked to be excused early and ran down to the cabin where she lived with Egyptienne and Marcelle and their children, to sponge the day's grime from her skin and put on a clean dress. She returned to the house gleaming like a new sovereign. She had oiled her body with coconut oil and had coloured her cheeks with rouge, she resembled a porclean doll with brown skin.

Nickola was no innocent. She already had a child whose paternity was uncertain and a catalogue of suitors from all parts in her nineteen years. The epitome of her ambitions was to be the mother of a white man's child. This she believed would help her to extricate herself from the miseries of hard labour and live the rest of her life with her legs up, on a reclining chair in his drawing room, polishing her nails all day. Her mind was already made up when Madlienne spoke to her that morning. Gimat's age would be immaterial, only his affections. Madlienne prepared the herbs in the traditional manner, calling out each one loud by name while Nickola watched. Madlienne went through all the stages slowly, commenting on the healing powers of each leaf. Nickola's other interests prevented her from readily absorbing Madlienne's instructions, in the beginning, but when gently reminded;

"This will be the only opportunity you get to be close to M. Gimat." She reconsidered and became a willing pupil.

"You had better learn fast, before somebody else take your place." The change was instant; her eyes glued even to minor details. Nickola accompanied her to Gimat's room with the basin of herbs, while she held the ewer. On seeing them come in, Gimat shot up and sat at the edge of his bed.

"Tonight you bring your apprentice, and a good looking one, I can see," he said, smiling.

"My hand don't have the strength in it anymore," Madlienne said. "Nickola will do a better job after I show her."

"Teach her well," Gimat said, looking into Nickola's eyes. She returned a shy smile, which made his body sing and the tiny patches of hair left around his temples stood on their ends. Madlienne began with the right leg instructing Nickola to work on the left following every movement she made. She learnt quickly. After the first week she was preparing the herbs while Madlienne watched. Within the month she was rubbing both feet with the skill of an accomplished masseuse. By the following month, Nickola was at the helm—she was now going into the room alone.

A lecherous gleam lit Gimat's eyes as it swept over Nickola's bosom as she bent forward kneading the fibres in his thighs. His hands twitched for a touch. Madlienne had been a good tutor. Nickola's natural aptitude, coupled with her panache, made Gimat's body tingle when her fingers brushed his skin. Visions of youth occupied his mind as he fathomed new depths. There was no further need for Madlienne, the apprentice had come of age. She felt she was intruding. Her pupil had unlatched the lever her hands had struggled to reach. Nickola's evening visits became longer, growing late into the night. She consulted Madlienne on other poultices, to rub other parts of the body to restore his youth. Madlienne gathered the herbs and prepared them. Nickola returned to the room with the new mixtures. Madlienne had heard the giggles and the laughter echoing off the rafters on many a night. She had seen Nickola decant sherry and take the glass to Gimat's room. These tiny bits of evidence were clues to a larger tableau, one she savoured; one that was germane to her plans. Madlienne remained discreet, pretending she had not observed, walking back alone at nights to her cabin, without Nickola's spirited descriptions of the days events.

CHAPTER TEN

It was coming towards the month when all the remaining cane stalks in the fields were burnt to prepare for the next year's crop. Everyone was in high spirits in anticipation of the celebration that followed on the night marking the official end of the crop season. The house was a hive of activity; every possible chore that could be imagined was being attempted in a single day. Gimat found some old clothes in one of his trunks, which he distributed among his workers for costumes. Nickola paraded as the mistress of the house, giving orders. It was common knowledge that she was the lady in residence by the haughty manner in which she behaved. She no longer spoke to Egyptienne and Marcelle as equals, but with gestures of superiority that made them squirm. She had however, a modicum of respect for Madlienne and never ventured near her. Their exchanges were brief and they spoke to each other only when it was absolutely necessary. Nickola seldom went down to the cabin to sleep with the other girls. She had hired a nanny, one of the old women who lived on the estate, to take care of her child. She did not have to visit them often, to face the daggers of envy that flushed from Marcelle and Egyptienne's eyes. They dared not confront her openly, as in the past, for they did not wish to lose their place at Moulin-a-Vent. The change in Gimat showed in the spring in his step. Miracle, or twist of fate, he had succeeded in shaking off the years that had overtaken him, quite probably, from mourning the death of his wife. Nickola dispensed the right medicines in their proper dosage, as instructed, to which his body responded like a flare. Despite this obvious transmutation there was still that small corner in his heart—unknown to Madlienne—open to her even when Nickola was in his arms: she appeared through its door in flashes, marshalling her forces to capture his soul. To him Nickola was a surrogate whose ministrations through a younger body, were conducted under directions of a superior force.

It was full moon; it was always full on the night they burnt the canes. They watched from the hills as the ribbon of flames swept through the valley, reddening the sky. The torches had carefully selected their spots. The dry stalks were thirsting for heat. They crackled and popped like firecrackers on a Christmas Eve night. Soon the whole valley was a seething inferno, much to the delight of Gimat himself. He had allowed the drummers at Nickola's request, to come to his yard, dressed in the "odds and ends" he had generously donated from his old trunk. Raphael and Phillipe came dressed as pirates and took turns at the *deux bottes*. They had learnt the native dances. Phillipe was particularly skilled at whisking to and fro between the skirts of the young girls, who had accompanied their parents for the first time to the house. Nickola forgot her status for the moment when she danced to the beat of her ancestors, the music swelling in her head. It was a rare privilege to leave Madlienne in Gimat's company undisturbed. Madlienne had deliberately avoided his presence, allowing Nickola to develop her liaison. Whenever he called for her she remained clinical and brief, particularly in the presence of Nickola, who had become his shadow. Apart from occasional greetings on the porch on early mornings or late evenings when their paths inevitably crossed, there were very few exchanges between them at other times. He was not pleased. The moment gave him the opportunity to tell her:

"You have been staying out of my way, you afraid of Nickola? It's you who bring her to me." His tone touched her faintly, deep inside. She could not remember when last this happened to her. She looked up at his face and smiled. It was a genuine smile, like the ones reserved for Raphael and Phillipe.

"You are not that old, you know," he said, almost admiringly.

"I feel old," Madlienne replied, "and nothing can change that." She hated the feeling of endearment; it gripped her and brought a sudden weakness to her knees.

"Maybe I could," he said.

The crackle in his voice reminded her of Theodule. It took her back to that evening in the river. She had not thought of Theodule in years. She found herself battling with her emotions, not knowing whether to cry or laugh. Briefly she had forgotten the man who had killed her father and was seeing a kinder, softer spirit take shape in his place.

Nickola, wrapped in the throb of the drums, did not observe Gimat swoop on Madlienne's hand, nor as she gently withdrew it.

"We don't speak to each other like before," he said.
"You been busy," Madlienne replied.
"With crop time over I will correct that," he said.
"Don't do anything to make you sorry," she said, struggling to appear firm. Inside, her fires were dousing.
"If it is Nickola, I can send her away," he said, his eyes fixed on the young sensual figure, caught in the magic of the drums.
"Nickola!" Madlienne exclaimed, "She's only a child."
Her mind went temporarily blank as the blood raced to her head. He mumbled something under breath, she did not hear.

The drums raved on, their beat tickled Madlienne's soul. She had come too far to surrender. She remembered a tale from old Monsieur De Brettes, about Napoleon and his grand army on the Steppes of Russia. He had crossed a thousand miles of mountains, rivers and forests conquering everything in his path, until he came face to face with the blank hostile coldness of the Russian winter. She felt a chill run through the length of her spine; it usually came with thoughts of defeat. She had to be close to him to execute her plan, but these confusing feelings that sent mixed signals through her body, warned to remain distant. A mist came over her mind; she could not think. Her feelings were softening towards the most repulsive, the vilest creature she had stalked for a lifetime and felt helpless to prevent. Would she ever find forgiveness in the eyes of Argos, Ti Frère and Jean, should she ever meet them again? The drums played on, their rhythm like a river crab burrowing deep beneath her skin. The urge to run away was strong. She wanted to go far away from Moulin-a-Vent where she could sift through the sands of confusion that were raging their dust storms on her mind. She remembered her hunting knife with its point tapered like the nib on a quill, waiting for a compass to steer it across his chest in a sign of the cross. The anger within her, returned. She got up from the small bench she had taken from the kitchen,
"*Excusez moi*!" She said, with a roll of the tongue to polish her French, "I have something to do."
She rose, stretching to regain her composure. Quietly, she walked away from the chatter rising above the beat of the drums. Gimat followed her with his eyes as she sauntered around the house, swinging her hips in that characteristic feline gate, swaying majestically, like a tall *palmiste* with the breeze.

Moonlight lit the narrow footpath which measured Madlienne's footsteps as she treaded lightly over sandstone and grit. She moved like a ship on the horizon, her white dress like a sail, drifting from port. She was heading in the direction of her cabin. In the distance, she was a spirit, an invocation of drums yet undisturbed by the music. She was absent for the better part of an hour. On her return, Gimat was holding hands with Nickola and Marcelle, part of a large circle around the drummers who were threshing their souls on goat hide in the middle. Raphael and Phillipe were in the group. They were chanting an old French madrigal about a lover pining for his heart that had gone away, hoping it would return before daybreak, so he could face the world and live again. They danced around the drummers, clicking their heels on the fourth beat. It was a new movement. They had never done the dance before. It was one of the improvisations Gimat had brought with him from France. Their voices rose in unison like a church choir, rendering their notes with sadness to bring tears to the tale. Madlienne watched from under the eaves, fascinated by the changes in rhythm and mood, jovial yet piqued with pain. It mirrored her own feelings with mysterious accuracy. She was beyond tears as she slinked along the the sides of the house, praying no one observed. She entered the the house through the kitchen. Inside she removed a flat parcel from her bosom, which was wrapped in a piece of brown linen and hid it behind the bottles on the ledge above the grate. She returned to her seat again on the small wooden bench, measuring her steps, like someone returning from a sudden call of nature. Her eyes swept across the faces reassuringly. No one saw.

It was Phillipe who first spotted her as she gathered the ends of her skirt and folded it between her legs in a gesture that was more erotic than modest. Breaking loose from the dancing circle, he ran towards her.

"Will you dance with me?" He asked, trying unsuccessfully to prise her from her bench, but she was contented to remain as a spectator.

"Come!" He pleaded, "Show us some new dances." But she continued to hold firm.

"I happy where I is; I can't dance. I will only mash your foot." She said. Disappointed, Phillipe returned to his place in the circle. There was a loud cheer when the singing was over; Gimat still holding on to Nickola and Marcelle by their waists. He seemed a bit tipsy, struggling to keep his balance, or maybe he was dizzy from dancing around in circles. One thing was certain; his feet did hurt. Flanked by Nickola and Marcelle, followed by Raphael, Phillipe and Egytienne, they walked towards Madlienne. He had them form a small ring around her. Nickola was singing: "*Levee, Maman, Levee!*" at the top of her voice. Everyone had gone deaf from the drums and the rum that flowed unabated from the two casks provided by M. Gimat. Madlienne held Phillipe's hand to anchor her to her spot while Nickola continued her taunts. She was in high spirits. The drummers whipped a new beat. Nickola turned to Gimat, grappling his lapels. He resisted. He had no desire to return to the arena and indicated to his knees. He gripped her hand firmly, and steered her to a seat beside him, where she continued to scream and giggle as he playfully tickled her ribs. 'This is not the same man I dream of killing all these years,' Madlienne thought. The Gimat in her mind's eye could not be domesticated. He was not friendly or responsive to his own kind. He could never be condescending to those he had persecuted his whole life. This was not the animal she had stalked at a distance hoping one day he would surface in her sights. A window revealing another being opened; one with a kinder, softer soul, she was beginning to like him although her conscience would not allow it.

Nickola was feeling light and could not remain seated. She was back again teasing Madliene before Gimat could stop her.

"We looking for you all night," Nickola said, bending down to hug her.

"You didn't look hard enough," Madlienne replied, drawing a smirk on Gimat's face through the wear.

"Come let's dance," Nickola said staggering; the drums had possessed her, she had become their slave. Madlienne shook her head, there was no need to speak, but Nickola was not to be defeated without a struggle.

"Ask her." She implored Gimat. "Ask her to dance; she can refuse me but she cannot refuse you."

Gimat was exhausted. The colour had drained from his cheeks. On ordinary days at this time, he would have been lost in sleep. He raised his hands in the age-old gesture of surrender.

"I've had enough!" He said. Nickola turned to Phillipe in an abrupt change of heart. He was thrown off balance as she lunged forward grabbing his hand away from Madlienne's. She dragged him into the open towards the drummers much to the amusement of the crowd, except Gimat, who remained unmoved. Phillipe was no match for Nickola's gyrations. She became a boneless wonder when the drums shook her body and their rhythms touched her soul. Conscious of eyes surveying his movements, Phillipe hid his face in his hands and wriggled his hips as best he could. He was the happiest man in the world to return to Madlienne's side when the drummers paused.

It was past midnight; Gimat blocked a slight yawn and asked Madlienne to call Nickola. Madlienne got up and went across the yard, where Nickola was frolicking with the other girls and their men, and whispered in her ear. She came without hesitation. Gimat rose as she approached and ambled towards the house. Nickola joined him as he crossed the threshold into the kitchen. There was a sting in the night air. It blew in Madlienne's face, gritting her eyes; it felt like being pelted with tiny flakes of sea salt. At Moulin-a-Vent, the breeze blew in from the sea. It simmered her senses and filled her limbs with purpose. Suddenly the noises of the night became clear, unimpeded by the drums. She had not heard them that loud since coming to live at Moulin-a-Vent. In recent years they were beginning to sound dim and she thought she was slowly going deaf. A surge of blood streamed through her sinews and her palms sweated. She knew her moment had come.

The yard was alive with frolic and laughter, the drummers untiring. The festivities would not end until the sun came up again, with the rum flowing from two casks at either ends of the yard; until everyone had fallen into a sleep of drunken stupor and revived again. Their world was twirling around them, faster than they could keep their balance. Reality had retreated through a back door in their minds; it had shredded its coat of consciousness to become illusionary. The momentum climbed gracefully towards its crescendo as the night crept on. She waited until she knew it was past the hour when sleep claimed Gimat; Nickola's youth having driven him beyond the point where exertion and stupor merged. She also knew that Nickola would succumb after having drunk in very generous terms, several potions and mixtures, all of them having rum as the base. She gulped faster than she was able to fill her glass particularly after draining the last fluid ounce of energy from Gimat's limbs on the dance floor. Madlienne stood up, tidying her dress, brushing the creases that could only disappear with ironing. She flashed a roving glance across the yard, surveying the faces that were only concerned with merriment. She waved to them and after ascertaining that no one returned her salutation, she folded the small bench under her arm and strolled towards the kitchen door, keeping within the shadow of the house, under the eaves. The moon was still shining brightly overhead.

Madlienne took down her parcel wrapped in the brown piece of linen from where she had hidden it behind the bottles on the ledge over the grate. She removed the hunting knife from its sheath and felt its blade with her fingers. She went through the dining hall where the lamps were burning low down to their wicks, following the row of chairs neatly stacked against the partition, her eyes riveted to the master's bedroom door. She paused, leaning against the mahogany panels, pressing her ear against the grain for a sign or warning in the rustle of bed sheets or the muffled change of beat in a snore. Searching for a sound, distinct above the drums, vibrating against timber; cold sweat oozed from her pores, dampening her undergarments. The world raced through her mind creating images that leaped and vanished before they solidified. Events from her own life unreeled in sequence like a piece of tapestry, beginning with her childhood, ending with the massacre of her tribe, not necessarily in chronological order, but as memory allowed. Each scene came with her father's name humming in her ears. She pressed her fingertips against the door, nudging it inward.

The light inside was a pale shade of orange from a lamp, its chimney smattered with soot spluttered to light the limp forms of Gimat and Nickola, across the bed. Madlienne saw him first, being closer to the door; old, emaciated, lying face upward absorbing the light with a twisted leer on his face, lost in his world where passion survives with the spent coin of youth in old men's dreams. Nickola was laying face downward beside him, one arm slung loosely around his shoulders cradling his neck—a bronzed nymph, in the pale light cradling her satyr. She snored loudly, her chest heaved as she breathed; her breasts hidden by the shadow cast by the lamp off her body. They were both naked. Nickola's fair-skinned complexion in the orange glow toned to bronze, the shade of *muscovado* and smooth like its taste. Madlienne's eyes were magnetically drawn to her shape. Almost immaculate, without blemish, bearing no visible signs of a previous pregnancy, not even the faintest stretch mark. It was in stark contrast to Gimat's wrinkled torso. Her body was moist, glistening in the pale light with remnants of sweat clinging to the rounded contours highlighting her curves, giving her the semblance of a brown goddess. Dark feelings which sometimes lurked in the depths of Madlienne's being were bristling under her skin. Nickola was beautiful, but Madlienne had never seen her in any other light than a meddlesome busybody poking her nose in conversations that were of no concern to her. A child trapped in an adult body with all its urges, deprived of the full bloom of womanhood by a quirk of nature. Seeing her naked, spent, after a brief moment of pleasure, thoughts wrapped in the mist of a distant past returned. She remembered Louise, curves meandering, like bends in a river, flowing along the ridge of a spinal column, rising to a soft clay mound of hills that sloped and merged into thighs. This was a landscape caught in the light of her past. Her body heaved. Madlienne's hands itched for a touch of that rounded symmetry that held her motionless. The forces were compelling. She remembered the night her hands wandered through those secret gullies in another body searching for peace. It bore the same complexion her eyes saw then. "Could it be?" No! No! She convinced herself, "it has been many years."

A warm liquid poured from her eyes, rolling uncontrollably down her cheeks. She was losing her sense of purpose, questioning her presence in the room, her motive for being there. She stood over them, like an avenging angel, the knife trembling in her hand, looking down at Nickola, but seeing Louise. She had lost her once and had never ceased blaming herself. She could not bear the strain of having to relive that moment again. She had to think. To strike would be to destroy them both. How could she execute, without drawing Nickola into the plot. To be safe Nickola would have to perish. A young life snipped in the bud of youth. It would be killing Louise all over again, a crime that would be too heavy to carry about on her chest. She wanted to scream. She had come so close. She shook her head to settle the tears that filled her eyes as she walked out of the room leaving the door ajar. She did not look back as she fled from the house as fast as her feet could bear: her white dress in the moonlight moved swiftly across the ridge towards her cabin. She hitched Clarissia to her cart, loaded it with her possessions and slowly clipped across the grass track towards the high road. The drums were still beating when she left. The merriment ringing through voices slurred by stimulants filled her with an inner peace.

She drove through the moonlit night at a slow pace not pausing for a minute along the route back to Trois Piton, lathered by thoughts that had kindled their fires forty years before, their suds smothering her with guilt. She cried all along the way. She wished deep in her heart that she had never come to Moulin-a-Vent, never pursued the man called Gimat, for having confronted her pain, she knew she would never be able to rid herself of it. The hatred that had willed her to live, the dreams that filled her nights with fantasies of a man begging for the life he had denied her father had mellowed into a bitter sweet feeling, the kind she had felt for Louise. The years had healed her gripes; even the pangs of jealousy that had driven her neurotic in a bygone age had lost their sting. She could have killed him with the same rage that seized her when she witnessed Louise's defilement. He had become the embodiment of Theodule in the same way Nickola had become Louise. She had grown to love them, not in vague intangibles of the infatuated, but with a deep spiritual feeling which old age brings— their souls merged. She had learnt to forgive. Forgiveness for her was a virtue that only the truly noblest of minds distill. She had found the corner in her heart where it grew like her herbs. She would not be able to blot them completely from her mind; she would see them in a new light. The phantom that killed her father would still haunt her until she destroyed it. She knew she would without harming the man. Meanwhile other thoughts were entering her mind—Argos, Jean and Ti Frère. Gimat the devil would no longer plague her. He was Theodule the man. She had come to grips with her pain, the inconsistent fragility of her own femininity and would outlive it. For the first time in years she would sleep well. She would awake to the new cause waiting to fill the void, to find the survivors of her tribe, to find them and free them. This would be her new mission. The journey back home was long and winding but her mind triumphed in the end over her wounded heart.

CHAPTER ELEVEN

Madlienne had never set foot on the deck of a ship before and as the brig *Reine des Antilles* rode at anchor in the bay at Port Castries she felt the world skidding under her feet. The churning in her stomach brought with it the feeling of nausea and she wretched over the sides. There were some slight remissions, regrets, particularly when she remembered it would be two days sailing before she reached her destination, with a stop at Martinique, but that indomitable will that was the backbone of her character would not surrender. She had sought the advice of her friend Duval the merchant, who knew Guadeloupe. He gave her a letter of introduction, for one Monsieur Raynal, a colleague, who would assist her on arrival. He was a ship chandler and was well known in Point-a-Pitre. He would direct her to Colombette, which she understood was some thirty miles from the closest settlement. In her own inimitable fashion she had gleaned all the basic information that Monsieur Duval could give, memorizing street names, parishes, names that were considered important, discounting all superfluous appendages that was of no help. She had began to recover from the shock dealt to her emotions by the experiences at Moulin-a-vent. For one who thought she had seen everything in life, these episodes were baffling to her psyche. She had discovered pity—an emotion nature had suppressed—in her yellowing years. It broke loose through her pores to blossom. Her mind was shaping new thoughts, like a horseshoe on a blacksmith's anvil. Though they suffered from lack of detail, they would become for her, her *raison d'être*.

The brig sailed just as the last rays of the setting sun sank below the horizon, the wind buffeting its sails. The promontories of Vigie to starboard and La Toc to port swept past. Gradually the weakness in her knees dissipated and the nerves of steel, the basic fibre of her psyche returned. She stayed a long time on deck watching the town lights twinkle in the distance until they shrank to the size of a tiny speck as the brig turned north. The ship rolled with the slow lap of waves, waiting to be swallowed by a dark void where only the wind played its violins. Night had covered the water with its cloak. Madlienne could no longer see beyond her nose. She sank down on her bundle and slept. The red and the green lanterns at opposite sides of the ship shared their light with the sea. All night at sea, the good ship rocked its timbers, slowly inching towards its destination, a strong breeze caught in its sails.

The lights of St. Pierre crept towards the brig as she drew closer to land. The early morning air with a sprinkling of sea spray stung the faces already awake on deck, looking over the sides. Madlienne awoke to the sound of voices across the water. Wiping the last remnants of sleep from her face in the hem of her skirt, she peeped through a bunghole on the starboard side. The mizzens of the fishing fleet caught in the first crimson streaks of morning streamed past, their helmsmen shouting greetings to the few sailors milling about on deck. To Madlienne, the town nestling between the folds of a huge mountain bore similarities to her Soufrière at home in *Ste Lucie*. She imagined Soufrière trapped on its riverbed, at the base of hills bordering the sea. They looked alike, except St. Pierre with its steeples, sprawled into the foothills was a much larger town. The wind was blowing across the land, seaward, the captain tacking leeward caught the gusts; dawn had not yet broken, though signaled behind the mountain's barrier. The voyage thus far was uneventful, her stomach had settled and although filled with anxiety at the sight of another country, her bowels felt at ease. The brig came alongside a wooden pier that jutted out to sea. There were other small boats already anchored there. A seaman standing in the bow with a brace of rope flung it over the sides fastening his end to a bollard on deck.

A bell rang from one of the cabins and the crew was busy fixing the gangplank for passengers to disembark. A white couple was the first to go ashore, followed by two mulatto women—one holding a child wrapped in flannel. She was the younger of the two. They came from the cabins where they had spent the night. Madlienne had not seen when they came aboard, she thought, until then, she was the only passenger. A member of the crew in whose care Monsieur Duval had painstakingly placed her like an invalid came with a tot of coffee and a lump of baked dough, ironically called a bake, which was made with flour kneaded to the density of a rock in salt water and finally firmed on a slow fire. A bake, particularly a seaman's bake had the capacity to dull the sharpest tooth.

"When you finish, you can go and see St. Pierre," young Flavien said, as he handed her a tot of coffee spiked with ample drops of cognac. There was the usual mark of reverence in his eyes. Monsieur Duval had told him her whole history and being of French descent, it had intrigued him and he repeated her story to the other seamen and the captain. *Reine des Antilles* sailed under the tricolour. The captain and crew were Frenchmen as well, who plied an honest trade transporting passengers and cargo between the islands, far south as Trinidad and north to Guadeloupe, stopping at La Grenade, St. Lucie and Martinique along the route. Monsieur Duval had mentioned to Madlienne, the brig was once used to smuggle guns and ammunition for the insurgents during the revolution and was quite old. Once he had owned a share in the boat, but had sold it to the present captain, who did favours for him from time to time in return. Two masts like a schooner, a set of square sails and a sleek hull. She hurtled through the water like a javelin, darting to and fro, between the islands' shoals with incredible speed, once the trade winds blew.

The sun was shining vaguely in a hazy copper shade over the slate rooftops that lined the promenade along the waterfront. A few town folk were hurrying about their morning chores, busy like ants, scurrying in and out of the narrow streets that ended abruptly at the water's edge. There was an innate beauty about this place, compelling almost. Madlienne, nailed to her station on deck, gaped with her mouth wide open at the quaint shapes of masonry with their rustic verandahs uniformly covering the edges of streets, forming a shelter from the sun. In the shade, citizens walked in pairs, leaving the centre of the road for carriages and carts.

The *Reine des Antilles* was scheduled to be in port for six hours. Flavien had repeatedly coaxed Madlienne to go ashore, but she decided to stay aboard. A new set of faces arrived haggling with their porters on a price to carry their trunks aboard. It seemed that they had packed the heaviest items in those trunks as each one took two men to lift, straining every sinew in the process. From their bulging eyes and taut veins in their necks as they struggled under their load to earn every farthing they charged, it was not difficult to surmise that those trunks were lined in real gold. Once on board with their trunks, the group continued their haggling with the porters, going back on their word about the fees. The Captain eventually intervened and decided on a fair wage, which was accepted. Madlienne found the entire affair comical, suppressing the laughter hidden in her cheeks. Carriages arrived at the quay, discharged their passengers and left, following in the rhythm of others before.

They came, clip-clop, clip-clop, along the promenade at the edge of the bay, smoothing the cobble stones as they chipped leisurely over them to disappear into one of the many side streets. Closer to the hour of departure, they came in threes and fours. The haggling between passengers and porters continued and the trunks came aboard after a few *sous* changed hands.

The deck was crowded with faces. Everyone seemed to know each other in a town of dandies and powdered women. No one paid attention to the old black woman in the corner, huddling against her haversack, pretending to be asleep, but all the while carefully observing them under her eyelids. Flavien visited her as often as he could between heaving the cumbersome monstrosities into the hold.

"We will soon be at sea," he said, "after the last passengers come aboard." Every conceivable shape and size was drifting about, their mouths begging for relief from the babble of hysteria sweeping the deck. It was like old friends greeting each other after twenty years' absence. There was not a black face among them, even the mulattoes passed for white as they too mingled aimlessly devouring the latest gossips. They were all over her, their spittle drizzled her face. Their conversations flowed like rivers after the rain; no one bothered with the animate lump of clay at their feet. She knew in that island her people were still chattels—traded like cattle, without name, without possessions. She clutched her certificate of manumission pinned to her bodice inside her bosom and smiled.

"*Merci Monsieur De Brettes; merci!*" She groaned. An elderly gentleman, astigmatic, stumbled over her.

"*Ah Merde!*" He exclaimed, after retrieving his leg stuck from her bundle, continuing with his business as if he had slipped on a stray dog without need for the slightest hint of an apology.

The ship sailed precisely at noon heading northward along a rugged coastline where mountains rose from sea to cloud. It was a clear day; in the distance the shape of another island appeared on the horizon, more mountainous than Martinique, which they had just left and was still within view to the southeast. They sailed the greater part of the day along the coastline of this island, which she would later learn from Flavien was called *Dominique*. Late that evening, with the sun already low down in the western skies, its orange globe washing its face in an amber sea; the azure light which blinded Madlienne all day gone, a calm ocean brought with it soothing winds that felt chilly when they ran across her skin along with sea spray. Another large landmass appeared on the horizon with the gathering sunset guarded by a sprinkling of tiny islands. It was a huge barrier rising over the bow as the ship inched forward, stretching as far as the eye could see. Someone among the passengers shouted, "Guadeloupe!" There was the usual scurrying of feet, everyone rushing for a closer look, causing a panic among the crew as the brig listed dangerously to starboard. It took the captain's twenty years' experience and a manta ray, which rose suddenly from the depths, darting through the air like the proverbial *gens gage* from their own Creole myths to get them to settle down again in their little niches on deck. Madlienne felt the collective fear pouring from eyes that had seen the devil; old women brought out their rosaries and blessed themselves as the ship passed through a minefield of scattered islets, some bare rocks, their bald-heads barely jutting above—Les Saintes. It was here, along this desolate strip of water, after passing Dominica *en route* to Guadeloupe, where caution became a watchword in the minds of sailors: never to be caught in a squall, or on a dark night, without the comfort of a full moon. The superstitious French always said silent prayers over the bow, remembering Admiral Rodney's encounter with Count De Grasse on April 12th 1782 in a decisive battle which gave the British dominion over the waves. The calm waters of the strait disguised these fragments of history hidden in the shallows. The flotsam of battle had long since cleared and the wrecks lodged in the watery depths had solidified like coral in their appointed lots. Waves no longer moaned for those bitten by the cannon and an ominous peace had cast her net in the place where the sea devil soared.

The sun that had gallantly held its head above the water took its final plunge below the horizon. Twilight, with its golden touch, transformed islands and sea into masses of gold. A sprinkling of hills appeared to the northeast as fins on a sailfish, bristled in anger at the sky. Twilight was short-lived. Soon the night was dotted with tiny sparks; a distant swarm of fireflies flickering on and out, signalling a town lay somewhere out there between the leaves. A brisk wind, blowing in spurts, fanned the sails pushing the *Reine des Antilles* towards the land that had grown into a gigantic black wall blocking the flow of the sea. Lights from the little settlements along the coast stretched across the water to bathe eager faces on deck with their light. The wind stopped when the *Reine des Antilles* entered Petit Cul-de-sac. There, it was guided by *flambeaus* strategically placed on stacks pointing to the narrow passage of deep water, taking the ship into safe harbour at Pointe-a-Pitre.

Pointe-a-Pitre was a shabby little town, prone to the wind blowing in from the sea, unlike St. Pierre nestling at the feet of its guardian mountain—*Mount Pelee*. Darkness had enveloped the huts, undistinguishable despite the combined effort of oil lamps spluttering behind the jalousies. Madlienne heard voices coming from the shore; but saw nothing beyond the radius of the ship's green and red lanterns, green for starboard, red for port. Flavien came to her after he and the other sailors had secured the heavy canvass sails and tied the ship to the old wooden pier that groaned when the waves rocked its wooden pillars. He had asked her to wait until all the passengers had disembarked, in order to accompany her to Monsieur Raynal, who had the responsibility of making arrangements for her journey to Colombette. Uncertain of her steps, but her mind alive with the memory of her brothers, she clutched the fretted rope that formed rails for the gangway to begin her slow descent to land. Flavien held tightly to her haversack, in which she had packed a few personal things, including a change of clothes. Crawling forward with the intrepidation of a solider crab, Madlienne appeared at the top of the rails directly behind him.

Monsieur Raynal was already in his nightclothes when Flavien rapped on the side door where he kept a small office to conduct his shipchandling trade. He was expecting them and was unperturbed by the apparent intrusion on his rest. He had made arrangements for Madlienne to spend the night with his housekeeper, Feyette, a huge *negresse*, who lived in the yard with her five mulatto children: local rumour insisted they were fathered by Raynal. The fact that Raynal was a bachelor did not help. Madlienne took an instant liking to Feyette whose arms reminded her of hams garnished for a Christmas table. Her smile was as soothing as the early morning love calls of *tourterelles* on grit roads. Flavien returned to his ship after pocketing a fat tip from M. Raynal; he had previously received a stipend from M. Duval in anticipation of his services to Madlienne. His ship would sail early next morning. "You can stay with me as long as you want," Feyette said, after they had returned to her little hut in the yard. The children were curious, the eldest not being more than eight and the youngest had just discovered his toes. Feyette was a voluptuous creature, with a loud infectious laugh; she had never ventured beyond the narrow alleyways of Point-a-Pitre. As far back as her memory allowed she had worked in kitchens and mastered her craft under the tutelage of many an accomplished *cuisinière*. By the time she was sold to Monsieur Raynal by an old retiring spinster, who had decided that it was time to return to France to die, there was not a meal she had not prepared under the careful eye of her mistress, who managed a boarding house for bachelors. It was there that she first met Monsieur Raynal—she was then barely sixteen. When the boarding house closed, on retirement of the spinster, Monsieur Raynal purchased Feyette at a bargain price of ninety francs, along with the house.

She prattled with Madlienne about her life with Monsieur Raynal, wiping the rosary beads of contentment that sprang from her pores. She spoke waving the hem of her skirt like a flag, transforming the most intimate details into jokes about herself. Madlienne was needling to ask her about Guadeloupe, but could not get her to pause, not even to catch her breath. It was clear that opportunities to speak about herself, were rare and she grasped this one with both hands. Her body reeked of leeks and thyme, the odour was not in her clothes. In the four hours they spent together, Madlienne was able to deduce that Feyette was the mistress of the household and maintained a firm control over Monsieur Raynal and his purse, although she knew he could not marry her even *in extremis*. She also admitted to Madlienne having several side affairs while Monsieur Raynal was away in the country gathering provisions for his trade. He was thirty years her senior and his appetite for her came only on those rare occasions when the wine had bolstered his urge and his energy allowed a brief respite. She knew all the sailors who worked the ships for which Monsieur Raynal took responsibility while in port and picked her men according to her fancy. Her laughter was like the common cold and the manner in which she told her stories had Madlienne in stitches. Not being a prude, Madlienne understood. The conversations were like a tonic, after a day of virtual silence among faces that did not acknowledge her, listening to Feyette was a hot *tisane*, which warmed inside. Sleep claimed her with a vengeance. They were not awakened until next morning by a loud rap on the door.

Raynal was up early and already dressed for the journey. He had decided the evening before; he would take Madlienne to Colombette himself, immediately as she arrived. This was but a small favour for his good friend Monsieur Duval who had stood for him in numerous transactions in his absence, which enriched his purse, also for the woman whom he had never met until then, whose name had been spoken in the same breath as Jeanne d'Arc, among the old soldiers of the revolution, regardless of race. She had carried the colours and restored honour and glory to his motherland from a small corner of the world. There was old Giles Du Prey at *Place les Cordonnières*, who plied his trade as a cobbler, praising each day he lived, the woman that gave him a drink of water and hauled him to safety in the bushes at Rabot, under the red glare of enemy flares. There was Pascal and Aphos, who had boasted how she had taught them to shoot, all wanting to see her again when Raynal broke the news of her intended visit. He was overjoyed. He had not taken part in the wars and was only a boy then, too young to serve. He remembered running about the streets of Point-a-Pitre, waving a homemade flag, when the wind blew news of victories. He had wanted to be a soldier, but his ailing mother protested. During the Napoleonic Wars, as a young man, he began as an apprentice in his trade, which over the years rewarded him with a small fortune.

Their names she did not remember; their faces buried deep in the folds of her subconscious and could not be resurrected. It was pointless trying to convince her that in faraway Guadeloupe, there were those who adored her like she was a saint. Raynal knew more about her life than she wished to remember. She had lived it and forgotten. It was difficult for her to believe all that was accredited to her, was true. A simple march under the cover of darkness had become a crushing defeat for the enemy, the defense of a garrison translated in time into a major victory, such was the reality of war; it was like a game of chance . . .

It was a good day to visit Colombette. Raynal had seen the *Reine des Antilles* sail at first light and consulted his diary at the office to verify that none of the ships in his care was due in port until later in the week. On their journey out of town, Monsieur Raynal passed through the tiny corridor that was *Place les Cordonnières*, where the shoemakers and cobblers congregated in a vacant lot, their heads bent nursing shoes in varying stages of wear, back to life on their lasts. He searched for Giles among the constellation of colourful characters inhabiting the place and spotted him digging into his box for beeswax. Giles looked up to acknowledge him, but his eyes darted swiftly across to the old woman seated besides Raynal on the cart. It could not be her, he thought, to himself. She seemed quite frail. There was no resemblance to the young buxom woman, whose eyes were ablaze, flaring like coal fire on the battlefield. She had moved with the swiftness of a mongoose, hands ripping through steel:

"Madlienne?" He asked, wiping sweat from his hands on the leather apron—the symbol of his trade. Madlienne looked down at him and smiled, she could not remember the face.

"This woman saved my life!" Giles proclaimed. "This woman saved my life!" He repeated, wanting everyone to hear.

The commotion attracted a few passersby and the shoemakers working adjacent to his stall, but none showed more than a cursory interest. It was pointless. History had closed its book on this minor episode. He alone treasured the memory. The pace of everyday life had deafened ears. The time for legend had passed.

Pascal, on overhearing Giles, came to the side of the cart where Madlienne sat:

"Thank God!" He exclaimed, "I live long enough to see you again . . . I never get the chance to tell you thanks."

Madlienne stretched out her hand and placed it on his head like a bishop. She said nothing, except gesturing to Monsieur Raynal to move on. Memories from the past weighed on her conscience, faces flew like bats from dark corners in her mind, both living and dead. She had long repented the evils of war, the atrocities committed in the name of liberty, fraternity, and equality. She had purged her body from the lust for vengeance that had driven her insane. She was sure that her father had forgiven her; she was seeing him more often in her dreams. The call of birds in the morning light took her mind back to the wilderness of her childhood and with it, came peace. The land was flat, the fields of cane stretched out before her, like the sea, billowing in an endless flood of leaves towards a green horizon. The unpaved road hemmed on either side by the tall grass stalks was littered with ground doves, pecking at the driblets of quartz ingrained in the clay marl. Although from the sea, Madlienne had seen the hills, under the shadow of night, it was difficult to believe it was the same country. A myriad of colour flowed before her eyes, the bold red of the flamboyant merging with light pinks of the gliricidia, flowing into the rose pink and whites of the frangipani, filling the air with a fragrance, thick and stifling, inducing sleep. The hours crawled by slowly. The sun beating on the dirt road sapped their energy. It was noon when Monsieur Raynal steered his cart in the shade of a mango tree, to water his horse in a nearby stream, running parallel with the road. When he dismounted, Madlienne led the horse by its bridle to the water's edge, while M. Raynal removed his jacket and spread it on the ground like a tablecloth. Feyette had packed a bottle of wine and a *baguette* broken in two, buttered and over brimming with ham, cheese and sausage—a hurried sandwich. Madlienne washed her face in the soothing water, before using the pail tied to the side of the cart—primarily used to mop up droppings when tethered in the town—to bathe the horse.

She sprinkled water sparingly on its head and flanks to cool the sweat which steamed from its body. When she returned, the bottle of wine was already half empty and Monsieur Raynal was busy demolishing the Feyette homemade sandwich. He offered the other half in the box to Madlienne, who daintily broke a small piece and nibbled at the edges. She did not feel hungry. The excitement of seeing the rest of her clan, before the day was through had drained her appetite.

She did experience a vague sense of nausea, brought on by the humidity that had stuck to her clothes. The wind blew hot across the pasture and in the shade. It did not affect Monsieur Raynal, for the minute he had finished his share of the loaf, he laid his head down on the grass and began to snore. Madlienne tied the horse in a patch of cane and returned to the stream. She soaked her feet in the water, wading through eddies until she reached a spot deep enough to wet her knees without bending. The day's warmth drove her to duck beneath the surface to wet her hair. Memories from a distant childhood flicked across her mind. She had done this on hundreds of occasions when drained under the weight of the day. She was usually surrounded by the cheers and laughter of those same companions she was about to visit. They were all young then, fired by the urges of youth and the novelty and salve of clear water against their skins; naked, soaked in the innocence ingrained in their lives. She rose, her clothes sticking to her body and walked up the little path in the sun towards the mango tree. Monsieur Raynal was fast asleep. She continued into the cane field watching the young stalks wave to the wind. She was feeling free as the birds quarelling in the shade. It was many years since she had been this happy.

Monsieur Raynal slept for the full two-hour siesta unperturbed by the occasional wasp or honeybee that hovered in his vicinity. He did not hear them. When he awoke Madlienne's clothes had dried, although the clammy feeling in her undergarments next to her skin was proving to be a slight but bearable irritant. He picked up his jacket and drank the last dregs from the wine bottle then ambled towards the cart where Madlienne had sat patiently waiting. The nap had refreshed him, there was not the slightest inkling of wear on his face. The sun had crossed the sky but was still high in the west as they continued on their journey. The cane fields patterned out into rocky grasslands where a mixture of sheep and cows were grazing undisturbed. Gradually, they approached some hilly terrain, where the road meandered to avoid crevices in the earth; deep fissures where water had eaten through the sandstone. It was a desolate country. The number of animal carcasses they passed putrefying in the heat endorsed that feeling. In the distance, the blue outline of mountains leapt like a tidal wave above the horizon. There were no rivers in sight.

"The river flows through at the height of the rainy season, but disappears as soon as the rains cease," Monsieur Raynal explained. He was familiar with the place. His frequent visits to the country to purchase produce took him to these parts several times a year.

They continued their journey through a small village. Monsieur Raynal did not immediately remember the name, except that it was in the middle of nowhere and populated by black faces only;

"*Gens Libre!*" He muttered sarcastically.

Madlienne became curious. The discovery of free blacks living in the middle of nowhere; on a God forsaken strip of land where nothing seemed to grow, had more than stirred her interest. Most of the country they had passed through was uninhabited.

"Why here?" She asked M. Raynal, "There is nothing here!"

The answer was probably in the opaque lethargic sheen reflected in their eyes when they looked up from their doorsteps, but Monsieur Raynal was content to say:

"I don't know."

"They half dead?"d Madlienne asked, observing the quaint phenomenon. 'Were these fruits of my labour?' She thought, chuckling to herself, 'they are my people too.'

"They have nothing to do," Monsieur Raynal said, giving his horse a slight twitch, quickening the pace from canter to gallop along the grit path that was both a street and a playground for the few shirtless children who lived there, in that village without a name, no name, like the faces closely resembling hers, except for their blank stares and the shifty strides casting long shadows on the ground they walked.

"*Gens Libre!*" Monsieur Raynal muttered again, the saliva foaming like venom on his lips.

"You hate them?" Madlienne asked, perceiving a quirk in character coming to the fore.

"No!" Replied Monsieur Raynal, "Only the system."

"The system?" Madlienne inquired.

"Yes," Monsieur Raynal replied, "the system that made them free, with nothing to do."

"I don't understand," Madlienne blurted out, looking back at the tiny huts huddled together like cattle in rain, with nothing between them and the elements except the wattle and straw.

Everything was clear—enigmatic, yet translucent. She saw through, but could not break the shell. Memories of her own conspicuous freedom, the war she waged for ten years without experiencing victory, the countless deaths witnessed on the battlefield, each one more hideous than the last. Her tortured mind reached for a principle beyond its reach; the migration of soul from body in search of an idealism that was not pragmatic, her own quest for vengeance in the end proved futile, evaporating with the steam of youth. She was one of those faces though separated by a mild contentment oozing from her heart. This faceless existence was hers as well as theirs. On deck, in the course of her journey to Guadeloupe she had shared their fate. Monsieur Raynal would never understand. He was of the opposite shade and colour. The village roamed through her mind, invisible only to eyes that were impervious to its plight. She knew the inhabitants were contented in their own peculiar poverty, they did not wish for change. They were happy in their state. Nothing else mattered. All this she saw in that fleeting second, passing through. They were mirrors reflecting her life. She knew.

Dirt tracks wound along the foothills, along the ledges and steep slopes leading into a mountain valley, magically green and isolated from the aridity around it.

"Colombette!" Monsieur Raynal shouted, "at last!" Breathing relief. The end of his journey was in sight, on the tip of this plain, smooth like a tablecloth on his dinner table laid before him. His eyes twinkled. A river flowed through the verdant savannah; the grass grew tall. It reminded Madlienne of that faraway country that Maitre Charle spoke of repeatedly in his bedtime tales when she was little. It was the largest pasture she had ever seen, with a sprinkling of houses, divided by acres and acres of green. A brisk trot down the slopes, carefully avoiding the loose stones flung in the air from the horse's hooves and the precipitous plunge to the sides, they progressed at a brisk pace. Soon they were under the sign marked "Colombette" entering the estate gate where two mulatto boys were outside the stables trying to force a colt through the turn-styles without opening the gates. Monsieur Raynal asked them for directions to the house and both pointed ahead without bothering to pause. Following their new found bearings, they cantered past a small sugar mill with stays on its sails, the last ton of cane having been threshed and ground into sugar for the year. An old labourer was pulling weeds in the shade. The air was thick with the smell of ripe *pomme cythérée*—golden apples, but there were no fruit trees visible within the compound, except for a tamarind tree laden with flowers and buzzing with the hum of bees. The unpaved road curved into a crescent leading towards the iron gates of the *maison blanche*, gleaming white in the afternoon sun under a fresh wash of paint.Behind it, the owner and his family lived in self-imposed seclusion from the rest of the world.

Monsieur Raynal stopped at the gates, dismounted and rang the bell. A young man dressed in the livery of a butler like those at the more fashionable houses he frequented in his younger years in Point-a-Pitre, approached and spoke to him through the grill. Madlienne remained on the cart, her mind was focused on the array of flowers blossoming in profusion in the garden that encircled the house. She identified petreas, ixoras, and hibiscuses of every conceivable shade, all in full bloom. She had become so engrossed in the surroundings, she did not observe the young man had opened the gates and Monsieur Raynal was signaling to her to dismount. She had become entirely enthralled by the sea of colours that greeted her and the tranquil haze, wrapped around the place. They followed the young man, walking behind him across a narrow strip of lawn; its impeccable sheen like a billiard table, made Madlienne tread lightly on the grass. He led them up a flight of stone steps, meticulously scrubbed and painted with no traces of moss. There an elderly gentleman in a light evening suit stood waiting.

CHAPTER TWELVE

"Monsieur Anoure Rochard!" The young man enunciated filling his lungs and expanding his chest like a true majordomo. He rolled the 'arrs' until they peeled off his tongue. Then, he withdrew nimbly, after an elaborate swoop of his body, meant as a bow, disappearing into the house. The place reeked of orderliness and discipline. The regimental rows in the garden stood like a guard of honour on parade, bearing the weight of the sun with an unnatural elegance, fearful of wilting to bring disgrace to the files. The freshly painted wooden walls were spotless. The wicker chairs on the porch neatly tucked under the tables and the curtains half-drawn in every window at the same precise angle gave further credence to this belief. There were signs of frequent brush marks under the eaves where the painters had retouched and blended to remove hints of discolouration. It was unusual for white lead to hold its colour for long in this part of the world, where heat and salt air browned everything fast. Monsieur Raynal made the formal introductions, slightly intimidated by the immaculate bearing of the man. When M. Rochard stretched out his hand to Madlienne, the tension in those opening seconds abated. The normal animated chatter for which Monsieur Raynal had been infamously venerated vanished with a note of surprise on his face.

"I have waited the better part of the day to meet you," Monsieur Rochard said. "It is an honour."
Madlienne curtsied, drawing on all the agility that was left in her bones; by this act of gentility, she returned his gesture in kind.
"We may have been in the field together fighting for the glory and honour of France, but I never believed we would have had the honour to meet."
He spoke his French with Parisian polish, forcing Madlienne to listen attentively. Although she knew the language and followed local accents without difficulty, the rhythm of the metropolis always sounded somewhat

foreign to her, particularly when the speaker addressed her directly. She thought deeply, before framing her words. The cadence of the Franks always brought to the fore an inherent complex she had noticed in most of her race, a feeling of inferiority, which she abhorred, but was powerless to dispel.

"You was a soldier?" The first few words trembled as they flew from her lips.

"I was with Comrade Goyrand in St. Lucia," he said, smiling through a flash of cane whitened teeth.

"Your bravery in the face of the enemy was an inspiration to every young man who fought under the tricolour."

"I obeyed my orders," Madlienne said simply, stifling the blushes that rushed to her cheeks.

"My wife will be down to meet you any minute, before I take you to your brothers."

"I cannot wait to see them," she said, "It's more than forty years."

"They are good men. They have been with me since I came to own this estate. I met them here. They never stop mentioning your name. They call you *Sais,* I believe."

Madlienne allowed the blushes to flow.

"They remembered," she giggled, looking away from Monsieur Raynal, to hide her tears. Her spirits soared as a reverie from a past unpinned from the tree of memory. A past that made her orphan, soldier, sister, mother, chief, before the years had pleated her forehead and crooked her limbs with the ferocity of winds was returning to the present. She splurged in the tide of an inner strength. She had outgrown its pain, too old for games; her short time left would be spent in search of truth. Rochard and Raynal would not understand her tears—there was no need to explain—they did not hold the key to open the inner chamber she called the heart.

Madame Rochard was petite and several years younger than Monsieur Rochard, although he had weathered well. She looked like his daughter rather than his wife. Her husband had filled her with the legends surrounding Madlienne, true or false; they had become like her Stations of the Cross and painted on her mind. She was visibly overwhelmed by the aura of Madlienne's presence, it made her appear timid, a trifle bashful. She glanced sideways in amazement at the woman who had defended the honour of France; who had brought pride to her race, curiously wondering the motive in God's plan to have chosen a black woman to do his bidding. France was a sacred country, before all things God came first.

'She must be a saint,' Madame Rochard thought. 'Could she be an incarnation of Jean d'Arc?'

There was no easy explanation. Madame had borne her husband four sons, who were at school in France. The eldest was at the Military Academy in Paris, hoping to follow in his father's footsteps. She was a proud mother, who observed her husband's proscriptions with probity, to the point of subservience. Her shyness in the company of strangers stretched to idiocy and there was no exception in Madlienne's presence, even though she was black: it seemed that the incubus had appeared to her in a dream and had neutered her voice. Here was a champion to be adulated, strong, cunning, armed with a quiet ferocity. Her eyes spoke. She wanted to reach out to Madlienne, but words never came. It was a moment of great joy, like the morning she gave birth to her first son and knew that her husband would be eternally beholden to her. Madame Rochard did speak finally on receiving a disguised signal from her spouse who stood with his arms folded like a chess player, tapping his fingers on his chest, contemplating his opponent's next move. Madame Rochard gestured with a gracefully rehearsed bow to Madlienne.

"My husband will take you across to your family—they wait for you." Without another word she melted through the doorway into the house. Raynal remained uncharacteristically quiet. His tongue stuck to his palate. He too had heard of the prowess of Madlienne and had been told firsthand by his good friend Duval of her indomitable spirit and her ability to will the order of things towards her design. He never suspected that her charisma would cross the colour bar with the force of royalty, where hardened republicans would forget their natural politics and afford her the courtesy they despairingly bestowed on kings.

Monsieur Rochard turned to Monsieur Raynal who appeared to have grown querulous, feeling a wee bit ignored.

"I am very grateful to you for making this day possible." He smiled, feigning good nature and quickly jumbled a few syllables.

"Before we go, I want you to know there are no slaves on this estate. I gave everyone their freedom five years ago."

"My brothers was born free!" Madlienne remarked with pride oozing from every pore.

"No! No! Not them, they were already freemen when we met."

Monsieur Rochard was at pains to explain. He forgot M. Raynal and had turned his attention to Madlienne exclusively. She was not quite sure whether he spoke to please her, knowing of her efforts in the earlier wars of liberation and the gallant support she had received from Argos, Jean and Ti Frère in her endeavours, not forgetting Constantin and Theodule who had gone on ahead (although M.Rochard did not know them). Her exploits would have been often repeated at Colombette by her three surviving siblings. For the moment she would remain silent. Her eyes would seek the truth. Monsieur Raynal felt vaguely out of place in the two warriors company and walked at a discreet distance behind, not wanting to hear snippets of their conversation, for fear he would shrivel and die of jealousy. He was a white man; the order of the day made Madlienne his subordinate, yet M. Rochard eyes saw her only.

They walked towards the back of the house, in the direction of a low wooden gate, ajar, propped by a plank. The gate was hingeless, securing nothing. They walked a short distance along a dirt track that was well worn from the frequent shuffle of feet until they came to a colony of huts, neatly laid out in rows like the garden plants.

'This man is a true soldier,' Madlienne thought, noticing also that each hut was covered in wine coloured shingles from the *Wallaba* tree and not straw as was habitual. It was evident that some measure of care had been afforded. The word that Madlienne had come had reached the huts and a small crowd had gathered to greet her. On seeing her in the company of Monsieur Rochard and another white gentleman, whose name they did not know, their expectations, which had already transported her, alive, up the ladder into the realm of myth, rose several rungs higher. Young mothers held their infants shoulder high for a glimpse at the living saint, who—in her youth—had dedicated her life to the cause of liberty and freedom. Three old men stood in their doorway and watched. Their failing eyesight did not miss the strut in her walk; they had all grown to love it. She had come: They knew from the proud strut she had. At last the leader had returned to lead what was left of the fold. The living embodiment of the Maid of Orleans had come in the flesh and not a minute too late.

Madlienne peeled her ears to listen carefully to the chatter, but was unable to discern a single word from the babble around her. Neither had she noticed the three old men walking with the empirical stride of elders towards her. Monsieur Rochard had seen them coming and paused, drawing a moment's silence from the small crowd, who were hesitant to intrude. Madlienne could not conceal the exhilaration that throttled her on coming into contact with the people. They had never seen her before, she had never met them, yet their faces, their eyes, their hair, and the colour of their skin was again, all too familiar. The joy in their eyes was the only stranger. It felt important being alive, if only to witness. The honour of the moment was hers alone, even the master walked in her shadow. Some stretched out their hands to touch her; but did not crowd, others crossed themselves with a sign of the cross, blessing their eyesight to have been allowed this one vision. Serene—almost saint-like—in a trance with the faint trace of a smile on her lips, she walked through the crowd and they parted for her to pass. A feeling of contentment rifled through the air; it came from the faces around her. This was not the features of a vanquished race. They were all happy, smiling people, a happiness that came only to a people natured in freedom. The crowd folded into two orderly rows. She walked down the middle flanked by their exhilarant faces on either side. The three old men stood patiently waiting their turn at the end of the aisle.

The first one she reached was Ti Frère, stretching out her hand reflexively with that far away look sealed to her face, his features never registered. She was turning to the next when she realized his hands were still firmly gripping her wrist. The slight receding line above his forehead, ash gray, caught her gaze. Nothing like the matted mass of black she remembered; she searched and found his eyes; the dark brown pupils had retained their colour. They were as she recalled. She watched them dilate, his heartbeat quickening as throes of excitement raced through his veins. He had always been the shortest and smallest among them. He had not grown an inch more in the forty years they had not met.

"*Sais!*" He said, quietly, almost under his breath. The quiet lisp was unmistakable even in that one word. So much she had remembered, they were never too far away from her thoughts.

"Ti Frère!" Madlienne shouted. "Ti Frère; that is you?"

They squared in front of one another like two fowl cocks bristling for a fight. She felt his hands grow limp on her wrist; in a rush of blood like the incoming tide at the mouth of a river where it vomits its bile into the sea, he swallowed her up in his arms. Argos and Jean joined him. She felt the weight of their bodies pressing her to the ground, three pairs of hands clinging to her shoulders. Their joy transformed into a raw energy, pulsating through her fingertips, it tingled her spine. She wanted to untangle herself, drawback and look at their faces to see how much they had aged.

"Argos! Jean!" She exclaimed, knowing the other hands could only be theirs. Their grip on her body was firm like the tentacles of a root, embracing its stone. They mumbled some incoherent jargon what could have been prayers as she felt breathe warm against her neck. A sudden wind filled with elation lifted her spirits, her head felt light like a feather and she soared through the air with the weightlessness of a bird. It did not matter if they drowned her with their kisses, or with the deafening slurp their lips made against her cheeks. It was eternity before she broke loose, gasping for breath. They had almost smothered her with their joy. She paused to regain her composure, then moved slowly from face to face, searching for a spark that would help her distinguish Argos from Jean. She had recognized Ti Frère in a flash. He could not disguise his height, or the lack of it and the lisp in his speech.

Nothing helped her to distinguish between Argos, and Jean. She tried to remember quirks in character, unconscious actions and strange mannerisms. Who picked nostrils or tugged at earlobes, some slight blemish on the skin, like a birthmark or a wound. She remembered Argos' birthmark and smiled. Its location could not be exposed in public.

"Where Constantin?" Ti Frère asked, breaking in the silence that was slowly forming a wall around them.

"First," Madlienne said, "Who's Argos, and who is Jean?"

The tallest of the three, raised his hand,

"I am Argos." This time it was Madlienne's turn. She embraced each one individually and then grappled with all three together, pretending to wrestle them to the ground, much to the delight of the crowd. Monsieur Raynal withdrew his timepiece from his waistcoat and consulted the dial. He turned to Monsieur Rochard whispering in his ear. It was time to leave if he was to reach Pointe-a-Pitre before dark. He had done his duty and would only be intruding if he stayed any longer. His awkwardness showed in the manner his limbs moved as he spoke. She broke loose from Argos, Jean and Ti Frère and went to M.Rochard and M.Raynal;

"Thanks for bringing me safe," she said to Monsieur Raynal, her face beaming with joy. "I am so happy to see my brothers again."

To Monsieur Rochard she simply bowed, acknowledging in her subtle fashion, she had confirmed his statement. The people on the estate were truly free as he had said, not only as a result of his actions, but in their hearts and minds as well. She felt their spirits like hers, among the birds. Indeed, they were one people, united by the same ancestral bond.

"I will get someone to bring your things. You will be with us a while I hope?" Monsieur Rochard said to Madlienne as he placed his hands on Monsieur Raynal's shoulder before leading him away. She looked across at Argos, Jean and Ti Frère: they were like three baboons grinning all over their faces.

"Yes!" She replied, "I think so."

A small crowd followed them to their hut and remained outside babbling, long after they had gone in. Ti Frère appointed himself spokesman for the trio—there were so many questions to be asked—he was frantically chatting his head off. He asked for Constantin, again, pressing Madlienne for a response. Obviously she did not want to give the bad news so early in the reunion.

"He is happy where he is," she said calmly.

"He beg us to come," Ti Frère said, "but, all our friends here."

There was no need to mention, the jubilation on the new faces Madlienne had met was ample evidence. They spent most of the afternoon exchanging anecdotes. Relating incidents each one remembered from their particular angle, clear in their own thoughts about the sequence of events; none in agreement with each other. They argued like children until the gray ash of evening settled on the huts. Argos lit the lamp and resumed his place. In her absence he was the one in control, although the line of authority appeared frayed by the argumentative Ti Frère who always seemed to be at variance with Argos.

"Monsieur Rochard is a good man?" Madlienne asked. For the first time, there was consensus.

"Tell me about him."

"Ask Argos," Ti Frère said, ceding his position for a change to the least talkative of the group.

"We meet in jail." Argos said. "The war was over. They had no use for us. I, Constantin and Monsieur Rochard was in the same cell. They separate us from Ti Frère and Jean. They say that Monsieur Rochard was an *Amis des Noirs* and a threat to the peace."

Ti Frère was priming to takeover.

"They beat the man so bad, his eyes was coming out of his head." He injected with the inimitable ease that was Ti Frère and Ti Frère alone. "How you know that?" Madlienne's alert mind prompted. This silenced him for a minute allowing Argos to continue.

"We didn't spend more than a week in that place. They come with a paper to say that we can go, but we must give our names to an estate. They want people to cut cane. Monsieur Rochard take us with him in the country. Not here, a next place they call Absyme. It was small. Monsieur Rochard got married there. His wife was still a girl."

"He make all of us learn a trade," Ti Frère butted in. "I was a carpenter; Argos and Jean learn to lay bricks," he added.

"But not Constantin," Jean said.

"His head was too hard to learn anything." Ti Frère edged in.

"He was a soldier," Jean said, "he know nothing else."

An image formed in Madlienne's mind, taking her back to that prison cell at Morne Fortune and that last conversation with Constantin. She had not attached much significance to his statement about the white man who came forward to save them, but having met Monsieur Rochard and listening to Argos, the gist of their story rang home. She sat musing over the fine details in this missing chapter that was being pieced together for her by Argos and the impertinent Ti Frère. Jean never said much, except to embellish details.

"He like you," Argos said.

"He take his gun and go for days," Ti Frère whimpered. "When he come back he would have wild goat and pig in his bag."

"Monsieur Rochard didn't mind," said Jean. "Between the three of us, we do all the work around the house."

"Where your children?" Madlienne asked them collectively. Argos bowed his head;

"I have one, a girl. She is a big woman now. The rest of us don't have."

"Where she is?" Madlienne asked, "I want to know her."

Argos shook his head. He was close to tears.

"She leave one day for Pointe—a—Pitre and never come back," Ti Frère said.

"You ever try to find her?" Madlienne asked him, but Argos only shook his head.

"Constantin use to tell her things that send her mad. He tell her about you, about us, about things that happen long, long ago, we want to forget."

"He tell her about Gimat and how he kill our mothers an fathers," Ti Frère said.

Madlienne was puzzled, they had not met to be briefed with all the facts she had learnt from Tergis, and yet they knew.

"Who tell you about Gimat?" Madlienne asked Ti Frère, bracing herself for his response.

"Constantin! He always was getting to know things," Ti Frère replied.

"From the *Negre Maron* he meet in the bush," Jean said.

"She make him repeat the same old story many times. Then one day she wake up and want to go to St. Lucie."

"She say one day, she will kill Gimat," Ti Frère added.

"Just like you when you give up the war to go and find them. She would help you do it," Argos said. "She just like you."

They knew of her pact to dispense death to the murderers of her race; like a solemn vow it had estranged her from them, it had prevented her from trying to find them after the fighting had ceased. She had become distant in an effort to protect them from any counter insurgence arising from her actions. They were all she had left. She was always petrified by the thought of being unmasked knowing that they would follow. Her captors would find them, for they knew they were inseparable: nothing under the sun could convince anyone she was acting alone.

It was that singular thought, which disturbed them too as they remembered her in their prayers on occasions like Easter and Christmas when they ventured the ten-mile journey to church. They had prayed for her safety and although they had no way of knowing the effectiveness of their prayers they continued, until it materialized into a habit. When Monsieur Rochard informed them of the impending visit, they knelt and sang the *Te Deum* together. At last the fighting was over. They knew she had come through unscathed, like she had done in battle, with rivers of perspiration streaming from all parts of her body and a smile coursing her lips.

"I wish I could know your child," Madlienne said, caressing the grey tufts on Argos' head.

"Her mother was a *mulâtresse*," Argos said. "Nickola is a *shabeene*."

The name fired a flare across her mind.

"Nickola?" Madlienne inquired; "I know a Nickola . . ." She stuttered, caught unawares in an atmosphere of growing uncertainty.

'It could not!' She thought, 'it could not be.'

Fireflies lit in Argos' eyes; "You know her?" He inquired.

The Nickola Madlienne knew had no pretensions to anything else but survival with her child who had no father. The one that Argos lost—from the little she had just learnt—was a compelling soul; a different being with a fixed purpose filled with grandiose ideas that could well have been a duplicate of herself. Although she had not met anyone called Nickola until she went to work at Moulin-a-Vent, it was unreasonable to believe, only one person in the world was known by that name. If the Nickola at Moulin-a-Vent was Argos' daughter, she was exceptionally cunning; a person as skillful as this would have the capacity to kill. A shiver wedged lengthwise between her ribs, remembering that last night in Gimat's room. The room and the two bodies, limp across the bed filled her head with frightful thoughts:

through *savonnette* leaves; its image fixed like a painting on canvass. Gradually, the image mutates to become Louise . . . Young, lithesome with the smell of lavender steaming from her body. These thoughts could not be shared. They were too sacred to be spilt, although her body craved for release, to forget, not wanting to be forgotten.

Ti Frère spoke of Constantin in a manner that recreated his presence, his brooding, bringing to life those long bouts with silence, which could not be punctured even if he was suddenly stuck in the buttocks with a thorn. Madlienne realized how much she had missed their company, tears of joy and pain streamed down her face, they warmed her cheeks. She was still their equal in a world which firmly proclaimed the dominance of men. More than this, she was still regarded as the leader of their lost tribe, they did not hide a single secret from her. It rolled back the years to when the mantle of manhood stole around their young shoulders prematurely and she was groping to understand the changes in her own body that made her suddenly different, they confided in her then, recounting their little liaisons in camp with all the details. Hearing them repeat their stories again, reaffirmed that trust, unshaken, despite the storms of time. That bond had painfully sealed her lips when Constantin opened up to her behind the cold walls of his prison cell with the enemy waiting outside. She had treasured their trust as her most prized possession; nothing could steal it away from her. That sacred bond, the mutual respect, the near obeisance, nothing had changed; nothing at all.

After a week following them to their garden plot on mornings, listening intently as they repeated themselves at nights—rehearsing incidents that had chronologically stuck to their minds in mortar, bonding firmer than lime—Madlienne began experiencing the nebulous pangs of homesickness. It came mid-morning after the night's proceedings had receded to an empty pocket inside, when Argos and Jean's heads reared above the steep slope they had been weeding for days. It was a Thursday. They knew the time from the height of the sun in the sky and from the subtle signals deep in their stomachs. She had not gone weeding; it was one of her idle days. She sat twiddling her thumbs, watching Ti Frère cook. Ti Frere had established his kitchen on three stones under a huge *Maubin* tree at the top of a lower slope on the humpback ridge and had peeled sufficient white Tania to feed a battalion. She saw vapour escape through the *balisier* leaves covering his pot, which was as black as the insides of a clay oven. The smell stroked her nostrils as her eyes sweeped over the brow of the higher slope, on a wave of nostalgia. The bugles at sundown returned with curious smells from the old camp; meat roasting on open fires, sweat mixed with gun powder and fresh cut logs from the *Laurier Cannelles* clutched under armpits and kindlings bundled and carried on the shoulder. A friendly shout, some deafening jeers, time could not erase these memories even when she no longer wanted to remember them. They reopened old wounds the years had healed. The ancient custom of cooking over stones, and the smell of the burning firewood, she had deliberately blotted from her mind was pulsating through her body with the urgency of drums. She was contented knowing that Argos, Jean and Ti Frère were still alive. The scars they strafed with their unending anecdotes were fresh but would not purify her blood. She had bled too many times before, dreaming of a vengeance that could not substitute for the return of her father. She would have to leave before she decided to start her crusade all over again. Argos was right. They were a family, united by pain, which like a stagnant river could not be purged by the sea. They were contented, like the sick river, wallowing in the putrid stench of its bile. The past pained. Louise, her beauty enthralling, yet her aura bred torment and disillusionment. In her old age, Madlienne did not want these unrequited dreams to mellow again into hate. The strain was more than she could bear. She ate the meal in silence, afterwards she stretched out on the grass allowing the cool breeze fanning the *Maubin* tree to seep through her pores. When she felt strong enough to think, after adjusting to her fears, she said aloud, speaking to no one in particular but addressing all:

"I have to go back. I have things to do."

They had taken the long journey from Colombette with her in their cart, drawn by their old mule whose whiskers had turned gray like their heads. They had not traveled that far in forty years, but they never stopped along the way to rest. It was one of those miserable November days, when the rain poured in fine grains like *farine* on their heads. Had Madlienne not made a special request before they reached Absyme, they would have passed through the place like it never existed. Her eyes searched and found the strange circular shapes that were the huts covered in *Kus-Kus* grass. The absence of smoke rising from their hearths although it was approaching the hour of the angelus, appeared more than strange, sporadic showers had cleared the street of any sign of life. This place, home of the *Gens Libre*, radiated a quiet charm; a quaint sombre warmth, only those who knew the price of freedom could see it; a dumb defiance stirred through the haze that perpetually smothered it, creating those clouds of solitude hanging from the eyes of the inhabitants she had seen when she first passed through. The solitude that epitomized

Absyme had been her life. It was as if she was looking into a mirror; a mirror reflecting her naked image, newborn and raw. They drove on towards the plains; the dry river had gathered its tears and was beginning to flow through the winding passes, the narrow dirt road, where the wheels sank in the slush, plodding on, until in the distance they sighted Point-a-Pitre, bleak, under its gray skies. During that week, the rain had come.

They stayed until the brig sailed; three scions of a dying race accompanied by Feyette and her brood and the ashen figure of Monsieur Raynal, waving from the pier through the light evening mist, becoming one with it when the wind in the bay lodged in the sails to drive the brig into the open sea. Argos, Jean, and Ti Frère, their features lean and haggard from the weight of their years, stood still in the hazy twilight gazing seaward, until a cloud strangled the light, drawing the final curtain on a past that poured its moments of joy and pain in equal dosage, becoming one with the night.

CHAPTER THIRTEEN

Dawn sprinkled its showers over the landscape as the sun crept from behind its cloud. Monsieur Duval, framed in the faint light, was at the docks huddled under a gray coat to protect him from the early morning chill and the slight drizzle. He boarded the ship as its agent as soon as the gangplank was lowered. After a few salutary endearments to the captain, in his infectious style, he came across to Madlienne on the fore deck, smiling nervously between his cracked teeth.

"Monsieur Gimat dead!" he said. "Your old boss."

He was agitated, not knowing whether to be sad or happy as he broke the news.

"Doctor say it was his heart. It stop beating." Madlienne felt the blood fill the hollow passages around her brain. She was lost for words. She stood, dumbfounded, gazing at Monsieur Duval with a puzzled look. Life and death had become companions in her mind. Age had willed it.

"When?" she asked, coldly.

"The funeral was at Gros Islet two day ago. Not many people came. Nobody really know him. But one thing strange, after he die somebody cut a tiny cross over his left breast with a sharp knife."

"Over his left breast?" Madlienne repeated.

"Yes," replied Monsieur Duval, "after he die, somebody made the mark."

The significance of this symbol was not lost. It was only a miniature version of the ones she carved on the breasts of Theobald and Valentine, but it was a cross no matter its size. They had heard the stories, whispered from ear to ear, years ago, after she had left camp and journeyed west to Soufrière. The news bristled through the undergrowth with its thick strands of lianas, finding the lips of the *Negre Maron*, who repeated it to Constantin during his sojourns deep into the woods, and he in turn to them. They knew she had embarked on a mission of vengeance. She did not withhold that secret from them. That last day, at the edge of the forest before they embraced her and she became one with the greenness, she reminded them. Unknown to her, they had followed her progress through the whispers Constantin confirmed. The marks on the bodies at Soufriere affirmed their suspicions. They knew the hallmark of vengeance; she used it like a seal to apprise the world, her father's death and their fathers, was being avenged.

Constantin had indoctrinated Nickola well in everything she should know. She knew the secrets of her progenitors, the essences that flavoured her race. A vague suspicion kept rolling—over and over—in Madlienne's mind. Though things are seldom what they seem, she needed assurance. She would learn the real cause of Gimat's death, even if it took one final act of defiance. It was her duty to know. The Nickola she remembered was young and frivolous at best, unskilled in the art of cunning, though shameless with her use of body as a tool for upward mobility. If she was Argos' daughter, she had fitted her disguises to another face, on another body and wore them well. Argos was versed in local poisons. As a boy, he gathered herbs and roots for his father, who was the shaman of the tribe. He knew how to mix them to extract their varying degrees of potency to taint the bait in his traps. The animals could be paralyzed for hours, their heartbeats fettered, in a state of oblivion where they were neither alive nor dead. Hours later, after he had secured them and the effects of the poisons had worn off they could be seen leaping behind the wooden staves of their cage, squawking in captivity. Her mind unraveled the long scrolls buried deep in her subconscious. She remembered the *jacquots* with their multi-coloured plumage; the red pockmarks under their throats, distinct in memory. He captured them by painting a thin coat of his mixtures on the red berries of the *gri gri* palm early in the morning, returning at a precise hour to collect his spoils. Although he could handle a gun, this was his method for hunting small game, the *agouti*, opossum, and even the *ramier* for which he set bait in the flowering white cedar trees. The more she pondered, the more elements of doubt helped feed her suspicions. She could not obtain the information she required from Monsieur Duval; the who and the why, the where and when, she already knew. He knew no more than he had already told her, although he remained strangely evasive when Madlienne asked him simple questions relating to Gimat's demise. He was the sort of man who never liked to say he did not know. Knowledge meant power and power wealth. They walked back together from the pier maintaining an uneasy silence. For Madlienne, the years of her youth again returned in a gush of tears to overwhelm her. The anguish flowing through her body at the sight of her father lying lifeless in his hammock was vivid like on the day it happened—too real to speak, but then she did not cry. The sudden news of Gimat's death had stirred these feelings back to life again. The hatred that burned inside for her father's butchers caused her lips to twitch by merely thinking about them. The hundreds that had died on the battlefield, in her arms and at her side, could not equal that singular loss. This coupled with the loss of the others of her tribe on that fateful day could never be erased from her memory. She would never be able to understand the senseless message their deaths were meant to convey; only the anger it bred. She had run from Colombette to escape from these memories, but, one by one, they were returning to haunt her. There was no place to hide. Monsieur Duval regretted breaking the news to her abruptly. His silence was his way of saying he wanted to kick himself.

Madlienne wanted to be alone; within the sanity of self she would find peace: Alone she would be able to think. She was confronted with an enigma and needed time and quiet to rip it to pieces, then put it back together again. She had refused Monsieur Duval's generous offer to let one of his handymen take her to Trois Piton. She preferred to walk. She hoisted her small bundle on her head and began the slow journey through Fond Marchand, up the lower escarpment of Bagatelle to her cottage, pausing along the route to inform her many acquaintances she had returned. Madlienne was back.

In the evening it rained. She looked out from her window; a thick white mist had enveloped the hills; it was the years clouding memory's dim maze as they floated by on low clouds, bringing the cold, which pained her joints. With Gimat dead—quite probably the last of the perpetrators who had plagued her days and nights—meant there was nothing left for her to do. She could not kill him. She had tried, but her nerve for blood had died with the years of revolt. Now, learning of his death, her old bones creaked with regret knowing they could not administer the final blow. Sleep soon claimed her on the sofa where she had laid her head on the old cotton pillow against the back rest; to dream . . . There were Constantin, and Theodule. They were children again, running up and down in the forest, the three of them. They were playing on a mountain ledge she had never seen before. They were enticing her to cross a bridge, which spanned a huge chasm where the mist was as thick as chalk. Beyond its white wall, faraway into a distant blue, blue like the sea, not the sky, lay the burial mounds of her ancestors. She knew instantantly, there was no need to be told; it was the other country; she knew she would visit soon.

Another urge came fast and furious; to exhume Gimat's body and search his chest for the sign of the cross.

'Who mark him?' She battled with her thoughts: 'Who else know?' There would be no peace until she unraveled this mystery. To reappear at Moulin-a-Vent after six months would invoke questions—some she would not be able to answer. She had deliberately avoided Phillipe and Raphael on the days she knew they would be in town. To visit them like a clear blue patch of sky at the height of the rainy season would require an excuse so tight, her mind could not begin to figure—what could she say? All night long the dilemma surged. It ate away inside. She could not quell the spasms that caused her heart to race with an unearthly curiosity, more painful than thirst. Next morning she collected Clarissia from the neighbour in whose care she had left her and took her down the gorge to the ravine for a bath. She was not gone long when she heard her name called and saw a young man edging down the slope in their direction.

"Monsieur Duval told us you come back. We come to look for you." It was Phillipe. He held Clarissia by the reins as they climbed the steep tracks at the back of the house—back to the cottage—where Raphael had dismounted from his horse and was waiting.

"Monsieur Duval told you?" He asked. Madlienne presumed he meant Gimat's death and nodded.

"He talks so much," Raphael said, "we have been asking him for you from the day you left Moulin-a-Vent, and when he tell us you go to Guadeloupe, we say you will not comeback."

"I born here," Madlienne said, "what I do to runaway?"

"When he told us yesterday, that you come back, we could not wait." Phillipe said genuinely, showing his joy in an exuberant flash of white teeth. Madlienne tied Clarissia in the broken down stable adjoining the cottage and when she returned, she ushered them into the house. There were things she wanted to know, but it did not seem right to tackle them in the steaming heat outside. Of the two, Phillipe was the most relaxed as he sank into the soft cotton pillow on the old sofa, which swallowed his weight. Raphael had remained unusually reserved, tugging at his lapels. He seemed reluctant to open the conversation.

"Papa wants to ask you to come back," Phillipe said, "but he is afraid you'd say no."

It was the gambit Madlienne feared, to begin the inevitable arguments for and against returning to Moulin-a-Vent. Raphael, being a matured man, had sensed this and was hesitant. He had been timing his approach, perhaps hoping to gain her sympathy, like he had done before, but Phillipe had bolted, like a horse from the stable, he had no choice in the matter but to listen. He knew Madlienne had a special place in her heart for Phillipe, even before the eventful day when she saw the first positive changes in his physique as a result of her potions. He knew Phillipe was no match for Madlienne's cunning. She would weave him around her fingers with the ease of cotton thread through a needle's eye. However if anyone could play on her senses and get her to return, it would be him.

"I am quite happy here by myself," she said. "I wake up when I want, and go out when I please."

"You can do the same thing if you come and stay with us," Phillipe implored. Madlienne shook her head. "I like to be by myself."

"With the old man gone, we will have to close up the house." Raphael interjected solemnly, keeping his distance. Madlienne spotted her opening and entered head first: "Where is Nickola?" she asked.

Raphael looked across at Phillipe with a dry smirk on his face. "She's there, heart-broken. He died suddenly and he didn't have time to make a will." "An Papa believe she going to make a baby. She always sick in the morning." Phillipe blurted innocently, racing through the words.

"She took it hard," Raphael said; "she was the last person to see him alive. She put him to bed. Next morning he did not get up."

"Nickola come an call us early," Phillipe said. "The sun did not well wake up, she say, when she bring him his coffee, she find his door wide open. He was kneeling down by the side of the bed like he was praying. When he didn't move she start to scream an run all the way up the hill and call us." "He wasn't sick before?" Madlienne inquired.

"He never complain, only the old foot that was troubling him again after you left, but Nickola was doing her best to ease the pain," Raphael said.

"By the time we reach, his lips was blue," Phillipe added, "and his body was hard like a statue."

"Nickola didn't sleep with him anymore?" Madlienne asked pretending that it was out of curiosity, there was a jocular tone to her voice.

"She say, her child was sick. She leave early, before Monsieur Gimat go to bed. She dress his foot in the room, and after she finish, she leave," Raphael said.

"You ask Marcelle and Egyptienne?"

"No!" Raphael replied sharply.

"Why?" Madlienne blurted out without realizing the significance of the question at first. She had slipped. She had no desire to squelch on Nickola, if at all it was she who had put out the devil's lights. Her blood, the blood of the tribe flowed in Nickola's veins. Nickola had done for her what she had failed to do despite her solemn pledge. In her heart a small voice spoke, more than ever she wanted Nickola to be part of her. There was no need to create suspicion in the minds of Raphael and Phillipe. They had accepted Gimat's death as a natural occurrence—he was old. Madlienne thought quickly . . .

"You didn't ask them when last they see him alive?"

"Before it get dark, they go to look for their children. That hasn't changed," Raphael explained.

"The doctor say, it was his heart," Phillipe repeated. Both were manifesting their childlike naivety; however Madlienne's natural inclinations advised otherwise.

'His heart?' She questioned, without asking.

It was too perfect for her mind to accept. Nickola pregnant, grieving like a widow, not running away; not afraid of discovery—this was an inborn skill; it intrigued her. She wished they could meet again.

Raphael and Phillipe were simple folk. They had not been tempered by the evils of life to understand that every action was matched by counter action, where covert acts bearing the sinister hallmark of hell became enigmas. They had not experienced crisis. Purity of thought revolved around natural events, which they accepted by the grace of God. Living and dying were natural phenomena that came to them like the sun with the dawn and the moon with night. The levels of subterfuge climaxing in the death of Gimat were beyond their simple understanding; only minds grounded in the mills of suspicion and hate could fathom such depths. That unwritten code to protect Nickola whether or not her apprehensions were real was foremost in front her like a Psalter before the priest. Madlienne took hold of herself, leading them through small talk about the funeral, limiting her interest to who cried, and who did not, who came and was present from the night of the wake, who bathed the corpse, who lowered him to his final resting place in the sand, with the crabs.

Phillipe enjoyed providing details of the minutiae, while his father continued fidgeting with his lapels until the drill began to fray. He was apprehensive about the future. Monsieur Cartier would be writing to the heirs in France. He feared that the estate would be offered for sale and he did not have the means to purchase. He knew of Madlienne's popularity among the French citizens in the colony. He had hoped that she would offer to open some doors for him. He hinted it, but Madlienne did not understand, wrapped in her own misgivings she did not perceive. He did not press. Instead, he allowed Phillipe the liberty of continuing to talk. It was not an easy thing for him to beg. The matter could wait. Madlienne's concern was for Nickola, young, already with one child and another on the way, none with a father's support. Was Nickola from her roots? Was she a branch from her tree? These questions could not be answered and yet they plagued her mind. Neither Raphael nor Phillipe detected the enormity of stress to which she was subjugated. She had learnt to disguise her feelings. When they were about leaving, Madlienne said, "you must tell Nickola to come and see me. Marcelle and Egyptienne too," she added, carefully considering the circumstances. It was then she observed the cold uncertainty in Raphael's strides as he slouched towards the door. She was looking directly at him and spotted an unusual reluctance in his gait. "You not well?" she asked. "It must be strain from the funeral." "I am well," Raphael replied, "it just have too many ends for me to tie." Madlienne did not pursue. They left, looking a bit down-spirited, Phillipe being unable to convince Madlienne to return to Moulin-a-Vent and his father not having the courage to explain his needs.

CHAPTER FOURTEEN

Life continued to unroll its pages for Madlienne, like the sea with its uneven steps. Blessed with good health despite her approaching years she continued to attend to her daily chores with a vigour that belied the age which piled on her back like a wagon heaped with cane. She restored her flower garden to full bloom and spent her afternoons until the brief twilight had vanished dozing in her rocker, intoxicated by the fragrance of *citronnelle*, frangipani and her hedge of pink oleanders that never ceased to bloom. She had also resurrected the beds in the kitchen garden and tended her crop of carrots, turnips, cabbages and beans for morning exercise. She no longer set a fixed day for town. She went only when there was need, when her provisions ran low and there were ample vegetables for sale. She avoided Phillipe and his father Raphael like fever, blotting Thursday from her list of days, fearing that she would wilt under Phillipe's constant bombardment; she knew he would not give in. She loved Phillipe and could not think of hurting his feelings. They could not understand contentment from solitude. They would continue their attempts to inveigle her back to Moulin-a-Vent, appealing to sympathy for support. She would be powerless to refuse.

Months went by slowly; her routine around the house had become a rigid military drill to which she committed her energy. It was self-imposed penance for sins forgotten. She worked with an intensity intending to shake off memories both pleasant and unpleasant that had become ingrained in her character molding her into the phenomenon she was. So intense was her dedication, she often had to remind herself of the days of the week. Her neighbours saw her as a recluse, but respected her privacy. They believed her self-imposed seclusion was madness from the wars and they pitied her. Madlienne, despite her untiring efforts, could not purge her mind of all the dark secrets it held. On evenings when it rained and the joints in her body creaked, the pain brought back the years of death and suffering through whose gates she had passed unscathed, remembering not only the chaos which reduced men to the status of beasts, but also the glory that lit smiles on the lips of the fallen, those who would never return. It made her toss and wrestle in her bed, fighting dreams that jolted her senses in the depths of the night, as she woke screaming, through rivers of sweat that drenched her nightgown and poured on pillow and sheet. However, there were lulls, through the eye of the storm her mind would shed its torment to usher in moments of calm. On such nights, visited by pleasant memories of childhood, during the interlude when pain and suffering receded to a dull throb in her temples, she would revisit that sweet idyllic innocence of youth, where forests transformed into the first garden that witnessed the birth of morning. She could not ostracize her past as distant as it seemed, from the present. It had helped her to understand the peace and tranquility she had uncovered in her twilight years in this little clearing at Trois Piton, among the trees and the vines and the occasional twitter of birds. Her mind ran through its phases until joy surmounted pain and sleep claimed her again. When she woke up next morning, it would be all forgotten, resolute in her chores another day would dawn as uneventful like the others before.

It was a bright Sunday morning. She knew it was Sunday, for the sun was shining with that peculiar glow reserved only for Sundays. She was in her kitchen garden, behind her house. She heard a rap on her front door, but could not bother. She was intent on feeding her plants some horse manure she had dried and pounded into a fine powder to spread between their roots. It was the middle of the rainy season, nevertheless she wanted to complete the task before the heat made it unbearable to proceed. She had decided to complete her task before noon. Someone was shouting her name, which caused her to stop impulsively, standing upright with her hands on her hips, feeling a slight jab of pain in her waist as she rose. She called it the weed's revenge, for she only felt it while weeding, an after effect from bending. She allowed the person to repeat her name several times all the while remaining silent, as she tried to catch the voice. It was familiar, but she could not place it. It was the voice of a woman, a young voice, she knew the owner but could not put a face to it. She waited until she detected a hint of panic, more like frustration setting in, before making a move. Even then she was in no great hurry. She gathered her tools in a small heap—her rake, her hoe, her cutlass and her garden fork resting them against the side of her house. She washed her hands in the hogshead that collected the water from the roof from a bamboo guttering she had fixed in place herself, but had turned black with fungus and mould, the growth of several years. As she came around the side of the house, she saw a woman standing on the steps clutching an infant tightly against her breasts. The child was asleep. The woman was desperate. She was bent on knocking down the door. She had not heard Madlienne's footsteps approaching, and was startled, accidentally brushing the flannel from the infant's face as their eyes met. Madlienne recognized her at once with the white child in her arms. She smiled.

"Nickola! You bring the baby to see me?" Nickola registered the same sheepish grin, like when they first met.

"Who tell you I have baby?" she said impishly, provoking Madlienne. Motherhood had not healed Nickola's girlish habits. They were part of her like the hint of a lisp in her voice when she spoke. It was the lisp Madlienne heard first, peeping through the soft-spoken tones of a good soul. It was the lisp she had always heard and never could determine what it was when they worked together. Nickola had worked hard at disguising it, although it fought back and gushed through her teeth whenever she became exasperated and momentarily forgot. She hugged and kissed Madlienne like she had met her long lost aunt.

"How old?" Madlienne asked, pointing to the baby.

"A month. Monsieur Gimat was his father." Nickola replied with a proud grin splitting from ear to ear.

"I can see that," Madlienne responded. "He has his marmoset face." One of the neighbours to the east was stewing the Sunday meat on a slow charcoal fire and the breeze fanned the scent, a mixture of seasonings and beef stew, to her yard. It was the customary odour that made Sunday mornings stand apart from other mornings. Neither commented but their faces lit as the odour settled in their clothes.

"I ready to go back to work." Nickola said. "I have nobody to hold the baby." Madlienne smiled, "At my age!" Mumbling to herself.

"I know how much you did like Monsieur Gimat. I want you to take him!" Madlienne took the child from her, covering him with the flannel shawl, which had slid from his chest as she lifted him.

"Let's go inside," Madlienne said, "the heat starting to choke me." They sat facing each other at either end, in Monsieur De Brettes' old armchair—in the drawing room—that sometimes became Madlienne's bed. Madlienne nuzzled the baby against her chin, peeping at his tiny face under the flannel shawl. There were questions she was curious to ask. She had rehearsed them for when she would meet Nickola, sharp pointed notes to guide her judgment.

"I never had a child in my life," Madlienne said, continuing from where they left off outside. "You think is now I will take on trouble?" Peeping at Nickola in her searching style, under her eyelids, looking for that opening, that drop in her guard. Nickola did not manifest the slightest hint of disappointment; she acted as though she had expected it. She took the baby from Madlienne and sat down again. She opened her bodice and bared her left breast, which she gripped between her fingers, placing the swollen nipple in the infant's mouth. He was hungry. Madlienne observed his tiny gums and throat moving in unison as he sucked and swallowed.

"I can't do that for you," Madlienne said, observing the instinctive reactions of mother and child.

"I know how much you did like Monsieur Gimat," Nickola repeated again, her voice droning with sensitivity like she was about to cry.

"He was a good man," Madlienne muttered, looking straight at Nickola, Nickola returned her stare with a smile. She was always smiling when she was not vexed. It helped to conceal her true feelings. Her thoughts were impossible to read. The old mongoose felt cornered, but she was determined to the end.

"Now tell me everything that happen at Moulin-a-vent since I left," Madlienne said in her loud characteristic tone, hoping to change the subject. Nickola giggled, returning to that girlish side of her personality that came to her at will.

"Nothing!" she replied. "The old man fold up and die an the estate just there waiting for his children to come."

"What about Raphael, and Phillipe?" Madlienne asked.

"They there spinning top in mud, Raphael hoping to make enough money to buy the place when it come to sell, while Phillipe hot behind any young thing with two legs and a crotch." Nickola continued giggling as she spoke making everything she said seem one big joke. Madlienne listened carefully, interjecting here and there, harmless but leading her through the paces. When she was ready she sprang.

"I hearing a lot of things!" She said, making her voice tail away like she was falling asleep.

"Like what?" Nickola asked, a bit anxious.

Madlienne paused for a moment.

"Like?" Nickola asked again.

"Like the way Gimat die." She had dropped his conventional title deliberately for the first time during their conversation.

"I hear he was poisoned." Madlienne was on the attack, her body tense, rearing to go. Nickola chuckled, forcing a smile through her teeth.

"Who tell you that?" she inquired. Madlienne was prepared for the long drawn out battle, for her it would not end until one of them had been outwitted.

"Bad news is like water. It does walk under the ground," Madlienne said. She was slowly assuming the mantle of the interrogator, against a skilled opponent.

"I never hear that!" Nickola said.

"You was the last person to see him alive?" Madlienne asked.

"Yes, I stay till he fall asleep," Nickola replied. She did not appear frightened by the questions. She was responding with an honest face. "Who would want to kill poor Monsieur Gimat? Everybody was his friend," Nickola added.

"The children and grandchildren of those he kill before," Madlienne replied. "I don't know nothing about what you saying there," Nickola said.

"You know a man they call Argos?" Before Nickola could shake her head she added, "Constantin; Ti Frère; Jean?"

"He kill these people?" Nickola asked. "No." Replied Madlienne; "But he butcher their mothers and their fathers."

Nickola was good, Madlienne thought. So far she conceded nothing; her eyes were dry although she spoke with feeling. Madlienne took out one of the dried goatskins she kept under her bed covering the boards to soften the sting from the coconut fibre in the mattress and spread it on the floor, with a pillow. The cool breeze coming through the half-opened door had lulled the infant to sleep. She placed him on the goatskin, his head resting on the edge of the pillow, still swaddled in the flannel, as she was fearful he would catch a chill and become ill. The two women continued the battle. "Who is these people?" Nickola inquired, her curiosity was aroused.

"Your father and his brothers and sisters, an mine," Madlienne replied. Nickola was neither stunned nor surprised, not even peeved by the remark. It appeared to her that the sediment of age was settling on Madlienne's brain causing a mild form of madness. She would be careful not to drive her to anger.

"Only one thing I want was Monsieur Gimat's child, before I get it he die," she said sadly, intoning regret.

"You didn't help him?" Madlienne asked.

"Help him for what?" Nickola responded with a question.

"To die," Madlienne said, finally.

"I don't know nothing about those things you saying. I don't even know the day I was born." The child stirred, Nickola bent and picked him up, removing the flannel, which was his only covering. Madlienne could not miss the tiny red circular birthmark at the top of his buttocks on the right side, the size of a farthing. A fever stormed in across her mind, scarring through the catchments of memory to drench her thoughts. Her mind rolled back to childhood, to the river where they bathed naked in the soothing waters; to Argos, remembering the white mark stuck to his body, in the same place. Constantin tried once to peal it off, but found it was part of his skin; he had inherited it from his father. Madlienne did not recall seeing the mark on Nickola the night she curled across Gimat's bed. She had not looked for it. At the time, there was not the slightest hint of suspicion in her mind—Nickola was just a frivolous, young girl learning the ways of the world. Madlienne stared at the birthmark. It was the signal she sought:

"What is this mark on the child?" She asked. Nickola smiled. It was deep, coming from inside.

"He get it from my father. He used to tell me, it is the mark of his tribe." There would be no further questions on the issue. Nickola had learnt her lessons well. Madlienne knew she would be unable to pry the tiniest morsel from her. It was best to let the past rest with the crabs in its cradle of sand. "You can go and lie down if you tired," Madlienne said. "An take the child with you." Nickola picked up the infant and the pillow and walked towards Madlienne's room.

"When you ready to go, I'll take you," Madlienne said as she stepped into the open air.

In the late evening light, mist covering the hills, the old woman seated quietly on her buckboard, musing, broke into an occasional smile. Memories of a past, still present, returned with vigour. It filled her with a strange but pleasant joy as the familiar landscape filed past. Nickola sat beside her with the infant in her arms as the old cart cantered into the driveway at Moulin-a-Vent. The haze thickened around her as daylight fled; it enveloped her body with its white sheet. They rode past the house; to them, it seemed not to have existed with its gables hugging the darkness; lamps had been lit. They stopped outside the cabin where Marcelle and Egytienne lived with their brood. Madlienne jumped down and walked to the other side. She stretched out her hands and took the baby from Nickola.

"Put Clarissia in the stable," she said, "I'll look after her later." Nickola took over the reins and turned the buckboard back in the direction of the house, while Madlienne walked towards the cabin.

"How we going to call you, boy?" she said, rubbing her cheeks against the infant's: "Argos? Or Desolee? We will ask your mother when she come." The infant wriggled in her arms as he heard her voice, baring his gums. A gurgle of joy broke like a smile through his lips. He understood. He already knew.

THE END

EPILOGUE

They hoisted the coffin—draped in the tricolour—shoulder high and marched up the aisle in unison to the muffled beat of kettle drums; the six young officers dressed in navy blue tunics, collars immaculately stiff and bristling from an ample dose of boric acid. Brass buttons dazzling even in the subdued light of a pale afternoon sun. The gold tassels from the flag tickled their earlobes with the persistent perversion of a swarm of flies, but, they never blinked or faltered in their steps. Their bland stares conveyed the impression that they had rehearsed their roles although there was obviously no time to do so. It was the Governor's wish that she be buried with full military honours. By this measure he hoped to cement a long and lasting peace in the colony between French and English residents. Also, to gain the confidence of the black inhabitants who were in the majority by a ratio of four to one, there were feelings of uneasiness among persons of different nationalities, but they were always united when confronted with colour. Since emancipation, this had become a necessity as freed men by self-proclamation were establishing a semblance of racial equality (among themselves) by creating their own social institutions: dance halls, rum shops, friendly societies, lodges and sports clubs, thus destabilizing the feeble balance of power, which had kept the inhabitants in check for generations, by what was considered acts of defiance. These subtle barriers from the past had been dismantled and freed men of colour were expounding their rights in the streets especially on Saturday nights after their fortnightly wages afforded them an extra tot of rum, to loosen their tongues. The French favoured the blacks in disputes with other nationalities, particularly the British, who were always pilloried for stealing their birthright. Abbe Lecailtel, the parish priest, was French and showed his favour particularly at high mass on Sundays when he allowed young black girls to sing alongside his lily white choristers in the choir loft, suspended like a floating mezzanine over the entrance on Laborie street. There were complaints from wives and mothers who secretly thought the timbre of those young black voices sexually alluring and could awaken dormant passions deliberately asleep within their feigning half-dead husbands. The Abbe remained unperturbed. He realized that the harmony rising from those rich young contraltos were superior to the squeaky sopranos, in pitch and scale and nothing of such rare beauty could lead to the unnecessary rivalry they imagined. They were outraged by his rebuff and quarreled under breath and badgered their husbands at will, outside the earshot of their housemaids, to no avail. The new order was fast becoming a reality, as was the word *égalité* they had muttered with honour as one of the endearing symbols of the revolution.

The tiny church nestled in the shadow of a gigantic teak with its wild pine saprophytes in bloom for the occasion, high up in its most inaccessible regions, enshrouding the steeple, muffling the sound of the tolling bell as it struck every hour on the hour from noon, until the last hour before the funeral when it tolled a double rhythm every quarter, in a style reserved for governors and kings. As they carried her body up the aisle in a slow march towards the catafalque, a lone flute from one of the back pews, played impromptu. It was an indecipherable chant between classical funeral march and Negro spiritual. Abbe Lecailtel stopped and turned towards the congregation with a frown. He had proclaimed *Sankeys* to be the music of the devil and never wanted to hear them in his church. Despite this, the soft sweet flowing strains continued to rise above the mass of humanity that had swamped the rear pews, pouring into the street with an ample mixture of body sweat and heat. The procession stopped briefly, until a restless feeling overcame the congregation and it reflected in their features, forcing the Abbe to proceed, despite his annoyance. As he resumed at the head of the procession, immediately behind the cross, the flute continued. It seemed to be in harmony with the kettle-drums.

Some had never met her, yet all present knew her name. She was their icon. She had become their holy relic, revered in the same breath as the crucifix or any other religious symbol or saint, to which they pledged their lives. For them it was not the end but the beginning of a new phase in immortality, where she would be worshipped and adored like Jeanne d'Arc before her. In death, the simple deeds in life are magnified one thousand fold and an ant can assume the stature of an anaconda, when ordinary feats of fortitude are recounted for posterity. It would be one new name to add to their litany of saints whose protection they craved at the crack of dawn before venturing out into the morning. It was for them, her final journey beyond beatification, an honour they had already accorded her, alive.

They had come from as early as noon to secure their stations. It was a Wednesday and as customary, the business houses in town closed at noon for the weekly half-day holiday. Phillipe had made all the arrangements and notified the mayor who in turn informed the Governor. The body arrived at precisely half past the hour of noon in a mule-drawn cart lent by one of the neighbours at Trois Piton. He had ensured that the coffin was draped in the Tricolour for its final journey along the Old Morne Road into town. Four young Subalterns, commandeered by the Governor—who was also commander-in-chief of the armed forces in the colony—from a visiting warship were to form the honour guard around the bier as it lay in state in the tiny town-hall at the corner of Corporation and St. Louis streets. Within the half hour, the Governor in full regalia filed past the coffin, accompanied by the Captain and senior officers of the visiting warship and the town's mayor, an arrogant snob, much disliked by the local inhabitants, both black and white, for his forthright abhorrence of Creole customs and practices. They knew that he had been summoned and that was the only reason why he was there, grinning like a marmoset lost in a bunch of ripe bananas. There were other dignitaries present, the seneschal or chief judge, who spoke only in French and whose job was to dispense justice, in civil matters relating to the French inhabitants of the colony. The Aldermen, whose job it was to advise the mayor in managing the affairs of the town and whose advice he often dismissed as puerile, because they were all products of the colony, not born like him, in England, the head of the Volunteer Guard, followed by the lawyers and doctors. Some white missionaries from the Methodist and Baptist faith, but no members from Anglican or Roman Catholic clergies; then came the masses, uninvited. The missionaries had time to say a prayer each over the coffin and walk out of the town hall towards their buggies before the people ventured in. It was like a prearranged signal in a play, as the last of the missionaries went out, they poured in. They swelled the tiny room with their numbers. Some wanted the coffin opened so that they could properly pay their last respects. Some commented loudly on the irony of a British Guard of honour paying respects to the French flag. As they filed past the bier, each commented with fear of incrimination. No matter the solemnity of the occasion they felt that their voices had to be heard. After all she had won for them that freedom, they would exercise it, with discretion. Unperturbed by the noise and hassle that continued until the final minute, the honour guard remained unnerved at their stations. Six young officers from the visiting warship entered the hall at the appointed hour to carry the bier on their shoulders to the mule wagon. The honour guard stood dutifully still, heads immaculately bowed in reverence until an officer shouted the command, which suddenly caused them to spring to life. They shouldered their arms and marched out in formation, behind the bier.

At the church Abbe Lecailtel preached a brief sermon and short-circuited the mass by not saying the prayers for consecration. Consequently, he moved straightaway into the blessing of the body and final benediction, much to the annoyance of those who had come specially prepared to share this final part of the journey with their friend. Then the six young officers lifted the coffin, turning in unison to ensure that the body proceeded head first down the aisle as the choir rendered the *magnificat* in a new format still unknown to the congregation, who could not follow. No sooner had the six young officers placed the coffin on the mule cart outside the entrance to the church and the Abbe had read the last rites, the four young subalterns fired a volley of blanks over the bier and marched away in the direction of the pier where their ship was moored. This was a signal to her people to take over the ceremony. Suddenly, a drum appeared with the drummer, a trumpeter with his trumpet followed by a host of minor instruments including bamboo flutes, *bahas*, kettle drums followed by an assortment of other handmade relics. In a brisk march, military style, to the rousing strains of '*Le chant de la guerre pour l'armée du Rhin*' they moved out of Laborie street turning left, up Rue Brazil. It was a bold move, this march not been played in public in the colony since 1814. It was banned by the British and any one found playing it in public could have been charged with treason. The dignitaries along with Abbe Lecailtel watched from the church steps. He was not quite certain whether they were aware of the march, but as a Frenchman, he knew what it was and fought to suppress the pride that wanted to swamp his face. He felt a strange qualm of conscience engulf him mildly, he nurtured regrets for not having consecrated the host to offer holy communion to the congregation, but Madlienne was not a communicant and it would not be right. His conscience pained him—greater than that she was a patriot, an honour that eclipsed all other temporal honours. He regretted being forced to judge. The Governor thanked him for the brief ceremony and took his leave, closely followed by his retinue, who ached for a swill of gin on his porch at Government House, while watching the sunset.

The procession stormed through Rue Brazil at quick march, then into La Chaussée, then on to L' Allez Marche, where the dead from the great cholera epidemic were buried in the sand, under the palms. As they lowered her body, the lone flute continued its mournful dirge and played on long after she had become one with earth—and Louise—to whom she had returned. At last, she was reunited with those she had never forgotten . . . Her father Desolee, Maitre Charle, Theodule, Argos, Jean, Ti Frère and Constantin. Even Gimat. Not to be forgotten and noble as all the others, she had finally returned to Louise. The earth lays lightly on her . . .

GLOSSARY

A

acajou	red cedar(creole); Mahogany(french).
affranchi	a free man.
agouti	agouti; a small tropical ruminant.
amis des noir	friends of black people.
attaque	attack; charge.

B

baguette	a long loaf resembling a baked rod.
bahas	a primitive musical instrument.
balisier	a tropical plant of the Canna family.
ballahoo	a small fish
belles aires	a traditional dance
bettes a feu	fireflies
blancs	white folk
bois d'amman	almond wood.(a favourite hard wood).
bolom	an evil demon, usually childlike.
boudin noir	black pudding (a local delicacy)

C

cabresse	a woman of mixed blood
Caille Parque	an estate in central Saint Lucia
Ca Ira	a french revolutionary chant

carres	a unit of measurement about 2.2 acres.
carte blanche	a free hand.
chapote	an aromatic spice. (almond flavour).
chemin Royal	In SaintLucia, the old main road.
citronnelle	a pungent aromatic weed.
citoyen	citizen.
colom	an overseer.
cristophine	a vegitable.
cuisinière	a cook.

D

dahs	wet nurses
décade	a ten day week, according to the French Revolutionary Calender.
deux bottes	an animated traditional dance.
diablesse	a fictional demonic female character.
diamante	diamond.
driette	an ancient local long skirt dress.

E

eau de bain	lightly perfumed water.
égalité	equal.
en route	heading towards ; going to.
excusez moi	excuse me, beg your pardon.

F

Farine	cassava flour.
fleur de lis	traditional french white lily.
Floréal	Spring, between Apr.20th and May19; French Revolutionary Calender.
Fraternité	brotherhood.

G

Gens libre	free persons.
gens gage	contracted souls
gri gri	a palm tree, its tiny edible red nut.
Gros Pichards	high folks, upper classes.

H I

inquisiteurs	inquisitors

J

jacquots	parrots

K

kus-kus	razor grass with aromatic roots.

L

La déclaration des droits les hommes et des Citoyen	The declaration of the rights of man and citizen.
L'Armée Française dans les bois	The army of France in the woods.
latanier	a variety of palm used for brooms.
laurier cannelles	a local hard wood.
Le chant de la guerre pour l'armée du Rhin	War chant for the Rhineland army.
Le Fleuve	The Fever, nickname for Sir John Moore.
levée maman levée	rise mama rise.
liberté	liberty
livres	pounds, currency.

M

Magnificat	canticle, "My soul doth magnify the Lord." Luke 1: 46-53.

maison blanche	the great house.
mammey-apple	tropical apricot.
maubin	hog plum.
mauby	a local bitter drink, made from bark.
ménage	household: matters related to.
merci	thank you.
merde	human or animal excrement.
Moulin-à-vent	an old sugar estate, north.
mulâtresse	a woman considered half white.
muscovado	raw brown sugar.

N

Negre Marron	runaway slave.
negresse	a black woman.
nom savane	nickname.

O P

palmiste	royal palm.
pauvre diable	poor soul(devil);a note of pity.
petite tasse	miniture teacup
petits blancs	poor whites.
piquant	an ancient sensual local dance.
pomme cythérée	golden apple

Q

Quartier de la Convention	Castries, during the French Revolution.

R

Raillon	An old sugar estate on the S.E. coast.
raison d'être	the reason for ; (illusionary).
ramier	a game bird
Reine des Antilles	Antillies Queen—a sailing ship.
Réveille	Wake up call: (in the milatary).

S

sais	sister
sankeys	spiritual songs, from the Deep South.
savane	an open pasture; a grazing meadow.
savonnette	a bush, its leaves used as soap.
serviette	a napkin.
sextidi	the 6th day in a ten day week; French revolutionary calender.
shabeene	a high brown skin woman.
su plais	please!

T

tambour	drum.
Te Deum	psalm; «We praise thee O God».
tisanes	bush medicines
tourterelles	ground doves
Trois Piton	An estate S.E. of Castries.

U V

Vétiver	same as kus kus grass.
Ville de la Félicite	Soufriere; during the French Revolution.

W

Wallaba	A local hard wood.

X Y Z

Xenon	An estate East of Soufriere town.